LONELY CROWDS

LONELY CROWDS

A Novel

STEPHANIE WAMBUGU

LITTLE, BROWN AND COMPANY

New York Boston London

Little, Brown and Company
Hachette Book Group
1290 Avenue of the Americas, New York, NY 10104
littlebrown.com

First Edition: July 2025

Little, Brown and Company is a division of Hachette Book Group, Inc. The Little, Brown name and logo are trademarks of Hachette Book Group, Inc.

The publisher is not responsible for websites (or their content) that are not owned by the publisher.

The Hachette Speakers Bureau provides a wide range of authors for speaking events. To find out more, go to hachettespeakersbureau.com or email hachettespeakers@hbgusa.com.

Little, Brown and Company books may be purchased in bulk for business, educational, or promotional use. For information, please contact your local bookseller or the Hachette Book Group Special Markets Department at special.markets@hbgusa.com.

Book interior design by Marie Mundaca

ISBN 9780316581332
LCCN 2024949127

Printing 1, 2025

LSC-C

Printed in the United States of America

For Elijah

When I think about it, I must say that my education has done me great harm in some respects.

—Franz Kafka, *Diaries*

LONELY CROWDS

1

◇◇◇◇◇◇◇◇◇◇◇◇

A PERSON DOESN'T choose when she is born. I was born in August and it was August. Since it was my birthday, I blew out my candles. The happy, off-key voices of my friends and neighbors trailed off and everyone clapped. They watched as the smoke rose faintly above the cake, dissipating before my eyes. And it isn't enough just to be born, either. There has to be something or someone that comes first at the expense of everything else, otherwise there isn't any point. Of course someone came to mind. That Maria wasn't here at the party was a source of great distress. When I met Maria, I learned that without an obsession life was impossible to live. I'd forgotten. Now, I remembered.

I sank a knife into the white frosting, and I could not understand what I was celebrating. I almost dropped the knife and ran out into the street, as you should run out and make yourself heard when an epiphany comes. But I didn't bolt since everyone was watching. I sat very still, reminding myself to smile, as my husband pulled the pink, spent candles out of the sheet cake one by one. Then, an acquaintance pulled me aside and touched my shoulder.

"Ruth, are you alright?" she asked.

"I'm wonderful," I said. "I'm having a really nice time."

"Are you sure?" she asked. She had a great mass of red hair that was piled on top of her head and secured with pins. Like most of the people at the party, she was also an artist and maybe thought of herself as a perceptive person. But I assured her there was nothing to perceive and smiled again, more convincingly.

"I'm fine." I nodded and made my way back into the center of the party. I fell into a conversation with my old professor, a painter called Moser, who was my mentor when I was a young woman. He walked with a stark limp, and because he could not keep his hands from shaking, he had recently stopped painting and had taken to making small collages, arranging cutouts together with glue to make simple landscapes that looked like dollhouse-sized mock-ups of the big, spectral canvases he was known for. I felt a lot of fondness for him, and it was natural to gravitate to him in an attempt to regain my bearings at the party, to retreat to a familiar figure of authority who had known me for many years. I perched on the edge of the wooden bench he was sitting on and told him that birthday parties were always strange, especially when you were the one being celebrated. There was this extreme pressure to feign happiness while at the same time you were forced to confront the passing of your life and what you had done or had not done up until that point. It was hard not to take the outcome of these short, overwrought celebrations as a referendum on your life so far.

"Sure," he said. "Plus there's the pressure of making sure everyone else has a good time since it's so inconvenient to find a sitter, or move your weekend around, or stay out late drinking. In that sense, your happiness is a sign of gratitude for all your guests who are going out of their way."

"Well, I hope you don't feel put out. I worry about you and your health, and I don't want you to stay out late for my sake if it would be better for you to stay home and rest or work."

"Don't be ridiculous," he said, "I'm glad to be here. I don't do anything I don't want to do. Last week it was my mother's birthday. She turned ninety-two and I didn't go to her home for dinner with all of our other living relatives. We aren't speaking and though we've been estranged for nearly thirty years, she still has my older sister reach out to me through my wife to invite me to her parties. The fact that she subjected my older sister to bitter verbal abuse makes no difference, such is my mother's power over her relations."

He continued, "Her ability to attack and mistreat, then drum up sympathy for herself, is unlike anything I've ever known. Though I've forgiven her for how cruel she was to me as a child, I want nothing to do with her. She knows I won't go or speak to her and yet she writes these long, demanding messages and uses my sister and my wife as go-betweens."

"Why didn't you go to your mother's party? What difference does it make?" I asked.

What I didn't say was that Moser's mother is so close to death and, relatively speaking, so is he, and forgiving her now wouldn't change anything. In fact, it might do both him and his mother good to reconcile and make amends as people ought to do at the end of their lives. I could understand being angry with your parents, but not abandoning them. As was the case for most people in my generation, there was a strain between my parents and myself. The generational schism was always felt. Naturally, there were things I wished they had done differently. But it wasn't anyone's fault; it was just the natural friction between those born at different times trying to talk across the chasm of their difference. It was perfectly normal. So what harm would it really do for him to go to his mother's party? Moser started to shake terribly when he heard my question. His tremor seemed to pass from his fingers and echo all throughout his body so that the wine in his cup spilled onto his tanned hands. When he spoke, his voice was low and desperate.

"I would never humiliate any child the way my mother humiliated me when I was a boy, never. While my father just stood by and watched. If he were alive, I wouldn't speak to him, either. I'll never speak to my mother again and I'll certainly never attend one of her parties. When she dies, I won't go to her funeral. And anyone who has felt the kind of pain I felt under her authority would understand perfectly why I won't. The entire purpose of my life, and of all my work, has been trying to escape my mother's cruelty. My mother isn't a sweet old lady who sits in a rocking chair knitting blankets all day. She's a remorseless abuser!"

By then the wine was all over his lap. I hadn't meant to rile him up this way. I put my hand on Moser's back and told him I was sorry, that I understood. He had every right to enforce these boundaries. What a strange word, *boundaries*. But in truth, it was hard to respect a man his age who blamed his mother for what had happened half a century ago. Moser certainly wasn't the only person I knew who had cut off his parents and foreclosed the possibility of repair, but he was by far the oldest. Admittedly, I found adults who went on not speaking with their parents because of the slightest offense to be frivolous and cruel. I was unable to liberate myself from my childhood, from my deference to my mother and father, my concern for them. Just that morning my mother called me to wish me a happy birthday and told me that even though I had never gotten a real job and was still "just painting," she was proud of me and loved me anyway. Should I have disavowed my mother for not taking my painting seriously enough? What good would it do? Everywhere I looked there were people walking out of the holds of their family's influence with a strong sense of finality. Estranged children were everywhere, spreading the good news of their estrangement. Why hadn't it ever occurred to me to try to emancipate myself similarly?

Moser said it was alright and stood up on his cane, drying his hands against his dark jeans. Even after so many years, he explained, the pain felt fresh. He would always be the little boy berated by his mother, every moment, forever. Again, I said I was sorry. He squeezed my shoulder affectionately and told me again it was alright. He walked over to his wife, Hildy. She was much younger than he was and her hair hadn't yet grayed, or she had dyed it diligently to keep her youthful appearance. He kissed her and sighed. Maybe it was because of his mother that Moser had started to shake and couldn't stop.

I was lucky to have such beautiful weather for my birthday. A warm, clear August night without rain. The guests ate their cake and set their gifts down on the kitchen table. Once they felt they had drank enough and smoked enough and exhausted the viable topics of conversation we had in common, they departed with kisses and hugs, saying that they would see me soon, though we probably wouldn't meet again until the next party. Everything went as expected.

The following morning I climbed out of my bed, no more weary than usual. I dressed, drank coffee, took my medication—these big white pills that were supposed to help with the dread. I wondered when these would start to work, since none of the others had. I drove down the road to the campus where I taught. It was not lost on me that the small town I lived in very much resembled the small town where I had grown up. It was a dull place situated along a river, just as the place where I had grown up had been a dull place situated along a river. Its best years were behind it, just as the best years were behind the town where I lived as a child. The houses that lined its quiet streets were like the houses I remembered, and scattered among these houses were plain brick apartment buildings like the plain brick apartment building I grew up in. I initially fled the backdrop of my upbringing so desperately, just to end up in this nearly identical place. Looking at the farmland lining the road, I laughed at the thought of Maria and me as girls, when we believed that New York City was the only place in the world worth living and if you ended up anywhere else you might as well be dead since the boredom would kill you.

I pulled into the quiet campus where I was to meet a colleague, Angelina, from the theater department, whom I had known for a few years and generally avoided. I didn't like her so much, but she was awfully friendly to me and sometimes had good recommendations for movies. She wasn't a very happy person, but then, neither was I. The only reason I was going to coffee with Angelina was because she said she had a project in mind and hoped I could be of help. She had won a grant that would take her back to the country she was from to stage a production of *Medea*.

Before the summer, Angelina had asked me to paint a triptych, three long panels exploring themes of madness and femininity, themes she hoped to emphasize in her play. My paintings would be used as a backdrop. I wasn't going to do it and I agreed to meet her for coffee so I could tell her so. We sat down with our coffees, and she caught me up on her summer. She apologized for not making it to my party, but she had recently stopped drinking and found it difficult to be around alcohol so soon. Her entire family was made up of terrible, violent drunks and now that she was going home to stage this play, she had to be especially careful about her own drinking, which couldn't be separated from that of her parents and grandparents. We spoke for nearly an hour before I realized that she hadn't brought up the paintings and I hoped that she didn't take my silence as acceptance. I tried to steer the conversation toward my busy schedule, but she didn't get the hint. She wanted to talk instead about what was wrong with her students. A favorite subject of conversation, I was learning.

"I can't stand this generation," she said. "Teaching makes me so unhappy. I'm so relieved this opportunity came and that I'll be away in the fall. I hope it isn't too much to say this but...I was feeling rather suicidal this past year."

I winced. She laughed and kept talking as though her admission were nothing. And I suppose it was nothing since she was in front of me in perfect health full of enough fervor to complain. The students took issue with the things she assigned. They wanted to make art without studying the past. At eighteen, they believed they were geniuses and that she was the stupid one for not giving them their due. Could I believe it? Their specific grievances were too frivolous to rehash and she didn't bother to go into great detail.

I nodded because nodding made people feel listened to and gave them a sense of inclusion, but I wondered if she wasn't the one who was being unreasonable or dogmatic. Which was not to say that she was, but you couldn't rule it out, could you? Who knew how deep our self-delusions went? Personally, I let my students talk because I was curious about the shape of their generation's problems, a shape that I'm sure resembled my silhouette against the blackboard. I knew my students thought I was too conservative, and I wanted to say to them that compared to my mother, I was a revolutionary. But I was careful about this impulse to defend myself, because no one was above critique.

Since I taught a painting class where I often expected students to critique one another, I felt I ought to embody the kind of humility I was asking of all of them. I ate my food and tried to participate in this conversation that I didn't find interesting. Bored, I looked beyond my colleague's shoulder at the oak trees outside the window and considered that decades ago, I must have looked at similar oak trees and felt just as dislocated and adrift as I did now, drinking that coffee. I stood up and told Angelina I had to go. I was sorry to be so abrupt, but I had to hurry because I was going out of town. It wasn't a lie. I did have a train to the city to catch, but not for several hours. For now, I needed to be alone.

"Ruth, is everything alright?" she asked. I nodded and grabbed my car keys. She looked at me like I was strange.

I wandered in the woods for a while. These weren't woods I could get lost in, like people do in stories, disappearing into the trees. I knew them too well. I walked to the north end of campus, where a philosopher was buried, and I looked at the trees that must have fed from her corpse once. I thought of my old friend Maria, and I could still see her face, vivid and unsmiling, hanging in my mind.

I came out from the woods and walked alongside the road, passing flocks of students dressed in loud clothing. They had such awful haircuts, but if that made them happy, then fine, what did I care? If some of the students I passed had been my own I wouldn't have remembered them, that's how dazed I was as I followed the gravel path back to my car. To think that once Maria and I were as young as these students and even younger, that once we did every-thing together happily. It was really all too much to think about, but I also couldn't help thinking about it like the delightful, sharp pain of pressing a finger into a freshly bandaged wound.

Nearing my car, I noticed Angelina across the road, and she waved and shouted in my direction. I tried to hurry and keep walking with my head turned in hopes she would give up.

"Ruth!" she said, waving and running toward me. "I thought you were in a hurry. I didn't say something to offend you, did I?"

She was standing right in front of me then, panting.

"No, no," I said, "I wasn't feeling well."

"What's wrong? Do you want me to walk you to the clinic?" She pointed in the direction of the small campus nurse's office.

"Sorry, no, I'm feeling fine. I just had an idea for a painting sud-denly and needed to be alone and jot it down."

"Why didn't you say! You've been thinking about the set. About the play. I completely forgot to mention it. Say, are you free right now? I got some early sketches from the woman who's designing the costumes; she's from the village I was born in. They're some-where here in my phone."

"I'm sorry, I really do have to catch my train now. And I don't think I'll be able to do the backdrops for you after all."

"Oh, so I did offend you. I shouldn't have mentioned that I wanted to kill myself. Or the drinking. My wife always says unhappy people scare others away."

"It isn't anything you said. Don't worry. I just don't want to work with you," I said and turned and walked to my car without saying goodbye. Angelina called after me.

"Where will I find another painter now? On such short notice."

I didn't look back and kept walking. When I got to my car, I saw that campus security had given me a ticket of one hundred dollars for blocking an emergency exit. I crumpled up the fine and threw it into my handbag. I drove home feeling uneasy. Back in my room, I stuffed underwear, a pair of high heels, two dresses, a cardigan, and a toothbrush in my weekend bag. When it came time to go to the station, I collected my luggage and went out to meet the taxi I'd scheduled. I watched the sun fall over the river as I waited for the Amtrak to Penn Station, and then rode another taxi to the restaurant where I met my husband and other strangers. We drank and ate oysters, then walked to my opening in a gallery staffed almost entirely by young interns in designer clothes. Going around like this, I forgot how poor I had been as a child. And Maria had been even poorer than I was. Poor, devout, ignorant, insular, reliable, modest, generous, beautiful people—a total thing of the past. None of them sat around the table eating oysters with me, that much I knew. I didn't even like oysters.

As I walked through the brightly lit gallery, people congratulated me, and some asked for pictures. We stood in front of my paintings and smiled for the cellphone cameras. This show represented two years of work. Very physical work because my paintings were so large and because I worked without an assistant, but I couldn't remember working on them. Wasn't that strange? Lately, the paintings looked as though they'd been made by another person. Another person I didn't know. Minor works by a minor talent. But it was a very good time to be an African artist, my gallerist explained. So I should be glad. In the small crowd streaming out of the gallery, I saw the back of the head of a friend I used to know very well, who had consumed my thoughts all week, all day.

"Maria?" I asked. Drunk, I touched the woman's shoulder and she recoiled. When this stranger saw it was me, she smiled and asked if I would be interested in an interview for her podcast about women artists. *No, sorry. I've mistaken you for someone else,* I said. I stumbled back, almost falling against one of the canvases, and several strangers rushed to help me back to my feet. My gallerist, a tall, white-haired, fit man with large, round glasses, pulled me to the corner. He was smiling and I realized he was trying to help me save face, spare me embarrassment.

"Are you alright?" he asked.

"Yes, I'm fine, but I have to go now."

I turned out of the gallery without saying goodbye, forgetting the people I came with, still holding my plastic cup of lukewarm champagne. I walked for however long up Canal Street. There were tall men there, Senegalese, totally modelesque, selling fake Chanel bags. They had them lined up on the street neatly atop white tarps. I felt that these men selling these fake designer goods on the street and the gallerist who sold my paintings were in essence doing the same kind of work and that if they were to switch places, no one would be able to notice the difference.

"I'll give you a good price, sister," a man selling wallets said. I smiled and nodded at him, pretending to look at the bags.

I knew that at that very moment, my gallerist was still back at the opening, working the room and securing a legacy for me, while I wandered the streets like a person without a name. Maybe I had been acting erratically, since everywhere I went people asked me if I was feeling okay, as you might ask an insane person as you led them gently back to a shared reality. I started to sweat as I walked, and I took off the blouse I was wearing over my thin dress and put it in my bag. My chest, shoulders, and legs were bare and covered with sweat and I was reminded of a recurring dream I had had for years of walking around the streets of a strange town naked, while everyone pretended not to see me.

Looking up, I saw that I was standing by the doors of a church called Most Precious Blood. I hurried across the street, feeling I would be found out if I went inside. Found out for what? Once across the street, I felt a strong urge to go into the church and I doubled back, unable to keep myself from walking up the marble steps and into the brightly lit cathedral where sculptures of the Virgin and angels hung above the lectern, their color as vivid as the day they were painted. The pews were filled with believers, mostly old women in long, plain dresses and flesh-colored stockings. I sat down so as not to fall. I was still holding the wine I took from my opening. I drank it and crushed the empty cup into my purse. I felt like a child, like one of God's many embittered children, desperate for love. It wasn't any comfort that all around the world, at this very moment, there were expectant people like me and these pious old women, sitting down in churches like this one to contemplate their deaths, their disappointments, all the mercies they'd been granted, all the people they were estranged from, all their unanswered prayers. Maybe some of the women sitting here in the pews were remorseless abusers with shaking sons like Moser's mother. Maybe some of them were violent drunks like Angelina's relatives in her village. Maybe some of them were very afraid like me. Someone sitting behind me tapped my shoulder. I turned around and saw an older woman holding out a black scarf to me.

"Cover your shoulders," she said. I apologized and wrapped the scarf around myself. The organ started to play, and the candle and cross bearers entered from behind a partition and the priest followed and I was ten years old dressed in my starched uniform, crossing myself with small hands. Suddenly I was in an early place, before I ever made a painting or knew a man.

I stared down at the white stone floors, and they were like the floors that lined the school I went to when I was a girl. It was a middling, old K–12 school for the religious education of girls. The tuition was low compared to other private schools in Rhode Island—no more than six thousand a year, one grand after the scholarship. It was important I go there.

My mother explained that at public school, Black children fell through the cracks. Private school was much better, since they didn't let children fall through the cracks. There was order. There was a structure to hold you as a noose holds the person wearing it. And that was good. I had to do everything my mother did because that was how it was. Each year, I posed for a photograph in my uniform that was sent to the Diocese of Rhode Island with a letter thanking them for their generosity. Would they be happy with the kind of adult their charity yielded? I pulled the scarf tighter around myself.

The stories, or the truths, of my childhood were lost in that ordinary, corrosive tedium that was time, that was my life. But the school was still right there on the same avenue just as it had been thirty years ago, painted white, just like the exterior of this church. There were some places for which rescue is impossible. It was said of many places and of even more people in the world of my upbringing that there was nothing that could be done. We seemed to address one another with an everlasting shrug, and if there were any permanent way that our childhoods were violated by our teachers, it was through their cynicism, which touched all of us. It was difficult to feel a part of my generation when so much of my education was organized by such atavistic tendencies and values. In my youth, I lived so much in a past that was decades and decades older than I was. I suppose this was one of the real ambitions of Christian schools, to slow time down for their pupils, to move more slowly than the world. But a person's will was easily overcome by those lagging histories, and I don't know if I will ever be myself.

After the mass, the priest sent us off with a blessing. The women filed out of the pews, their heads slightly bowed. I pulled the scarf off my shoulders to return it to the woman behind me, but she had already left. I started to walk back to the hotel but grew tired. I hailed a taxi, even though it wasn't a long way. I couldn't walk any farther. Up in my room, I checked my cellphone and saw that my husband had called and texted. As had my gallerist. He was throwing an after-party at a nearby bar in my honor. A big party, open bar. Lots of fun. Every last one of my paintings sold. It was cause for celebration. I was the woman of the hour. Everyone wanted to see me. *Did I want them to order for me? Did I want coke? Ketamine? Where was I? Was everything alright?* I undressed and then I swallowed two small yellow pills, antihistamines for sleep, washed down with a cup of tap water. I said a quick prayer, for what, I didn't know.

I started the story from the beginning before falling asleep.

2

IT WAS LATE August. Girls and their mothers queued up in the little storefront on Pawtucket Avenue for new cardigans and polos. That particular Saturday morning, the line stretched out the door. I saw a girl there standing under the shadow of her mother: a tall, frail, light-skinned woman, her hair slicked back with a waxy sheen. The woman pleaded with the shop owner to let her take the uniforms home. She would come back and pay for them once her disability check arrived. No, the shop owner said. He made a big show of casting her out of the store. I pulled at the hem of my mother's skirt and asked her what was going on, why was he shouting at that woman.

"Mind your business," my mother whispered back. Minding one's business was the foundation of my mother's worldview. A person should mind their business, be quiet, iron their clothes meticulously, wash until their skin feels raw, visit the salon every two weeks for a perm, attend mass three times a week, not be greedy, not call attention to oneself, not show weakness, not show love.

The young girl and the woman with her crept out of the shop as though they'd done something terrible. People stared as though they had, attesting to the power of the shop owner. We were all recruited to silently take part in the condemnation of this woman and child who could not pay. Why should they be allowed to take the uniform on credit when everyone else's father had worked hard and saved? Why should they expect mercy? Or a handout? I saw these questions in the unblinking eyes of the other mothers. I stared along with them, but my staring had nothing to do with their reproaches. The woman held the girl close to her thigh.

"Let's go, Maria," the woman said.

So her name was Maria. I'd never seen her before. Everyone in the town stared. People lived for those small controversies, the mothers especially, as many of them didn't work and had even less to talk about than their husbands, who had obligations outside the home. Without shame, Maria looked back at me as she crossed the threshold, wide black eyes, perfect. Then she was gone. I felt doomed. My mother stood over me, inspecting the manicure she'd done at home, with the burgundy bottle of Revlon she'd bought with a coupon at the pharmacy. I turned my head and watched Maria grow smaller and smaller in my view. My mother pulled me along as the line moved. Once it was our turn, the shopkeeper asked for my name and I felt I'd forgotten it. My mother answered for me. I couldn't wait for the first of September and felt the days leading up to it were a waste.

We drove home and I modeled my new uniform for my father, turning at the end of the hall so he could see my newer, larger clothes. He furrowed his brow and sighed when my mother told him how much it had all cost, but he said it was worth it. My mother and father slept in different beds in our small apartment. The floral sofa pulled out into a queen-sized mattress. That was where my father sat awake at night after he worked and ate. He spent decades working and eating and keeping things to himself.

"Will I ever have a brother or sister?" I asked my parents as we ate dinner silently around the table.

"A brother or sister means half as much food for you. And half as much love," my mother said.

"And half as much for school fees," my father said. On that they could agree.

"When I was pregnant with you, there were two babies on the first ultrasound. Twins. I went back for my next appointment and there was only one left! You ate her alive. I already gave you a sister. Look what you did with her."

"Don't tell her that, you'll make her feel bad," my father said, looking afraid himself.

It did make me feel bad. So there was my one chance at companionship and I had killed it before it even had an opportunity to develop. If it was true that we were all born with sin and we could only rid ourselves of it through humble atonement, then there was mine. Why did I eat my twin? Because I was a greedy, careless child who couldn't be trusted. That summer had been full of lonely days when I waited out the sun in bed and didn't go outside. There was no one there to play with. We lived on the edge of a white neighborhood in Pawtucket between an Irish cemetery and a factory that used to make textiles but had switched to bottling beer. Though I felt alone, I was curious about the girl I had seen in the shop and the brief memory of her was enough to pass the time. I had been nervous about the new school, and knowing that Maria awaited me had transformed my anxieties into pure interest. There was no question that we would immediately connect and fuse together, becoming inseparable. All we needed to do was see one another again and our lives would begin.

"Aren't you very excited you get to go to this wonderful school?" my father asked.

"They won't tolerate any nonsense," my mother said, "so you'll have to be on your best behavior."

My parents continued in this vein, but I wasn't listening. My mother was working as a secretary then and my father was bouncing around from one job to the next; couldn't hold anything down. *Racist bosses, no room for growth, the hours were too short or else they were too long.* Though it seemed my mother was the one being mistreated and never said so. She stayed late at the doctor's office where she worked and sometimes alluded to bad actors there. Mostly, my mother said nothing. My mother was a quiet person. She needed long silences to consider things alone. She was a woman who absorbed great quantities of information to kill and memorialize inside herself. A sort of funereal air mixed in with the White Diamonds perfume she wore, photo albums full of dead relatives buried abroad. Now, I'm sure there were many others like her, but as a child I found her strange.

So my mother went to a mass in town. Closest thing to Anglicans. Roman Catholics.

I have to get my Eucharist. My father stayed home and didn't bother with American churches. My mother admitted that the Catholic mass did nothing for her and most days she "slept with her eyes open" while the priest went on. If anyone could go through the motions it was her. I never witnessed her do anything with a drop of enthusiasm in my life, except shop. She liked the big box stores best, where you could buy a frying pan and a blouse on the same floor. *I don't feel God here,* she said once, coming back from mass on Sunday with a big plastic bag from Filene's full of Spanx and blouses. She didn't say it to anyone, she said it to herself. Confirmation of the sense I had later on, that God had turned his back on America and Rhode Island in particular, that we were living in a cold shadow of that fact. But it had to be Catholic school. She insisted.

Now that I was going to this special school I could be trusted with new responsibilities. I could separate my own laundry, I could go down to the first floor to bring the bank check to the landlady, and I could be sent to the store. As an only child, I lived like a queen, never cleaning up after myself or anyone else, but it was a cloistered existence, disconnected from the world. I preferred these obligations that allowed me to think of myself as having a purpose in the grander scheme. My mother handed me two small bills and sent me to the store on the corner for milk.

"Keep the money safe in your pocket and don't look at anyone in the street. If anyone tries to talk to you, tell them, 'My mother doesn't let me talk to strangers.'"

I nodded and ran out, the money secure in my pocket and my gaze straight ahead. A woman waiting for the bus smiled at me and I averted my eyes, remembering what my mother had said. Hoping to prolong my outing, I went past the store on the corner and walked to the larger grocery store several blocks down instead. It wasn't so far that my mother would notice what I'd done, and when I reached the store I saw that they had a special on milk and I could save the change for myself.

Was it stealing if I kept the money while my mother thought I'd spent it? God would probably be happy I was so frugal and had taken advantage of the deal. I walked down the neat aisles, excited to be free in the world. This was just a taste of the independence to come. I took my time looking at the bright boxes of cereal my mother would never buy. My mother felt that Americans were gluttons and that sugar was one of their favorite indulgences, along with alcohol. They made the boxes and bottles so bright so that you didn't know you were eating and drinking poison.

No poison for me, I thought, since I had so much to look forward to. Once September came, I'd go to Our Lady and Maria would be there. No more loneliness or insularity. I continued to walk down the aisles, checking my pocket every moment to make sure the money was still there. Stopping every so often to count it and place it back where it was. I was stopped at the end of an aisle, confirming the money was all there, when a woman pushing a cart walked past me. I stepped back to stand out of her way. As she turned to pick up a bottle of soda, I saw that she was the woman from the uniform shop and trailing some steps behind her was Maria. I ducked behind a display and watched them intently. From the summer sun, Maria's skin was almost the same shade as her dark hair. She could have been cast from bronze. The disability check must have come and now they could do their shopping. The uniform shop owner wouldn't cast them out of his store anymore.

I was glad to see that life was improving for Maria and her mother, even if they did drink soda, which was gluttonous. I thought to say hello, but what if she didn't remember me? Also, how could I say hello when my mother had told me clearly not to talk to strangers? I longed for September when Maria and I would meet and I wouldn't have to regard her with this caution reserved for people you didn't know. I told myself that I could watch Maria and her mother from a distance as they did their shopping. I'd just follow behind them and watch them from down the aisle.

It was my mother's day off and she was probably busy at home scrubbing the baseboards or darning old socks. She never sat still for a minute, never let a moment go by without being productive. She wouldn't notice if I stayed out at the store a bit longer. I watched Maria and her mother walk toward the pharmacy counter and pick up a prescription. I stood behind the tower of reading glasses, poking my head out just so. When they moved to the frozen foods I carefully studied their choices: mixed vegetables, Salisbury steaks, French fries. Maria and her mother didn't speak, but as one placed the items in the cart, the other crossed them off the list. I was enraptured watching them work in tandem. I couldn't believe that someone like Maria existed and I had not seen her until yesterday. In September we would meet. I expected instant intimacy. Ruth and Maria. Maria and Ruth? I recited our names silently as I watched them shop and was satisfied by the sound. I continued to trail behind them, reminding myself all the while of the milk and the special and the change I would keep for myself. I was in a daze and felt that catching them in the store, seeing them without them seeing me, was the greatest part of summer. I quickly forgot the long days spent in isolation. Just this proximity to her in the supermarket was enough. Maria turned around and stared at me curiously. I was following too closely. I looked back at her.

"Hi," she said.

I ran out of the store, grabbing the money in my pocket. I ran all the way home. My mother had told me not to look at anyone, not to talk to anyone. I ran. When I got to our building, I saw my mother standing on the lawn, her hands placed on her hips.

"What took you so long?" she asked.

"I got lost."

"Where's the milk?"

"They didn't have any left," I said, staring at my tennis shoes.

My mother was suspicious and told me to give her back the money. I reached into my pocket and it wasn't there. I turned my pockets inside out searching for it, but it must have fallen while I was running. If it fell somewhere in the store, then maybe Maria could hold on to it. She and her mother could save it toward the uniform, so that things were not so scarce until the next check came.

"Ruth, you know how hard I work. How hard it is to make money and pay for all the things we need. You're so irresponsible. You can't be trusted. I knew you weren't ready to go off on your own."

My mother walked me inside, where I got into bed and came to understand the magnitude of my irresponsibility. A nine-year-old girl should have been able to go to the store for milk alone, and yet. Would Maria find me irresponsible? Would my irresponsibility repel her? She had been so diligent in crossing off the items on the list; she could be trusted. I'd have to wait and see what she thought of me. At least the day was nearly over and it was one night closer to the first of September. Over dinner, my father told me that if I had stolen the money for the milk, I should say so. That it wasn't too late to repent and that he and my mother were forgiving people. I didn't have anything to say for myself. Too bad that I had lost my mother's money and hadn't even remembered the milk. Yes, I was irresponsible. No, I didn't know the value of money and how hard-won it was. But it was one night closer to September, so what did that matter? I was so thrilled about having seen Maria, but I had to conceal my excitement and put on a sorry expression.

3

◇◇◇◇◇◇◇◇◇◇◇

IT WAS THE first day of school and my mother parted and reparted my hair several times before she was satisfied the lines were straight. We took a picture on the cracked, sloping sidewalk. First, my mother and me. Then my father and me. Then me alone.

"Pull up your socks," my mother said. I did.

"No, not so high." I adjusted them until she approved. I would do whatever she said. I was eager to get to school, to be the first one there, to be there when Maria arrived and watch her come in. She would be wearing a uniform; she might have changed her hair. Would I recognize her, only having seen her twice before? Of course I would. There weren't many of us.

"There aren't going to be many Africans," my mother said.

"Okay," I said.

"So you should do your best to fit in," my mother said.

"She doesn't need to worry about that," my father said.

"She absolutely does," my mother said. Then she straightened out my collar and helped me into the back seat of my father's silver station wagon. He bought it cheap in hopes of doing the repairs on his own, but it was slow going. He could never find the parts and when he found them it turned out they weren't any good. Going forward I was to ride the bus, but since it was my first day, he insisted on driving me. I felt so important being driven to school two towns over. As we turned onto a tree-lined bend on a back road nearing the school, the car lurched forward and slowed to a stop. My father quickly turned onto the grassy, narrow shoulder. Smoke rose from the front of the car and we stepped a few feet away from it. I watched him perch beneath a tall yellow birch, shaking his head as the car became shrouded with dark exhaust. He seemed so irresponsible to me then. Could a girl ever recover from seeing her father's imprudence? I didn't think so. He took my hand and we walked the rest of the way to the school, my father carrying me part of the way since there were ditches in the ground and cars speeding past. I didn't understand how someone like my mother came to be with someone like my father. My father was lonely, mercurial, romantic. He hummed to himself while doing things around the house or just sitting alone, which my mother said men shouldn't do. And when my mother scolded me, he intervened to soften her criticism, which she also said wasn't normal for a man. I turned back and looked at the station wagon. Its smoke blew up into the trees. Cars were slowing to look at the breakdown and the traffic we had caused made walking faster than driving. As we were crossing the road to the gates of Our Lady, I saw Maria walking across the courtyard alone with a large red backpack. She dragged her feet as she walked up to the schoolhouse. I told my father to put me down and I trailed behind her. He followed after me with his hands in his pockets, looking out of place. In a crowd of mothers dropping off their daughters, he was the only man. A blonde nun ushered me through the white double doors with the rest of the children. I waved goodbye to my father and he waved back to me.

"Will you be alright with the car?" I asked, suddenly very worried about how he would fare alone.

"I'll be fine, Ruth, you go ahead."

I squeezed through the line to catch up with Maria, who was up by the front. A young teacher with straw-colored hair listed out names from a clipboard. Maria's name was called and she moved up to her assigned group. I was at the end of the alphabet and I waited fretfully, hoping I would be placed in the same classroom. When my name was called, my shoulders tensed and I walked toward the line Maria was standing in. I stared at the ground as I walked, counting the small white tiles. I looked up and saw that she was looking at me. She moved closer to me, direct and unshy. I was struck by two things: her dirtiness and her tremendous confidence. I noticed that her shirt was soiled at the collar and it stood out to me because my collar was very white. How had she already gotten so dirty on the first day? Maybe the shirt was secondhand. My parents would never let me leave the house that way, even if my shirt were secondhand. They washed and dried and folded my clothes with a passion they didn't extend to anything else. I was always very clean. I didn't mind that she was dirty. Actually, the fact that she had gotten away with it, had undermined authority in a way I couldn't, made her more attractive to me. Just as I was staring at her, thinking of something fitting to say, we were herded into our classroom, where she rushed to a desk by the window. I tried to go for a desk in her row, but other groups had already formed and a group of friends filled in the chairs beside her. The only empty desk was the one directly in front of her. I figured I would just move the following day, but our teacher explained the seats we were sitting in then would be our assigned places for the rest of the year.

"My name is Sister Paulette."

"Hello, Sister Paulette," we said in unison.

"You'll come to understand that I like order. Order, neatness, and cleanliness delight our Father."

We went around and said our names and favorite colors. Lilac was a frequent answer. I could barely open my mouth when it came to my turn, and the thought of Maria staring at the back of my head mortified me. I managed to say my name was Ruth and didn't bother with the color since my voice was already barely audible. We rose to recite the pledge, following along with the staticky rendition over the intercom. After the pledge to the flag, there was mass. When we walked down in single-file lines to the chapel, I tried to hang back to be in Maria's vicinity, but I was shouted at for walking out of place.

"Do not slow down the line! This is a serious occasion. Not a time for playing. You'll all learn to respect the Lord."

We filed into the rows of the church and were silent. The entire school was there and no one spoke above a whisper. A few hundred girls shifted in the wooden pews. As the service began, two young boys in milk-colored robes carried burning candles on iron holders. The priest stood over a long table and his thin, white hair made him look weary. He led us through the motions. My mind wandered as he licked his lips and began his homily.

"We're all born with sin. Everyone here is marked by a debt that God has paid and we owe all our lives in gratitude to Him. There are things we do that dishonor God. Things we do in haste, in the heat of the moment. Things we do out of what we believe is love. Some of you young girls might be pressured to give up your virginity. Some of you may have already done the deed and deflowered yourselves outside of the sacrament of marriage. While it is unfortunate, and while it disappoints God, for you to violate yourself and your honor in that way, it isn't too late. Just as God forgives our sins, we can pray to Him and make penance, and He can forgive us for our sexual transgressions. If you've lost your virginity, you can pray to God to restore it. To restore your beautiful, physical purity. Because God is merciful and because you as women and girls have a precious gift and it is up to you to safeguard it at all times for the loving union of marriage with your future husbands."

The feeling in the room was mixed. I saw some teachers nodding, while others looked very displeased. Some older girls held back laughter; others rolled their eyes. The younger ones' mouths hung open in awe. I looked back at Maria and she was grinning. I smiled, too. I didn't understand why I was smiling because I had no idea what kind of restoration the priest had in mind. I often listened without understanding, hoping someone would enlighten me. I wasn't sure if awareness would come with age or if I was just dull. We got up and snaked around the pews in neat lines to receive Communion, bowing slightly and opening our mouths. Quickly enough, we were back in our classroom and everyone was whispering about the priest. Our teacher wouldn't have it and told us that if there was something we wanted to laugh about, we should come to the front of the room and share it with everyone. She said that we had no respect, no humility, and that she'd make decent women out of us yet. I looked into the frosted window and saw Maria's faint reflection. She was listening intently, nodding along to everything Sister Paulette said.

"Is that Ruth who's turned around? Will I have trouble with you this year?"

"No, Sister," I said.

It rained the first day of school and every day that week. A heavy, sudden downpour that came unexpectedly and never stopped. We weren't let out for recess; instead blank notebooks were handed out and we were expected to write or draw quietly. I didn't understand how writing in silence was consolation for not going outside to play, but I didn't ask any questions. We were instructed to write a story of what we did over the summer and draw a picture to go along with it. The best stories would be hung up on the wall. Since I didn't do anything that summer, I drew a person sleeping in an ornate, tall bed and underneath the drawing I wrote, "I didn't do anything. I slept." My story wasn't chosen for the display, but I thought my drawing was pretty accurate, for what it was worth.

By the third day, I was used to the monotony. I called no attention to myself, standing when others stood and being quiet when others were quiet. In the morning we stood for the pledge, we walked down the narrow corridors to mass, we studied numbers, spelling, the life of Christ, the geography of our country, and the names of the planets, in that order. There hadn't been any opportunity to talk to Maria. Every minute of every day was accounted for and, anyway, we weren't in the same row. It wasn't as though I could just turn around and start a conversation with Sister Paulette watching me.

In the evening of the first day, I went home and my parents asked if I had learned anything and I said I hadn't. *Nothing at all?* they asked. Finally, I told them about the priest who said that if we lost our virginity, we could pray and God would give it back. *He'd restore it,* I said, just the way the priest had said it in a low, droning voice. *Restore.* My mother looked at my father and they both looked at me without saying anything.

"What happened to the car?" I asked.

"Ask your father," my mother said.

On Sunday I washed laundry with my father. Laundry was my father's chore, his only one. My mother reasoned that since he was the one who bought the lemon, and left us without the car, he would be the one to carry the clothes down the road to the wash. If I went to evening mass with my mother, she didn't bother me on Sunday. She preferred to go to mass alone anyway. She felt I got in the way of things, I knew. While all the other men and women and children in our neighborhood went off to church, my father and I enjoyed the empty laundromat. It didn't occur to me that everyone in town was Christian and took to heart the idea that a person didn't work on the Lord's day. I was proud of the laundromat as the one place my father and I had any sway. Later, I understood that it stayed open on Sundays only because the Bengali family who owned it was Muslim, but back then it felt like they kept it open for us especially. There was something dignifying about that, whether or not it was real.

So that he wouldn't have to entertain me, my father gave me a sketchbook and a tin of colored pencils that kept me quiet for hours. I spread out across the countertops and drew simple reproductions of my surroundings that were more real once replicated. Things seemed to exist only once I'd drawn them. I adored my father for giving me those materials and leaving me alone. I loved him, though I knew he wasn't strong. He definitely was not strong. I understood that, watching him work at the week's worth of dirty underwear.

Since the car couldn't be fixed, I rode the bus, which I was meant to do in the first place. I was the first stop on its route since I was the only girl from the school who lived in my neighborhood. It picked me up just after sunrise, and as we got nearer to the school, moving from suburb to suburb, it filled with girls who lived closer by. One morning the bus spun out in the rain and the driver started to yell and told us to hold on to one another. I was sitting in a row alone, so I just held on to my seat. Finally, the driver got control of things and he told us we were fine, but there had been an unavoidable accident and he had killed a person. A church van came to retrieve us and we got to school early since the van was faster than the bus.

Finally, the sky was clear and it was as though it had never rained at all. We were let out to roam in the schoolyard after lunch. Sister Paulette let us know that any nonsense and we would spend the break sitting with her on the steps, discussing what was and what wasn't appropriate behavior for young pupils at Our Lady. Maybe being punished would have been a mercy, preferable to sitting alone on the far bench without the courage to approach anyone. Maria stood across the yard, flipping through a picture book. Here was the opportunity I had dreamt of all summer. I was right on the precipice of the friendship I wanted. All I needed to do was stand up and go over to her. You couldn't follow people in supermarkets and stare at them all day and think that your work was over. In order to have a friend, I had to speak. Why couldn't I act? *Hello* would have sufficed. *Hello* would have been effective. I closed my eyes and counted, telling myself that when I was finished counting I would stand up and walk over to her. Then, as I counted, it occurred to me I could go on indefinitely and delay action for however long, so that's what I did. I was somewhere in the forties and counting slowly when I felt something tap my knee. I opened my eyes.

"What are you doing? Praying?" she asked.

Maria had red mulch beneath her fingernails. She looked me up and down. She sat on the bench beside me, her legs spread wide open, making her skirt fan out like a plume. She had a glossy book in her lap and a pen she had just pulled out of her skirt pocket. She took to drawing in the book like I wasn't there. Her grip on the pen was forceful and her movements on the page were urgent and repetitive. She was drawing on all of the pictures. I saw that she had taken the book out from the library. We had been told to return the books as we found them and I figured the librarian had neglected to remind Maria of this rule.

"Can't you get into trouble for that? With Sister Paulette?"

"There isn't anyone watching. We can do whatever we want to do."

That alarmed me.

"Look," she said, pointing at the steps. Sister Paulette was in the hall, standing out of the sun, gossiping with one of the other sisters. She wasn't watching us at all.

"They're barely ever paying attention."

Maria slid the book in front of me and I recognized it, *The Velveteen Rabbit*. Except in Maria's version, all of the eyes had been colored in red and horns, like a devil's horns, had been drawn over all of the people's faces. She had also put large red crosses through the bodies of the rabbits and she drew little drops of blood spilling from their mouths and eyes, which I assumed was to show that they were dead.

"What do you think?" she asked, smiling.

I looked at the pages. "What about other kids who want to read it?"

She paused and her expression changed. "When you put it like that, it makes me feel kinda bad."

She got up and threw the vandalized book into the garbage with great force. Then she walked back over to me and gestured heroically, leading me out to the playground, where I watched her hang upside down from the monkey bars by her knees. While the other girls perfected fishtail braids and brokered gossip, I stared at her, her knee-high socks loose around her calves and her underwear bright in the late summer sun. Her black braids hung upside down and her face was flipped so that it looked, somehow, both sullen and ecstatic. I didn't know how she was getting away with it. When she came down from the monkey bars, she brought her face close to mine in the middle of the sandbox.

She pulled back her braids and turned her face so I could see the small, bright pearl studs in each of her small, black ears.

"Aren't they beautiful?" she asked.

I nodded, ran my finger over them. The pearls were hard and cool.

"They're a gift from the music teacher. I sleep with them on. One day I'll let you borrow them if you're careful."

"Oh, I'm not careful," I said. I couldn't lie to her. I was transfixed.

"I'm careless," I said.

"That's too bad," she said.

"Yes, it is," I said, grazing the slick pearls again with my finger.

4

◇◇◇◇◇◇◇◇◇◇◇◇◇◇

"YOU GIRLS ARE in for a real treat, I've got a big surprise for you all," Mr. Fournier told us. I sat with my hands folded in my lap. I needed to first hear what the surprise was before I got my hopes up. I hated to sing, but it was the elective my mother chose for me. She'd had a beautiful voice as a girl. Her primary school's choir had sung for President Jomo Kenyatta, and it almost brought him to tears. I wanted to take the arts and crafts elective because I'd heard you mostly just made origami and once you were done folding however many cranes, they let you read, draw, or do whatever you wanted. The teacher was a young married woman who had never taught before and she never shouted. My mother told me that she didn't send me to school so that I could learn to make paper airplanes. *Singing*, my mother said, *is a good skill for a woman to have. You can sing to your children when you're older, you can sing in church. You won't look back when you're a woman and think,* I wish I had learned to make origami. So music it was. Maria was also in the class, which was a relief, but she usually sat up at the front with Mr. Fournier since she had a beautiful voice and often sang the solos. Though it was only the first month of school, Maria and our teacher, Mr. Fournier, seemed to already know one another, to already have a silent understanding. Just as I'd heard rumors about the priest on the bus, I'd also heard rumors about Mr. Fournier. But the problem was, I hadn't actually heard the content of the rumors, I had just heard that there *were* rumors. No one told me anything.

We all looked at Mr. Fournier expectantly, waiting for the big news.

"We're going on a field trip!" he said.

"A field trip where?" asked Camila, without raising her hand. Camila's father was the mayor of Providence and every morning she was taken to school by a black car with tinted windows. Cars were supposed to go through the back lot, but Camila was always dropped right by the front gates behind the moss-covered statue of Mary, then the car would wait until Camila walked inside and then turn out of the roundabout slowly, the mayor's wife sticking her hand out the window to wave at Camila, one of those awkward waves politicians did on television.

"I said, a field trip to where?" Camila repeated herself.

"A concert. The first one all year," Mr. Fournier said.

"Who'll sing the solo?" Camila asked him.

"Maria will," he said.

Camila wasn't pleased and said she'd tell her father.

"Who's your father?" Mr. Fournier asked. Camila told him.

"I've never heard of him," Mr. Fournier said and handed out the tattered songbooks we'd be singing from.

We started practicing the songs right away, because the concert was only one week down the line. Even though I generally mumbled and didn't really pull my weight in the alto section of the choir, I felt compelled to at least try when Maria led us along in preparation of the songs for the concert. I wanted her to hear and see me. If she trusted me, she would tell me how a person went about getting older. I was drawn to Maria and her knowledge about Mr. Fournier, and about the adult world. Why had he given her those earrings? What else didn't I know? I stopped Maria after school let out and asked if she wanted to come to my house for supper. I didn't know what gave me the courage.

"Sure," she said, with total indifference.

"How do you sing like that?" I asked.

"Singing's the easiest thing in the world," she said, looking over my shoulder.

Maria boarded the bus home with me without any issue. She usually rode the number four bus home, while I rode the number three, but there was no one there to tell her where she was supposed to be. How could it be that as children we felt that on one hand there was always someone scrutinizing us and on the other we were totally unaccounted for?

We didn't speak much on the bus, but I silently rehearsed how I would lead her through the apartment. I had to be careful how I framed myself. I had to come across as measured, impassive, and confident, like she was. I couldn't seem too interested in my toys, I couldn't come off as someone who was sent to the store to buy milk and came back with neither the milk nor the money I was sent with. Then the bus stopped and we were on my street. I led the way. We walked shoulder to shoulder down the sidewalk. Maria whistled quietly. We climbed up the stairs to my apartment and I pulled the key out of the flowerpot. My mother and father wouldn't be home until five, but the landlady knew what time I came home and usually peeked through the blinds to make sure I got in. I never saw her, but I knew she was there because she said thank you when we dropped the check through the mail slot and I often saw her bony fingers grabbing at her white blinds to watch what was going on in the street. The landlady had no reason to go outside. Her husband was dead and she had already finished raising her children, who brought her groceries once per week. Her income was dropped through the mail slot and we never asked her to fix anything since we didn't want to call attention to ourselves. Maria and I stepped inside, then sat down on the linoleum floor and took off our shoes. I carried them over to the pile by the door and we went to my bedroom.

"This is my bedroom," I said.

"I can see that," said Maria, looking around.

"Who do you live with?" she asked.

"My mother and father," I said. I thought it was a strange question, who else would I live with, but I didn't mind telling her what she wanted to know.

"I live with my aunt. My mother's dead," said Maria.

I didn't know what to say, so I turned away from her and opened up a plush chest in the corner of my bedroom. I let Maria take the first pick of my toys, but none of them seemed to interest her.

"You sure have a lot," she said. "I don't usually play with toys."

"Because they're for kids?" I asked, closing the chest.

"No," she said. "My aunt can't afford them. We're poor. My aunt's sick."

"Sick how?" I asked.

"She's bipolar," Maria said plainly. "My mom had it, too. She killed herself."

I must have been afraid then. What did that mean for Maria, that her mother had killed herself? Mothers went to work in the morning and came home in the evening, they cooked supper, and died only in terrible accidents. It seemed outside of reality for a mother to not only die, but to do so on purpose.

"You do have some really pretty dolls, though," Maria said indifferently.

I was losing her interest and needed to act quickly. I took her into my mother's bedroom. My mother had a coat stand draped with scarves and hats of all different colors. She didn't care if

I played in her clothes, so long as I put everything back exactly how I found it. My mother had all of this wonderful evening wear she bought from consignment shops in wealthier neighborhoods in Warwick or Barrington, things she never wore. I didn't know why she bought them, since the doctor's office where she worked as a receptionist only allowed plain skirts and blouses. Maybe my mother was saving her best clothes for someone else. Just as children had to dress nicely to impress adults, women dressed nicely for men. Though I couldn't imagine my mother taking interest in someone, even in the childish way I had taken interest in Maria, I sensed that my father wasn't the great love of my mother's life. But I wasn't sure if they'd even invented love yet by the time my parents came of age. Maybe she was one of these women who saw themselves as constantly on the verge of a beautiful evening that would change their lives and believed that if they didn't start hoarding cocktail dresses, they'd miss their only opportunity.

"I'll leave this all to you when I die," my mother would say about her best clothes. I wondered what Maria's mother had left for her. Certainly, she hadn't left her any money.

A noise came from the kitchen and it startled me. We walked to it. It was my mother, home early, standing over the sink, washing a bowl of lentils, her hair parted in the middle and tied back at the nape of her neck, conservative silver hoops in each ear. She was mumbling to herself, but she stopped when she saw us. Drying her hands on her apron, she walked up to Maria, bent down, and shook her hand. I overcompensated, telling my mother how beautifully Maria sang and how well she did in school. Maria was at the top of the class, I told my mother. I figured this would reflect well on me and assure my mother that I chose friends well, that I was worthy of friendship. My mother said that Maria was welcome to stay for dinner. She almost smiled. This was the most enthusiastic response I'd seen my mother give.

My father came home and I heard him set his thermos on the

coffee table, then his house keys and his tool bag, familiar sounds that evoked dread. I braced myself for Maria's judgment. If she didn't like my father, I'd have to find a new father. The table was covered in mail; bills, I figured. My mother said hello to my father. She picked up his thermos and lunch pail and began cleaning them out. He came up behind her and hugged her and her arms were frozen at her sides. My father bent down and kissed me on the cheek. Then he noticed Maria, as though he'd been moving through the domestic fog and was forced out of it by a visitor. Strangely, he bent down and picked up Maria. He tossed her over his head and caught her twice, the rough way men played with small children. This stole my mother's attention away from the dishes. I couldn't believe it. My father never played with me. Maria laughed politely as my father tossed her in the air, but she couldn't have been impressed by him.

"Put her down," my mother said. "You'll make her sick."

My mother pulled off the pair of soapy yellow gloves she wore. My father looked ashamed, but maybe that was me seeing myself in him. He was working at a laboratory that ran tests on urine samples then. He made twelve dollars per hour. It was his tenth job in as many years. He was a gentle person and my mother hated his gentleness. Or he was not a gentle person and my mother hated that he pretended to be one.

We all went into the living room and watched *Jeopardy!* In the rare event that I thought I knew the answer to a question, I'd never say. Neither would my parents. We'd all sit there quietly concealing what we knew. A contestant, one of these unassuming ladies from small towns who win everything, chose Words That Start with the Letter D for one thousand dollars. Alex Trebek read the clue in his confident voice that conveyed familiarity with whoever it addressed:

"A texture so fine, it's transparent," he said.

"Diaphanous," Maria said. My parents looked down at her. They were sitting on the couch while we sat cross-legged on the rug. My mother was darning a sock. My father had his hands folded in his lap. The heat was up high. The broken thermostat was burning us out. The teacher on the screen offered Maria's answer seconds after she did.

"Good job, Maria," my father said.

"Look how smart your friend is," my mother said. "Why didn't you know the answer, Ruth?"

My mother and father seemed to be speaking through Maria. Not talking to her, but using her as a conduit for which they might speak to themselves. I tried not to draw any attention to myself by crossing my legs and staring ahead at the screen until dinner. When the moment passed, I turned to look at Maria and couldn't yet assimilate the image of her in these familiar surroundings. After *Jeopardy!*, we ate dinner at the table. The adults drank water and Maria and I drank milk. It was very important that children drink milk, according to the doctor my mother worked for.

"What does your father do for work?" my mother asked Maria, staring at my father.

"I don't know. I never met him."

"And your mother?" she asked.

"Dead," said Maria. She moved her rice around in the stew, then shoveled a bit of food into her mouth. She seemed to enjoy it. I didn't want my mother to know these morbid details of Maria's life. My mother believed that all bad news was retribution for something someone did. Even if she never said it, I thought my mother would look at Maria askance for her misfortune. My mother put her fork down and placed her hand on top of Maria's. My father and I watched her stroke Maria's small, clenched hand. He shared my disbelief.

"I'm sorry," my mother said. "My mother died when I was a little girl, too. We were on a holiday on the coast and she drowned. She couldn't swim."

"You weren't a little girl," my father said. "You were seventeen years old. Practically a woman."

My mother stood up and pushed in her chair. She was angry. Her anger came as silence.

"All I'm saying," my father called after my mother, "is that there's a big difference between a nine-year-old orphan and a person whose mother drowned when she was seventeen."

I didn't understand why my father wanted to die on that hill. He was nonconfrontational when it mattered, but now he wanted to prove that having a dead mother was a contest Maria had won over my mother. In the cool exchange between my parents, I forgot to consider the confession my mother had made. That her mother had drowned. She'd never bothered to share that detail with me, but after a half hour she'd poured her heart out to Maria for reasons I didn't understand. I suspected later that my mother wanted corroboration. Someone to know what she meant when she said she was an orphan. *I'm you* was all she wanted to say and hear. I wanted the same, but we could not give that to one another.

The doorbell rang an hour later. When my father opened it, there was a skeletal, sad, fair-skinned woman standing on the steps. She was the woman from the shop. Dark circles under her eyes, so uniform and black, like she'd painted them on. I looked at Maria. She looked down at her scuffed-up patent Mary Janes.

"Come on, Maria, hurry up," the woman said with a tired voice.

Maria said goodbye to me. She thanked my father. Then Maria turned back to me.

"What's your name again?" she asked.

5

◇◇◇◇◇◇◇◇◇◇

THE FOLLOWING DAY we filed into a small yellow bus. Mr. Fournier hadn't told us where we were going on our field trip. Those days, there were no permission slips. What happened when we were in the school's care was outside of the scope of our parents' concern. The bus ride felt ominous, but that wasn't unusual. More than innocence, we radiated the fear and the power of exclusion as we sat in the cramped rows, gossiping as we rode through suburbia. I sat between Maria and another girl named Jane, whose plain looks and long hair seemed then like the most tremendous, unattainable privilege. Jane was considered one of the prettiest girls in the class and was ostracized for it. But I preferred Maria. I didn't really care for the white girls at school; most of the time I couldn't even tell them apart. I only knew those who were well-known, the ones with important parents who made sure you knew their parents were important.

Maria hummed to herself and brushed her shoulder up against mine. On the surface she smelled like baby powder and almond oil, but beneath that there was the stale, hardened smell of a woman, not a girl. Like perfume that had set in somewhere deep in the fibers of an article of clothing and would never fully wash away.

The bus driver let us out in a round driveway in front of a cathedral in downtown Providence. The tall, heavy glass window-panes cast strange blue and yellow shadows down onto the spotless white marble floors of the large church. As we walked down to the altar in a single-file line, it seemed we were at the center of something sentient and cavernous. Not necessarily in the presence of God, but in something equally ominous and endless. There were so many short, cryptic doors and halls along the walls. I pictured God running in and out of all those little doors, as I wanted to at that moment. Anything to get out of singing these dreadful songs again.

Mr. Fournier led us through a corridor that went on forever. We all wore black dresses, black stockings, black shoes—like small little chess pieces, moving around someone's board. We turned into a smaller chapel that had deep red carpets and smelled like damp wood.

Mr. Fournier's young, demure wife lined us up in the pews across from the altar, placing Maria and Camila front and center. Fournier explained that new arrangements had been made for them to sing the solo together, and it seemed that Camila's father, the mayor, had used his influence here simply because he could. If that had been a lesson about the world, I understood it only vaguely. We rehearsed for half an hour, accompanied by the slow, unsettling music of the organ. The room grew darker as we sang, or it felt darker as we sang. Mr. Fournier watched Maria as he conducted the choir. I stood in the back beside the other altos and listened to the somber music fill the crypt-like room. We sang "Pie Jesu" in our bad Latin. Camila's nerves overtook her and she wet her pants. She had to be led away by Mrs. Fournier to be cleaned up in the bathroom. We laughed, of course, except for Camila's followers, Debby, Susan, and Jane, who gave us dirty looks from the soprano section. We left the cold, dim room and went out through the bright, open sanctuary. Maria turned back and stared at me as we walked. We lined up in the pews beside the organ and lazily continued to warm up our voices, sighing and humming more or less in tune. Camila was badly shaken by it all, so Maria had to do the solo alone. I was nervous myself, but watching Maria helped. Mainly because as I watched her, I realized that no one was going to watch or listen to me. Anonymity came as a relief.

"Settle down, girls, settle down," Mr. Fournier said, standing up from the organ and quieting us with a wave of his hand.

A somber flock streamed into the church, all dressed in black. They walked weirdly. They staggered. Years later it would occur to me that they were drunk. That nearly everyone in town was most of the time. A woman who wasn't old and wasn't young leaned on two men for support as she walked to the front pew of the church. The light from the windows refracted against her glossy pink lipstick. She cried so hard that it was difficult for them to keep her from falling down. She was almost doubled over as she moved across the marble floor.

All of us girls watched her in unison, captivated not only by her outsized emotion, but also by her lipstick. And for weeks after the fact, you never stopped hearing about that pink lipstick. The music from the organ started up and Maria sang. Her voice pierced the heavy atmosphere in the room. It traveled far and it was frightening listening to her sing so convincingly in Latin, which was foreign to all of us. Mechanically, we joined in, our voices traveling far above our heads and all around us, creating a sad aura. From the tall double doors across the church, I saw a coffin lifted into the air. The pallbearers moved down the aisle, some in tears, some seemingly indifferent. I'd never seen a coffin, except on television, on my mother's soaps. I didn't know anyone dead. What it reminded me of was the way ants came together to carry away a crumb of food. A silent, efficient, united front carrying something away, forever.

That's when it occurred to me that this was the field trip. The big surprise was a funeral.

The following morning, I woke up and discovered I'd lost my voice, though I had hardly sung, mostly mouthing the words.

During recess, Maria sat next to me on a splintered bench, our thighs touching. My navy blue stockings against hers.

"I might have to go back to Panama," she said.

"Why?" I asked, my voice hoarse. I didn't know what Panama was.

"Why do you think?" Maria asked, expressionless.

I shrugged. I didn't know.

"My aunt can't take care of me. I told you. She's too sick and the disability check isn't enough."

"You can stay with my family," I said.

"And what happens when they can't take care of me anymore?" she asked. I'd asked the same question privately on my own behalf. When school let out, I asked Maria if she wanted to come over to my house to play and she said no. She was too tired. I boarded the bus alone. I worried I'd squandered a friendship that had the potential to be my only way out. I feared Maria would go back to Panama and forget me. At nine, I wanted love as a kind of corroboration of my own existence. I didn't get it at home. I didn't get it at school. The path home seemed arduous, biblical in scale, like going up Mount Moriah. I'd have to ride the bus all the way to the end of Pawtucket Avenue, then turn onto my street, walk four blocks past the man who neglected his dogs, climb the crumbling cement steps to my apartment, fish the keys out of the pot of dead marigolds, turn the lock, push the door open, and face the empty apartment that looked like a close replica of a place where people lived but wasn't one at all. The wait for my parents to get home from work would be long, and when it was over, they'd offer me no consolation.

The bus door opened. I saw Maria's small outline walking

down the row. I was elated. She sat down beside me and put her bag down at her feet.

"I changed my mind," she said.

"Thank you," I replied.

Once home, I oriented myself around Maria. I acted as she did: sitting when she sat and standing when she stood. She sang while she drew and because of the nature of our school, she only sang hymns. I was better at drawing, but then again Maria never seemed interested in demonstrating her ability to draw. She wasn't interested in laboring over colored pencils to represent anything clearly, as it might exist in the world. She didn't draw the sofa like I did, with no one sitting on it, just to show I could. Drawing was what Maria did to pass the time as she sang and, more importantly, as she thought her thoughts that I was eager to know.

"Is your aunt getting better?" I asked her. She stopped singing.

"She's never gonna get better," Maria said with finality. She didn't feel like talking. I knew enough to be able to sense when a person didn't want to speak to me. I could almost hear my mother telling me to mind my business or my father setting a piece of paper in front of me and telling me he needed quiet as I sat across from Maria and sketched the scene available to me through the dirty window, obstructed by a jagged circle of yellow leaves.

6

∿∿∿∿∿∿∿∿∿

MY MOTHER TOLD me she and I were going away, without my
father. On a vacation. I called Maria to tell her the news.

"I'm going on a trip, so I won't be around for two weeks," I
said.

"Two weeks?" Maria asked, over the static on the line.

"Yeah, it's a big trip."

"Is someone dead?"

"Not as far as I know."

"Usually when you go on a big trip out of the blue, it's because
someone's dead or gonna die."

"I guess I don't really know. My mom didn't say. Maybe someone is dead?"

"Probably." Maria put down the phone and I heard a muffled
movement in the background of her apartment. "I've gotta go now.
I have to go down to the pharmacy for my auntie's Zoloft."

"Okay, bye," I said. Then strangely, "I love you."

My mother did crosswords at the airport bar. She rarely drank,
but when she did, she got cheery and then she got sad. We boarded

the plane and stopped in Amsterdam. I drew in the margins of my illustrated Bible all the way to Nairobi. The open-air baggage claim at the airport was small and the weather was dry and hypnotic. My mother waved down one of the taxis parked in the arrivals area. The driver took us to a white hotel, lined with tall palms.

We slept by the pool for a while and when we woke up, my mother stood up and gathered our things. Her one-piece bathing suit was too big for her, as she'd lost so much weight working, working, working. She took off her sunglasses and told me that she had someone to introduce me to.

"Who?" I asked.

"You'll see."

We walked into the restaurant at the top of the hotel. The dining room overlooked a main street, and its balcony rested above the date palms and below, through their fronds, the tops of people's heads could be seen getting in and out of cars.

My mother walked us over to a table where a man sat with his three children. She hugged him.

"This is my brother," she said. I didn't know my mother had any brothers or sisters. She seemed to come out of the blue, but then, nobody came out of the blue.

I shook my uncle's hand and sat down.

"These are my children," he said and the boy and two girls introduced themselves, making me immediately feel welcome and part of their fun. But I didn't feel like having fun. My cousins wanted to go swimming. I told them that I'd just been at the pool and that I'd come meet them in a little while. My uncle told them to eat first, but my mother told him to let them go. Things between them were tense, cold.

My cousins stripped down to their bathing suits. It was a hot day. Nearly one hundred degrees. The sky was blue. It was a week from Christmas.

"Don't you want to go and swim with your cousins? In the

pool?" my uncle asked. I stared back at him blankly, and smiled, waiting for my mother to answer for me. She shrugged. I had no interest in anyone my age, aside from Maria. Nothing in this country appealed to me. I wanted to be back in my apartment on Pawtucket Avenue, watching Maria draw, watching her sing, watching her watch *Jeopardy!*

"It's nice to have other children to play with. Wouldn't you be happy if you had a brother or sister?" He smiled at me as he spoke. "It's lonely being the only one, isn't it?"

He looked at my mother as he said this, but she wasn't smiling.

"You aren't lonely, are you, Ruth?" She turned to face me; I shook my head. My mother looked at her brother. "Anyway, who's to say having a sister or brother would make her less lonely? I had you and it made no difference."

My uncle, my mother, and I drank our tea and ate our sausages. My uncle asked me questions about school, about our president, about winter. I gave quick, one-word answers and scarfed down the rest of my food. My mother pulled my plate away before I had a chance to finish. The server cleared everything away and my mother asked her to charge it to the room, but my uncle took out a crisp green bill. This wasn't American money. It occurred to me that here the presidents were Black. For some reason, that made me very homesick.

An hour or so later, my cousins ran back into the restaurant, the oldest holding the youngest, who was bleeding badly from her mouth. She'd cut her lip open while diving into the pool. My mother took off the white robe she was wearing and cleaned up the blood. Then my uncle said goodbye in a hurry and told the children to say goodbye. From the balcony, I watched him carry his daughter into a taxi. I could still hear the girl crying.

My mother and I rode the elevator down to our hotel room and ordered sodas from room service. She opened a brown bottle of milky liquor from the mini-fridge and poured herself a glass. She combed my hair as we watched soap operas on the small television. She put my hair in pink rollers and tied it up in a satin scarf printed with white flowers. When the sun was setting, very late in the day, she ran me a bath. She told me she needed to go down to the small kiosk in the hotel lobby that sold cosmetics and toiletries and told me not to open the door for anyone.

I lowered myself into the bath, careful not to submerge my hair. Some time passed and the bath, which had been hot, grew cold. I stared at the clean blue tile that lined the walls of the windowless bathroom. My clearest memory of the country overall was of those blue tiles. I dried myself off and put on a dress my mother had packed for me. I toyed with the television remote, but I couldn't find any programs for children. So I just watched the news. The anchor was a pretty brown-skinned woman with straight teeth so white they looked artificial. She read off the week's weather in a bright voice, pointing to numbers that floated behind her head.

My mother came back with two bags and a box of pizza. She said grace quickly. We spread out napkins on the spare bed and ate while the television played in the background. She patted my head and left the room to run herself a bath.

"I got you a bottle of nail polish," she said. We weren't allowed to paint our nails in school. It was too suggestive, but it was a holiday and we were in another country where there were different rules.

I got up from the bed and sat on the blue porcelain toilet and painted my fingernails. I watched my mother in the tub, submerged up to her neck, shrouded by a film of white soap. She kept her eyes closed, but every so often she opened them and asked if I was alright. I nodded.

"Is anyone dead?" I asked.

"What do you mean?"

"Did we come here because someone died, I mean?"

She sank deeper into the bath.

Later that night, my mother and I went out on a walk. She needed to buy Kotex. We went up a dim street. My mother pointed at a large, beautiful, old building that looked like something left over from a lost time and she told me that it was where she went to school when she was a girl. She lifted me into an opening in the building's fence and followed me inside. In the middle of the courtyard there was a tall bust of a man's head: European, thin nose, neat hair, frightening eyes.

"That's the founder, the old headmaster," she said. "He went on to be the archbishop of Mombasa."

"You went to school here?" I asked. My mother nodded. I never considered my mother as a girl before then. I imagined she was born thirty years old, the rollers already pinned into her hair. Had my mother also been young? Had she also felt alone? Had she also been childlike and afraid? Was it possible? The thought of my small mother in a uniform, walking through the tall iron gates of this school, left a dull, old feeling in my chest. I felt a closeness with her and thought to naively confide in her.

"The music teacher, he gave Maria a pair of pearl earrings."

"And why did he do that?"

"He loves her," I said. "Big pearl earrings, as a gift."

"You shouldn't latch on to people so easily," my mother said. "Did it ever occur to you that maybe Maria isn't telling the truth?"

I shook my head. I didn't push. Maybe my mother had a point. She pushed herself through the fence and led me back out to the street, and we walked on to the supermarket where she bought herself tampons and a bottle of orange soda for me. Those were my memories of Kenya: the Kotex, the sickly sweet orange soda, the blue bathroom tile. That was all. Not a country so much as a small hotel room. Back at the hotel, before I shut my eyes to go to sleep, my mother turned to me. My mother spoke carefully, as if trying to justify how she'd spoken to me before. Not to apologize; she never did say *sorry* to me. I didn't expect her to.

"My brother's wife," my mother said, "killed herself. She hanged herself. Do you know what that is?"

I nodded. Something in me absorbed those words and all her other language, too. Dead like Maria's mother, dead like the saints.

"If only she'd been stronger," my mother said. "What will her children do now?"

I shrugged.

"You should be grateful for me, Ruth, for all I do for you. I'll never leave you."

"Thank you," I said.

"Being a mother isn't easy, but you don't just up and kill yourself at the first sign of difficulty." My mother paused. "How selfish. Now none of those children have a mother. Without a father, you can manage, but no mother?" She was no longer talking to me. "How will those kids ever know who they are?"

And who was I? A tourist in a hotel room in a hot city whose native language I did not know. I shrugged again; I carried out that one-sided conversation with my mother. I thought of Maria, her dark blow-dried hair. I thought then that if my mother killed herself, at least I'd have Maria to tell me how to live.

We spent the weeks of the holiday traveling from one relative's home to the next, not turning down the food we were offered, though we had no appetite left. Not wanting to offend anyone, we accepted whatever we were offered and expressed gratitude. When an aunt or uncle asked my mother how my father was, how her marriage was, she said it was very good. She said she was very happy. When I was asked how I was, I said that I was very happy, too.

On our final morning, my mother packed up my bag and was especially kind to me. *There was no funeral because when you kill yourself, they don't give you one,* my mother explained as she covered my face in Vaseline and tied my hair back. We scanned the small hotel room for things we might have forgotten, but we hadn't brought much to begin with. I followed her to the elevator. She pulled the pins out of her hair and smoothed it over her shoulders as we rode down the floors. Her hands shook noticeably. I looked at her and felt that I knew nothing about her. And what's more, I didn't want her to explain herself to me.

We stood in the circular driveway watching a heavy European couple smile in lieu of conversation as dark bellboys loaded their luggage into a cab. My mother hailed a car and spoke to the driver in Swahili. He had a soft voice and nodded attentively as my mother told him where we needed to go.

"Did you have a nice time in Kenya?" he asked me, in perfect English.

"Yes," I said, "I did."

My mother and I flew out from Nairobi. After a long layover in Heathrow with many delays, we watched the Atlantic pass under us and then we were home. She made a phone call before we boarded the Greyhound back to Rhode Island. She told me that my father would like to say hello to me. He missed me, apparently. I didn't want to talk to my father. Up to you, my mother said. My mother didn't insist, characteristic of her strange way of parenting where she had no strong opinions about the important things but she'd die on the hill of my skirt being unironed. She offered me a turkey club and a bag of potato chips from the kiosk in the bus station, but I couldn't eat. I told her I'd wait until we got back home and saw Maria for dinner. I didn't want to be away from Maria again. Back at the apartment, I rushed past my father and ran to the phone. I called Maria and when her aunt picked up, she sounded afraid. Her paranoia had progressed and she didn't trust that you were who you said you were. She would ask a million questions. I resented her then for the wasted time spent telling her it was me, Ruth. Ruth from Our Lady. Ruth who lived on Pawtucket Avenue; yes, my mother worked for the ear, nose, and throat doctor on Mineral Spring. Yes, I was the Black one. Yes, I was in Maria's class. I'd come over for supper last month and we'd had mackerel.

Her aunt had overcooked the small fish and they were tough and bland. I responded calmly to the interrogation. She handed the phone over once I'd answered the questions to her liking.

"Maria," I said, "guess what?"

"What?"

"My aunt hanged herself. Someone *did* die, that's why we went on the trip," I said.

"I knew it!" said Maria. I was glad that Maria and I shared this morbid way of looking at the world. I would have been glad to have anything in common with her. My father sat in a wooden chair by the kitchen phone and watched me as I smiled. I was sad about my aunt's death, insofar as a child could be sad about someone dying whom they never knew, but I couldn't help but laugh hearing Maria's voice. I asked her if she wanted to walk over for dinner. I hung up the phone and stood in place. My father reached out his arms.

"Give me a kiss. I missed you," he said, beckoning me over. My father was the more tender parent. But that was not saying much. Still, I didn't trust him reaching out for me. There was no precedent for hugs and kisses. Sometimes, if he had change in his pocket, my father would give me a dollar for candy. I would use this money to buy Maria soda, stationery. She never thanked me. Sometimes she'd look my gifts over and hand them back, saying they were wasteful or too much.

I wondered what my father did the days my mother and I were away in the Kenyan hotel. I had a very flat image of my father. As someone who worked, ate, slept, and retreated into himself more and more extremely. I was more concerned with how Maria fared while I was gone. I climbed into his lap and kissed him on the cheek. I put my own desires aside. I had to be on guard. Here was another mother who had taken her life. Did fathers kill themselves, too? I put my short arms around his neck.

"Don't hang yourself," I whispered.

"What was that?" he asked.

7

MARIA SLEPT OVER my first night back in the country. She'd changed since I saw her last, grown into her features in a way I hadn't. My mother, who never smiled, smiled at her across the table. It wouldn't be unfair to say my mother wasn't a friendly woman. She seemed to have her sights on Maria, almost as if she'd use her to get to heaven. Finally an orphan she could put all her kindness into. My mother wanted more out of life. More than I could offer. I was spoiled and lazy in my mother's eyes, Americanized. She ladled another spoonful of beans over Maria's rice. Maria ate quickly. She was hungry. My father poured her more milk. I sat across from her and served myself. It felt like us girls were at the head of the table, but the table was square and had no head. The head was wherever I looked. Maria appeared in charge. As my parents filled her glass and her plate, it was like they were placing their best things down at a shrine. I wasn't jealous. I had the sense to know that if you find someone better or more beautiful, you support them. The fourth chair at the kitchen table was finally filled.

There's a photograph taken around that time at Maria's tenth birthday. She's sitting at the table in our kitchen, frowning before a birthday cake lit up with those trick candles that never go out. Her bottom lip is a bruised shade of pink and her eyes are wide, but not fearful. She sits up tall in a way that's natural to her. She conceals an awkwardness that belongs to girls in the window of time after their sexual organs develop and before they know what to do with them. I'm not in the photograph because I'm the one behind the camera. My mother and father are cut out of the frame, but I recognize their bottom halves. My mother's hands are clasped together and my father's arms drape against the back of the chair. There are kids from the neighborhood scattered in the periphery, faded by light leaks. We didn't know the other children well because we didn't go to the public school down the road. The other people there were interchangeable to us anyway. Or to me, at least. These pictures were kept in a shoebox in the bottom drawer of my dresser. I looked through them sometimes as a teenager, as one looks through the detritus from childhood, searching for some well of emotion to provide, in order to make art after a dry spell or to craft workable self-mythologies. But there are few photographs of me, apart from the ones taken at school. There's one I remember, from when I turned eleven, snapped at the clean, mostly white beach in Charlestown where my father took us one Saturday each summer. Maria and I are holding each other at the waist, standing in the sand. A few minutes later, a mother starts shouting and approaches groups of tanners, looking more and more desperate. The woman runs back and forth from the shore, her breasts spilling out of a too-small Hawaiian-print halter top. In a frenzy, she loses her footing and falls in the sand, while calling out a name I can't remember. Strangers stand up and help her search the coast, but the beach isn't crowded to begin with and even the children understand what has happened. Maria pulls her arm away from my waist and is frozen in shock. We each consider the limited possibilities. Either someone took the child or she is dead in the water. My father takes our hands and shakes the sand from our beach towels. I've never seen a person's face contort the way that woman's does as she pleads with the lifeguards to scan the beach again. People stand up and get into their cars and we follow suit.

Why did driving home feel like a total desertion of that panicked woman who we did not know? A part of me was left on the beach, a part the photograph captures and also marks the dissolution of. The part that believes in coherence, resolutions. A new understanding: that a parent brought a child to the beach and left childless. Childhood was the apprehension of these lacunae, these unfillable gaps. Maria held my hand as we drove up I-95, and my father wiped his face as he drove. When we neared our neighborhood, we stopped at a Cumberland Farms and he bought us hot dogs and root beers.

"How was your day at the beach?" my mother asked when we returned home. He told her it was very good.

During that summer, Maria came over for dinner almost every night. Her aunt weighed no more than ninety-five pounds and looked like she was vanishing into herself completely, very eager to disappear. She was a very bleak picture of womanhood. Maria really was an orphan. Maria and I bathed together after we ate. Maybe that was strange. I didn't think so. There were still these other stories about the Fourniers and Maria, but I didn't ask. I couldn't stand to hear Maria talk about anyone else. My mother never listened to (what she called) secular music, but she loved Billie Holiday. In retrospect, Holiday was a very Catholic figure: long-suffering, impoverished, schooled in a convent as a child. With Maria, I was reminded of the song "Don't Explain," where Holiday sings to her unfaithful lover who comes home with lipstick stains on his collar, asking not that he stop wandering, but that he be discreet. "Hush now, don't explain," Holiday sings repeatedly. It's a sad, defeated song, a song about looking the other way, about being unable to bear knowing what is already obvious. When Maria didn't come home with me on the school bus, the Fourniers drove her where she needed to go. They paid her a meager allowance, even dropping off groceries to Maria's aunt on occasion. I suspected they weren't just being charitable. Those nights without her were painful nights. The happiness of my days with Maria overshadowed my days without her. The only significant marker of time that summer was how tall Maria grew, at first imperceptibly, then rapidly, like a shoot breaking through the surface of the earth. I must have grown, too. In school that autumn, someone mistook me for Maria from behind. Sometimes, in the intervening years, I forgot I was a girl and the fact struck me unawares as I caught sight of my varnished toenails in plastic sandals. Later, I'd forget I was a woman.

8

◇◇◇◇◇◇◇◇◇◇◇

GROWING OLDER FOR Maria was a constant disavowal of her old self. *This is who I am. No, correction,* this *is who I am,* she said in her phases and experiments in self-construction. I could scarcely keep up. My inseparability from Maria was not something I took for granted. I felt it could be dissolved at any time, so I didn't question the qualities she claimed for herself or consider the fact that I might have qualities that didn't agree with hers. She was the first person I knew who made assertions about her own personality. This was the first I had heard of carefully wrought self-mythologies apart from the half-living, half-dead realm of literature and the Bible—works of fiction that I read as being for and by men, with marginally important feminine interlopers that had nothing to do with me. My mother and father never made these kinds of generalizations about their inner lives or ways of being, except for my mother being an orphan, which was more a fact than a disposition.

"I'm an extrovert," Maria decided at the start of sixth grade.

Extrovert—is that a medical condition? I didn't know.

"Meaning, I thrive off of attention from others and being around others."

That struck me as inaccurate, but if she said it about herself, it must have been true enough.

"Also, I'm not the type of woman who gets married," Maria said, over the sound of the lecture going on.

"*You're* the type of woman that gets married," she told me. This was said during the sexual education class all the middle school girls had to take. Or it may be more accurate to call it lessons in abstinence, since chastity until marriage was the only 100 percent effective birth control there was.

"She doesn't know what she's talking about," Maria whispered to me across the double desk as the gym teacher, Ms. Myles, flipped through her slides. "*She's* a lesbian."

More a hiss than a whisper.

"Maria, quiet down," the young, overzealous teacher's assistant said.

Maria rolled her eyes. *Lesbians, extroverts.* There was apparently an entire world that I was totally ignorant of. The reason I didn't know anything was because my parents didn't allow me to read the women's magazines Maria had access to through her aunt. As the health class spun into quoting verses from the Bible at length, I tried to arrive at ways to describe myself, but could go no further than the pronoun *I. I am. I am.* That was a start, wasn't it? Class droned on. I didn't know how we could be subjected to such routine boredom and also be expected to use our brains. The fact that not using one's brain was the point was becoming clear, even to me, who arrived at the facts so slowly. If I didn't know who I was, or was on the trajectory to become, I was sure I only needed to be attentive since Maria would be more than willing to tell me. She'd already explained that I was the marrying type. The bell went off, school let out. A couple hundred girls were ejected from the old brick building like mourning doves freed from cages they'd been trained to fly back into.

9

◇◇◇◇◇◇◇◇◇◇

BY THE TIME we were in middle school, my parents had really taken Maria in, doing for her the things a parent does since her aunt was in and out of the hospital, increasingly paranoid and depressed. Maria and I both got our physicals for free from the doctor my mother worked for, and when Maria started to wheeze when the dogwood trees bloomed in spring, my mother snuck an inhaler out of the office for her. Maria's aunt, on the other hand, had shirked, or was no longer lucid enough to understand, her responsibilities as a guardian. Rather than protecting Maria from the world, her aunt spent all her energy protecting herself from other imperceptible forces. Taping cardboard over her walls and cutting her wrists with dull blades. She believed there was a conspiracy to bring her to hell. She turned on the gas on the stove and tried to suffocate herself like in an old-time movie. The downstairs neighbors intervened and she chased them away with a knife. Maria tried to conceal it all from me, but I saw. I only went to their apartment on the other side of town a handful of times over the years, and what I

60

witnessed in her aunt was enough to show the situation was dire. Sometimes I wondered if Maria wasn't in danger. If, during an episode, her aunt would not pull a knife on her, too. I went over once to help Maria relax her hair. We bought a box of the white chemical straightener, gloves, and Vaseline, and spread out on the bathroom floor. Maria took off her shirt and her jewelry. She was naked in the afternoon sun and I parted her hair into four plaits. As I smoothed the Vaseline over her hairline, her aunt burst into the bathroom, shouting, holding a box of tampons.

"What the hell are these?" she asked Maria. Maria's hands shot up to cover her bare chest.

"What do you think they are?" Maria asked.

"Virgins can't use these," her aunt said. "You having sex?"

"No. Are you?" Maria asked.

"Don't be fresh. If you get pregnant, I'll kill you. I don't want any fucking babies in my house."

"You're nuts," Maria shouted back. I sat there in silence, my latex gloves resting in Maria's hair.

"You're just like your mother. Can't keep your legs closed."

Maria's aunt was the first adult I knew whose death I could picture with perfect clarity—corpse, casket, and all. I had no idea, before her, what it meant for a person to be completely doomed, to be so close to the precipice all the time. Her name was Jocelyn, but we seldom used it. It was mostly reserved for extreme situations, like shouting *fire* or *he's got a gun*. Less an identifier and more a final warning in an extreme situation. Hard to know as a child when you're in an extreme situation. Jocelyn thought the FBI was following her with satellites planted in trees, so she lined her windows with tinfoil to block the rays and bought a gun. Jocelyn cut up her thighs with a razor and said God told her she could save her soul with twenty slits on each leg. That, according to the messaging we received at school, was the most sane of the outbursts. You couldn't totally write self-flagellation off or say it had no precedent. These things had a way of normalizing themselves.

One afternoon Maria and I walked to the pharmacy. We were off to get her aunt's lithium. Jocelyn was often short with the pharmacists and quarreled with them, and to avoid those kinds of scenes, Maria picked up her medicine for her. The medication was supposed to be ready when we got there, but there was some sort of shortage or delay. The soft-spoken brunette who took care of us at the counter told us that she would be able to fill the script, but it would take her a moment and we should wait. Maria and I wandered the aisles of the drugstore, trying out nail polish in the cosmetics aisle. I painted my left hand red and she did hers silver. Later we would have to take it off since we weren't allowed nail polish in school.

We waited a long time, looking at boxes of condoms and finding them very funny and mysterious. What was especially strange about the boxes of condoms was how they promised safety and peace of mind, which wasn't true since the only effective contraception was abstinence. I told Maria we should go check on how the lithium was coming along. We had been gone too long. Jocelyn would start to worry if we weren't back soon, I reminded her. Generally, she didn't keep very good track of Maria's comings and goings, but if Maria was out running an errand for her she needed it to be done promptly and would complain if it wasn't, accusing Maria of sneaking out to see boys, which, like most of Jocelyn's assessments, had very little to do with reality. Maria asked the pharmacist how much longer she should expect to wait and the woman walked off and came back with a pill bottle in a paper bag. It wasn't a long trip back to Jocelyn's apartment and we walked quickly with the medicine in tow.

As we climbed down the steps to her unit, we heard a strange sound like air hissing out of a tire. Maria went ahead of me and opened the door. We stepped over the threshold calling Jocelyn's name. There was a damp smell and a strange quality to the air. We looked at our feet and saw water up to our ankles, papers and silverware floating on its murky surface. We waded across the apartment and assessed the damage. Each room was flooded. From the bathroom, we heard the sound of running water. On the edge of the pink bathtub Jocelyn sat, soaking wet, staring past us. Maria rushed to shut off the faucet and Jocelyn grabbed her arm. There was a sort of milky, there-and-not-there expression in Jocelyn's dark eyes. Maria struggled against her and turned the knob. Remanent drops of water leaked into the overfull tub and we helped Jocelyn out of the room and onto the porch, where we hoped she would dry off and grow lucid.

There was no use talking to her then and we didn't feel licensed to scold her since we were only children. I told Maria we should call my mother and father or the fire department, anyone. She said we couldn't call anyone since they'd put Jocelyn in the hospital and take Maria away from her. Maria explained that Jocelyn needed her, that without her, things would only get worse. I saw that Jocelyn was the only relative Maria had and she couldn't abandon her now, seeing as abandonment had already been so rampant in her life. But the flood had done a lot of damage. Most of Maria's belongings were destroyed, some clothes could be cleaned, but her photographs and books were now lost to time. Maria didn't even have a moment to account for her devastation, all her irretrievable possessions, because she had to deal with fixing the problem at hand. The landlord came down and Maria finally alerted him to the flood, having no choice. He said he would bring a cousin of his in to fix what he could, but that they would owe him; he would tack it on to the already unaffordable rent. Fair was fair, he said. In fact, he was being generous, and he was only being generous because he was a good Christian, but the next time something like this happened, he would put them out. Maria thanked him. Later, wrapped in a stale-smelling blanket, Jocelyn tried to explain herself.

"I was only trying to fix this mess," said Jocelyn. "Everything is so dirty. I turned on the water because it's all so dirty."

10

<small>◇◇◇◇◇◇◇◇◇◇◇◇◇◇</small>

PEOPLE LIKED TO see their children performing. Parents cleared their evenings for an opportunity to see their children play even minor parts. Even a child playing a minor part badly elicited tender pride in their parents, who couldn't resist the timeless pleasure of seeing their dressed-up offspring nervously reciting simple lines. So it should have been easy and painless for Mr. Fournier to put on the annual Christmas production, but he was temperamental and exacting, airing frustrations that were older and more remote than any of the students he was in charge of directing. It was supposed to be a musical nativity scene with a twist, but wasn't the point of the nativity scene that there was no twist? That the birth of Christ was evergreen and that we could always only aspire to this perfect physical embodiment of the divine? I was involved in the production because Maria was involved. But Maria was unreachable and hard to access during these rehearsals—so much scrutiny fell on her from Mr. Fournier while everyone else ambled about, waiting for instruction that never came. It was a demanding schedule, five afternoons a week, but little was accomplished. There were interminable conversations around choosing songs, choosing costumes, choosing a backdrop. Mr. Fournier had found a young woman who went to the Rhode Island School of Design to paint a dark, celestial mural that would hang behind the actors, but as the rehearsals went along it became apparent he had promised her money he then refused to pay.

"I'm afraid you just don't have any talent," he told her. "I thought you'd be grateful for the exposure you're getting here, but you've been nothing but nasty to me and you're really wasting this opportunity."

"You sought me out," she said. "Either you pay me, or I'm leaving."

"And how do I know you aren't going to go off with my idea and give it to someone else?"

"You don't have an idea."

"It's nasty to talk to me like this in front of my students," he said. "It's very unbecoming."

The art student stormed out. I admired her resolve. Unlike Maria, I didn't think Mr. Fournier was a brilliant, misunderstood artist. I thought he was an old man who hadn't been able to accomplish what he wanted and had retreated into education because children couldn't recognize him for what he was. Maria felt that because he came from Canada and worked as a musician, he understood her feeling of being outcast, unmoored. He was so generous, giving her special attention, singling her out, and she didn't want to consider that maybe he was just stupid or crazy. I didn't want to argue with Maria, who had so few people in the world, about one of the only adults who seemed to show her kindness; and if the school hired him as a teacher, maybe he did have some merit that I was just too young to understand. So I showed up to the rehearsals, agreeing to work with the wardrobe department. It couldn't really be called work because the production wasn't going anywhere, but I was content to sit around drawing sketches of Maria from the wings of the stage.

We were one month into the rehearsals when I made plans to meet Maria in the auditorium after school on a Friday in late November. She absentmindedly nodded and told me she would see me there. We went our separate ways to our respective classes, and when the bell rang in the afternoon, I carried my things to the auditorium. There was no one there and I figured I had arrived early. I took out my sketchpad and my charcoals. I began to draw the pews in front of me and the stained-glass windows that hung above them. I didn't wear a wristwatch, but when I saw that I had made a lot of progress in my drawing, nearly filling up my page, I figured quite some time had passed. I walked into the hall where I knew there was a wall clock and I saw that the passage was dark. It was evening. I went back into the auditorium and quickly gathered my things, then turned back out into the empty corridors. I ran outside, where I saw my mother leaning on her car in the parking lot, her breath white in the cold. When she saw me she looked like she had seen a ghost. I ran to her and she grabbed both my shoulders.

"Where were you? I've been waiting for two hours. I went home and called the school. No one picked up. I thought you were missing. Where's Maria?"

"I'm sorry, I was drawing. I didn't notice what time it was. I don't know."

I realized that they must have canceled the rehearsals. Why hadn't Maria said anything? I turned and looked back at the school; it was deserted. They must have come around and shut off all the lights without checking the auditorium, leaving me alone for hours in the empty building.

"I haven't seen Maria since this morning," I said. "They must have canceled the rehearsals. She didn't tell me. She's probably just at home."

"Maria never went home. I called her aunt thinking you were there."

"Well, she could just be imagining things; she could be lying," I said.

"That's what I figured. I stopped over, I told her I was in the neighborhood. She wasn't there." My mother opened the door and told me to get in the car. Snow started to fall as we drove down the main streets slowly, trying to spot a familiar figure in the dark. There were bright candy-colored decorations on the dead lawns. Trees were tied up in white string lights that flickered in dizzying sequences. I didn't allow myself to think of the worst. What was the worst? She could have gone home with someone else, it wasn't inconceivable. We had been talking less during the rehearsals, since I was offstage and Maria was onstage with the talent. It was possible that she had befriended someone else, but it wasn't like Maria to go off without saying anything, and I hadn't noticed a rift. If she hadn't gone home with someone else and something had happened to her, how would I know? Would I feel it? If she was out alone in the snow then she must have planned for it, wearing warm enough clothes. You couldn't get far in this kind of weather, particularly as a young girl with very little money. But then a girl could use her body to get from one place to another. A girl could go very far without money.

"What will we do if we can't find her?" I asked.

"We just stay calm and look. I'm not going to call Jocelyn and set her off. She's a fragile person. We shouldn't act in haste."

"But what if she's already dead?"

"Ruth, calm down!"

The snow came down unrelentingly and we could not see very far ahead of us. My mother drove slowly and looked ahead calmly so as not to frighten me, trying in vain to conceal her own panic. Still, I saw her alarm as she squinted at the road. She sat with her chest perched on the steering wheel, wiping the foggy window with her left hand, a focused, repetitive gesture that made her vision no clearer. There was nothing to be seen aside from Christmas lights strung along identical houses. We drove from one town to the next, until an orange light flashed on across the dash, signaling we were low on gas. It had been an hour and we knew our search was fruitless. The heat was off in the car to conserve fuel. We trembled as we passed over the icy road. My mother turned to me and suggested we go home, warm up, then try again once the snow settled down. I understood that this was a gentle way of telling me our search was over. We were nearing our neighborhood and I knew we would have to go home, but I protested. I told my mother to circle the block again.

"I can't see anything, Ruth. If I keep driving I'll cause an accident."

We turned toward our apartment and parked the car in the street. My mother took the key out of the ignition and we looked at one another, silently drafting the story we would tell my father. I knew we couldn't worry or involve him too much. My mother took my hand and helped me over the slick curb. Then she let me go as she led the way up the stairs and down the hall, where we found my father waiting by the door. He looked over my mother's shoulder. He hugged me and was relieved, but his expression changed when he saw that Maria wasn't there.

"Where is she?" my father asked.

I looked at my mother. She shook her head, whispering to my father that we didn't know.

"We need to call the police," he said. "We need to tell her aunt that she's missing. She must think Maria's here with us. I mean, it's been hours. If she doesn't turn up, they'll think we did it."

"Did what?" I asked.

"Relax, you're scaring her," my mother said. "You need to be calm and be an adult for once."

"We're expecting two feet of snow. If she's outside, and that's the best-case scenario, then she'll be buried in the snow by morning. That's if no one picked her up; then she'll be halfway across the border by now. You watch the evening news, you know."

"Ruth, go in the living room," my mother said.

"Yes, go in there and turn on the evening news. I'll call the police," my father said.

"Do not touch the television. Go sit down and draw with the charcoals you got."

I stood frozen, unsure of whose authority I should believe in. I sensed that neither of them knew what to do. That we were, all of us, afraid and at the mercy of stronger forces: the weather, the whims of strangers, the night, the evening news.

"Ruth, is it possible that Maria could be with anyone else from school? Anyone at all?"

"I don't know," I said.

"Well, of course she isn't with anyone from school—she's spent every day with us for years. If she didn't come home, it's because she's been abducted. We have to call the police!"

"I told you not to scare her," my mother said. She turned toward me. "Think hard, Ruth."

"There's a teacher. Mr. Fournier. Maria likes him." I explained the music class, the rehearsals. It surprised me how little my parents knew about the hours I spent at school; the complete trust handed over to teachers was careless of them.

"It's always the teacher," my father said, reaching for the house phone.

"Put down the phone," my mother said. She opened the kitchen drawer and pulled out the wrinkled phone book. "How do you spell *Fournier*? What's his first name?"

I told her how *Fournier* was spelled. I told her that I didn't know his first name. We weren't told the first names of teachers since we'd never need them.

"Here. He's the only one with that name," she said. She pointed at the open page. The phone was balanced on her shoulder as she waited. Her hair fell over her face. She had just had it styled, but the snow had ruined it. Her lips were chapped and pursed, but her eyes stared ahead serenely as though she could ward off bad news with a confident look. I wondered how my mother had been when she found out her own mother was dead. Had she, around the same age I was then, faked resolve and looked ahead calmly? Someone answered the call. She put on the voice she used for bank tellers.

"Hello. This is Mary. I'm a mother of a student at the school. My daughter, Ruth, is in your class."

"Oh, I'm sure you'd know her if you saw her."

"Yes, we are excited for the nativity play."

"Well, we are sorry to hear the production's been canceled. My daughter was looking forward to it."

"I'm sorry the school has been so unsupportive."

"I'm sorry to interrupt you, but I sometimes look after a girl named Maria, since her aunt is sick. She and my daughter are very good friends."

"It really isn't any trouble. Two girls are easier than one. They entertain one another, keep one another busy."

"Yes, Maria *is* very bright."

"I hope I'm not being too forward by asking if Maria is there with you…in your home?"

"You haven't seen her since yesterday…"

"Right, of course, I just thought I'd ask. She must just be with another classmate."

"Good night, stay safe in the storm," my mother said.

My mother set the phone back on the hook and wrung her hands. No one spoke. We all just looked past one another, tending our own guilt as if we'd all colluded in something awful and we all knew it. I remember thinking then that that was how it must have felt to kill a person inadvertently, like turning your back while bathing a toddler and finding they had drowned in the shallow water. There wasn't anything that could be said. My mother felt responsible. She put a hand on my father's shoulder and on mine. The snow fell steadily outside the window, accumulating without any sense of what it was falling over, just falling.

"It doesn't mean anything happened to her. Maria is smart. She could just be trying to get some attention. Children run away from home. They come back."

"You shouldn't give her false hope. If Maria's missing it's better to rip the bandage off," my father said. "We all lose people. We lose everything and everyone. Things never stop getting taken away from us, until even our bodies are taken away. Eventually, Ruth, we all die."

"Will you be quiet?" my mother asked. "I'm going to go to sleep. I've worked all week. We'll keep looking in the morning."

My father told me I could stay awake with him on the couch. He figured I wouldn't be sleeping that night. My mother allowed it, cautioning him again against saying anything to worry me. But I couldn't be more worried than I was. I kept staring at the front door hoping she would knock.

If Maria had gone off on her own accord, were we the ones she was trying to get away from? Was there something wrong with my family that would make someone want to flee? And if so, why didn't I want to run off? Was it because there was also something wrong with me and so this was where I belonged?

I followed my father to the sofa, watching him in the nightly routine of unfolding the mattress, securing its legs, pulling out the sheets, throwing the couch cushions down on the floor, unfolding the comforter, slowly smoothing it across the couch-bed. Content with his work, he turned on the evening news. They were only concerned about the snow. No mention of Maria, of course, since we hadn't told anyone, not even Jocelyn, which seemed wise. Her mind would invent something awful and conspiratorial, but the strange thing was that in this context, she might not sound so insane. Maybe we needed the insane in times of high stress to translate our contradictory impressions and concerns. If we listened to them, we might become legible to ourselves in all our uncertainty.

But I wasn't one to override my parents' guidance, not even my father's, which was hardly guidance. I sat down and stared at the screen; a red-haired weather woman smiled in the snow. Her smile, and it may as well have been a dispatch from another planet, said that everything was fine: we would have a white Christmas; all festivities would go on without interruption, without pause, rain or shine, no matter who came home or didn't come home; the world would keep eating and going shopping; our hearts and smiles would be as pure as freshly fallen snow.

"It isn't because your mother and I don't love each other, that I sleep out here. It's that I wake up in the night, from bad dreams. And you shouldn't think that we don't care for you."

Did he worry that I would run away, too? He spoke without looking at me, watching the weather forecast, the small-town news items. I told him I didn't mind where they slept.

"You don't spend that much time in your father's house," he said. "When you count all your years, the married years, the working years, you only spend a short time with your parents. Then you go off to school and marry and you never go back home, never."

"I can visit. I'll visit you," I said, sorry for him.

"You say that now," he said. "The other day I read in a magazine at my doctor's office about something called trauma. Horrible things happen to you as a child and you never forget them. And they make you act the way you do, make you become an alcoholic or get divorced. I thought, *That's a lot of hog. That can't be right.*"

I told him I didn't know. I had never heard of it.

"And I wondered, *When Ruth is gone and she looks back, will she see this as a good time or bad time?* Was this trauma? Right now, tonight, is it a trauma?"

"No, I don't think so," I said.

"Good. You might feel now that Maria running away is the worst thing to ever happen to you, but one day you'll forget it. Because the suffering never stops, Ruth. It never stops. There's a bit of mercy and you think you're out free, then you're hit with something else and it's worse than everything that came before. You didn't ask to be born and yet you have to bear it. Blow after blow."

I nodded, looking at my father in profile. If I were to draw him, I'd make his eyes oversized and glossy. Teary and cartoonish, like a caricaturist would. He spoke as if he were on the verge of some great discovery, the fact that life was subjection to cruelty. Adults spent their lives trying to remember what they knew originally as children and in the same breath they dismissed children's insights. It was the first time my father had really asked me what I thought. When children stomp their feet and say the world is unfair, they're written off as naive. When a man says it, he is on the verge of liberating himself.

"I'm saying this to comfort you. It will get worse," he said. "There's nothing you can do."

I thanked him for warning me. An infomercial came on for a new kind of blow-dryer. My father dozed off. His mouth hung open and his eyes twitched as he sat back slowly and pulled the comforter over himself. I crept down to my room and took off my uniform, placing it neatly in the hamper, making sure to separate my long underwear from my pants, to pull my shirt out of my cardigan. I climbed into bed and I heard my mother call down the hall in a muffled voice.

"Brush your teeth. And say a prayer."

Looking in the mirror as I brushed my teeth, I saw there was no use in crying. I prayed that Maria was only lost and not abducted. I prayed she was warm and not afraid. I prayed it was only a misunderstanding and that she was not so unhappy as to run away. I lay in bed with the quilt pulled over my face, but I did not sleep. Sometime between night and morning I gathered my materials and began to draw a portrait of Maria. I drew her in the style of missing children on milk cartons, with heavy lines and an innocent, smiling, permanently frozen expression, like a face in a funeral program. Dead or missing people were always shown smiling, maybe in order to make us miss them more than we already did. I smudged the dark lines to create a haloed effect of shadows. Fitting for a picture of a runaway or an angel. Then I took a pencil and wrote a small caption: *Name: Maria. Height: 5 feet. Last seen wearing an Our Lady uniform consisting of tan slacks, a navy blue sweater embroidered with school insignia, and a white blouse.*

At the top of the page I wrote MISSING in a bold, official-looking script. Strangely, I felt nothing as I drew. All feeling was drawn out of me and compressed in the fibers of the page where I sketched Maria's likeness. I added more and more detail to the round, young face of this person who caused me such joy and distress. As I drew, time did not pass and I was not myself. It was wonderful to vanish in this way. A night that should have been characterized by desperate searching and waiting was instead spent fervently transmuting pain into a satisfying picture, so much so that I fell asleep with my sketchbook in my lap and slept so deeply that I didn't wake up even when my mother came to my room and pushed the curtains open, letting in the light. She shook me awake. Through the window, cars were covered up to their sun-bleached roofs in snow. The roads were unplowed, and I could see that until someone came to clear the way, we would stay trapped inside. Then I remembered what had happened the night before and I stood up in a panic. My mother, trying to comfort me, explained that we could look once the town cleared the streets. She pulled back the quilt and lifted up my sketchbook. She puzzled over it and held it up close to her face. I moved to pull the book out of her hands. She handed it back to me with a look of real revulsion. An outsize reaction. It was too much, I later thought.

"How awful. To draw something like that. Go show your father what you did."

Hearing himself mentioned, my father came into my bedroom and asked what the matter was. I lowered my head and showed him my sketchbook. He took a look at the page and beamed at me approvingly, holding the drawing up as if it were a shining example.

"It's very realistic. We can show it to the police. She could be one of those artists who work for the police!"

"You're both crazy," my mother said. "Throw that drawing out, Ruth. How do you think your friend would feel if she found out you were drawing pictures of her missing?"

"I'm sorry," I said. "But I don't think Maria will see my drawing since she's dead in the snow."

I ripped the drawing out of my book and handed it to my mother. She sighed and went to the kitchen to pick up the phone, which was ringing. My father patted my back and said nothing. I knew he would not be as talkative as he had been the night before. But I sensed my father understood that by giving me that sketchbook and pencils he had opened a hatch that would not close again, and maybe he felt sorry. He left the room and I stood alone, and my being alone felt final. I brushed my teeth and tied my hair back up neatly. I sat at the table and drank tea and ate bread with my parents while the plows went by, flashing their white and orange lights. We decided finally as a family that we should call Jocelyn. Who would be the one to do it? We volunteered my mother, of course. Then we heard a hard, heavy sound against the living room window, and another. Someone was throwing rocks from the street. The stairs were slick with ice and unsafe to climb. We huddled together at the ledge of the window and looked over one another's shoulders. There were two figures in the freshly cleared streets swaddled in heavy coats. One wore a large hood and the other was wrapped in a tartan scarf: a man and a child. We couldn't hear their voices through the window and over the plows, but when we looked at their mouths, we knew that they were shouting. We put on our coats and shoes, moving in unison down the hall. We stood at the top of the stairs, watching my father go down first, sliding his body against the railing.

"It's me," Maria said. Then the man took off his hood and I saw that it was Mr. Fournier. Maria ran to me and I was elated. I felt it was a beautiful reunion like the story of the prodigal son, that we would all go inside and celebrate that she had come home, since as far as I was concerned, this was her home and she was entitled to whatever we had. Suddenly I felt guilty that I had drawn her as I did and that I had entertained the thought of her not coming back. She draped her hand across my shoulder. My father sprinkled salt on the stairs and my mother talked to our teacher. She had questions for him. She would not be inviting him inside. I tried to listen to the exchange they were having in low tones. I didn't understand why my mother didn't look pleased. Maria was back and it was a cause for celebration.

"You're lucky I'm not calling the police," my mother said, turning away. Maria looked up at her knowingly. Again, I didn't understand. My mother took my arm and Maria's arm forcefully and led us up the stairs. Inside, she ran us a hot shower and told us we would spend the day studying while she cleaned the house. Going forward, she would rearrange her schedule so that there was always someone to pick us up from school and bring us home. I didn't think that would last long since her work was demanding and not very flexible at all, but I was glad that Maria was back and that all that trouble and sadness had been averted, if it could be averted at all.

I put out a set of warm clothes for Maria. Until then, we had communicated only in silent, familiar glances and gestures, but I sensed there was something within that silence that she was not saying.

"What happened?" I asked.

"I went off alone. I was going to take a bus to New York. Then it started to snow and all the buses were canceled."

"Who do you know in New York?"

"I think my father's there," she said. "But all the buses were canceled. So I called Mr. Fournier and asked him if he would drive me home, since he lives close to the station, but the roads were covered in snow."

"Where'd you find his number? In the phone book?"

"He gave it to me. In case I ever wanted private lessons. Now that they canceled the musical."

"Why didn't you call us?"

"I knew your mother would tell my aunt. My aunt hates my father," Maria said. "She thinks he's the reason my mother killed herself."

I could tell that Maria was tired and didn't want to say more. Maria, who was so intelligent, didn't know that New York was a massive city swarming with people from all over and that she couldn't just show up at a bus terminal and expect to see her father there? And if she did happen to figure out where her father was, how would she know him when she saw him, if she had never met him before? In any case, it was true that if she had known, my mother would have told Jocelyn that Maria tried to run away by bus in the middle of the night. My mother couldn't be trusted with information like that. Even if Jocelyn was crazy, she was entitled to know when things became extreme. Maria shouldn't chase after her father. What did Maria need her father for anyway? He hadn't wanted her. I put my hand on her shoulder to comfort her.

"If your father wanted to see you, he'd know where to find you. Since he hasn't looked for you, he probably doesn't want you. Aren't you happier here with us?"

Maria looked at me with her eyes widened and didn't say anything. I hoped what I said would make her feel better and see the reality of the situation. We put on our clothes and took out our books to study. Judging by how angry my mother had been, I thought drastic consequences were in store for us. I figured my mother would take me out of the school and place me in another one, and encourage Jocelyn to do the same to Maria. I assumed Mr. Fournier would be replaced by another teacher, maybe an American instead of a French Canadian, someone local and less strange. But I was no one to be the judge of what is ordinary and native to this place. There was so little I understood and my drawings were also a problem. Was it because of my constant drawing that I was missing the details of what I was meant to understand? Maria's disappearance and her return in the morning were definitely momentous, definitely a shock, but I didn't know what would come of them. I waited for the consequences to come down, but then they never came. On Monday, we returned to school. Mr. Fournier was there and acted no differently than before. In fact, he was in an excellent mood because the nativity play was back on and they were giving him the funding he needed to really make it a success. Rehearsals resumed and my mother temporarily moved her schedule around to see us home, but then that became untenable and we just took the late bus home like before. Events accrued and it was hard to know what to make of them, apart from pictures. Time passed without any concern for its inhabitants who were lodged in it through no choice of their own. I thought often of my father's question: No, it was not a trauma.

11

◇◇◇◇◇◇◇◇◇◇◇◇

"IF YOU DON'T believe what you're singing, why would anyone else?" Mr. Fournier asked Maria, over the old speaker system. He turned to one of the Magi, a tall middle school girl in a long robe, and gave her a disapproving look.

"You are the most wooden actress I have ever seen. You're bringing gifts to the son of God; act like you want to be there." We had a quick, tense final rehearsal and Mr. Fournier didn't appear satisfied with his players. He put his head in his hands and said that there was nothing left he could do for us. I cleared off the props along with the other crew members and we prepared for our opening night, guests already arriving and settling into their seats.

Maria was dressed in a leotard and a heavy, modest robe that was supposed to make her look like the Mother of God. My parents sat in the front row, looking all around silently. They stood out in the pale crowd. I watched them from the wings and resumed my place with the rest of the stagehands, all of us dressed in black. I had learned all of Maria's gestures and lines. Frankly, I was bored by the production, having seen it so many times, disrupted relentlessly by

Mr. Fournier's pedantic interjections about the spirit of acting, the obligations we had to an audience and so on. But watching Maria hold the bundle of linen that stood in for the infant Christ, something stirred in me. After her performance, Maria cut through the throngs of parents and teachers to find me. She asked me what I thought and I told her I found it very touching. She nodded graciously, thanked me, and asked if she had seemed nervous. Immediately, I said no. I was surprised by the question. Maria wasn't a nervous person. She had a deep reservoir of confidence that she could always access, and I had rarely, if ever, seen her appear to be shaken or afraid. She thanked me again and mentioned that Mr. Fournier was throwing a party in his condo.

"Do you want to come?" Maria asked, cradling a flashy bouquet of roses.

"Do you want me there?"

"Why wouldn't I?" she asked.

"You're secretive about him, is all."

"I'm not secretive; there just isn't anything to say," she said.

I pleaded with my parents to let me go. I lied to my mother about who was throwing the party, knowing that she would remember Mr. Fournier from the morning he dropped Maria off on our doorstep. I told her that a classmate's mother was hosting us and that she would watch us the entire night. It was my father who persuaded my mother to let me go, reminding her that I was old enough and could be trusted. On the quiet highway, Mr. Fournier smoked with the windows rolled up and ranted manically about how good Maria was, how she really nailed it. His wife nodded along in agreement. He seemed foreign somehow, impossible to categorize. I felt he came from somewhere far away—not Canada, but a quaint and callous past that was much, much further away than a neighboring country.

The Fourniers' condo looked like it belonged to much older people. Its walls were covered in flat, floral prints, its rooms filled with plastic-covered furniture. Surprisingly normal. As soon as we got inside, Maria was in their liquor cabinet. A few senior girls that I recognized came by in their own cars. Mr. Fournier put on a record, jazz for a hotel lobby, and Maria oscillated between an air of tremendous comfort and a dazed look of inebriation. She was hitting the bottle of vodka hard, and after passing around a second tray of sandwiches, Mr. Fournier walked up to her and whispered something in her ear sternly, sensually. Then he took the bottle away.

I couldn't believe what I was witnessing. This merging of the worlds of pubescent girls and adults was bizarre in its ability to neutralize itself and somehow feel normal. I had a drink to be polite, but I didn't get drunk because I felt I had to keep it together for the both of us. The strange salon taking place in the Fourniers' living room in the heart of their eerie suburb resisted interpretation. All of the girls seemed so happy. Mr. Fournier and Mrs. Fournier, his young wife, were the portrait of a solid marriage, a marriage happier than any of the homes I'd witnessed thus far. Something moved in me. Longing? Recognition. Maria sat down on the sofa beside me, the plastic foggy from the warmth of all our bodies indoors. Her eyes, which had looked so clear and open before the show, were bloodshot. I could see her and Mr. Fournier stealing glances at one another, his reflection straightening itself out in the mirror in the china cabinet. He held his wife's hand as he smoked a thin, long cigarette, but he looked at Maria unabashedly. She wore a faint pink leotard, a black skirt, black stockings. As she sweated, the strands at her hairline reverted back to their original pattern, and it was clear that she noticed this. She ran her hand over her forehead, wiping it dry. She ran her tongue over her teeth to check for lipstick.

Five times at least, Maria crossed and uncrossed her legs as though she were rehearsing the gesture. I looked down at the glass in her hands, which had been full of dark liquor but had become nothing but a pool of dissipating ice cubes. I still believed then that mixing dark and light liquor was a violation of some sacred rule and led to sickness, but in the volumes that Maria drank that night, it clearly didn't matter. I watched her pick lint off of her dark tights though there was no lint on them. She resembled the people I saw sometimes at the bus stop or in front of the market, who spoke excitedly, hand gestures and all, to people who weren't there.

"You look fine," I said. Maria didn't answer me but smiled politely in a way that made me think she wasn't well, in a way more serious than I'd realized before.

I called a taxi from the phone in the kitchen. It cost all the money I had saved: small bills my father doled out on payday and birthdays. The cab driver's voice was kind and hoarse; his car interior smelled like pungent fast food. Maria was slumped over in the back seat; the driver looked at her through his rearview mirror without a trace of desire. I was grateful for that. I helped Maria up the steps to my dark apartment. My mother had gone to work, doing her rounds in the hospice where she picked up extra shifts. I didn't know where my father was. He should have been home, but I was glad not to find him there. By the time we got to my bedroom, Maria was talking in her half-waking state. I helped her out of her clothes and threw them into my hamper. As I tried to pull the cotton nightgown down over her head, she became alert and whispered to me, "I'm sorry I got so drunk. You're such a good friend. You always take care of me."

"Don't be sorry," I said. "We shouldn't have gone there."

"I'm sorry I don't do anything for you."

"I don't need anything," I said.

I pulled the covers up over Maria. I went into the closet for a change of clothes. I smelled like liquor and cigarettes. I supposed that meant I was no longer a child. I felt myself capable of sex and rebellion. But rebellion against what? My parents were too tired to chase after me, and whatever you did at school was fine if done in secret. You could have sex if you really wanted to, but you had to be quiet about it and not say a word until you started to show, then you had to rush the wedding, and every baby was a gift from God anyway. I had this sobering feeling that there wasn't any template for living. That we were alone in the world and no one watched us. Was that why we clung to customs, tradition, and the past, because we knew we had no control over what happened to us and even less control of what happened to others? I wasn't yet ready to grow up. I was not yet ready to accept my innocence had vanished and Maria's also, if she ever had it.

As I straightened out my closet, I found a children's book on the floor in the dusty corner beside a box of outgrown plaid skirts. The book was tattered from so many years in the corner of my closet. I handed it to Maria. It was the one she'd drawn on the day we met. Did she remember? For me it was a relic, for her a scrap. I'd gone back to the garbage to retrieve it after she'd thrown it out, I hadn't known why, but now I understood. I excitedly handed it to Maria. She constantly said she'd lost everything that meant anything in her aunt's flooded apartment, but she was wrong, she hadn't lost everything. There was still this book. Everything wasn't lost.

"You didn't lose everything," I told her.

She looked the book over, visibly confused, unsure of how to respond.

"What is this?" she asked, then handed it back.

12

◇◇◇◇◇◇◇◇◇◇◇◇◇◇◇◇

MY FATHER TOOK a job working night shifts at a group home for children with special needs, though I'm not sure if that's what they were called then. My mother began looking after an elderly couple down the road who loved pudding, the five o'clock news, and racial epithets. Her job was to help them to the toilet and do their shopping. And to hang around in the next room in case one of them fell, which they often did. My parents were sick of having no money. Sick of not being able to go to Florida (Florida was an Eden to working people in our town) or buy a car that didn't shake when you drove it over forty miles per hour. Like a person shaking in the cold, the car trembled going down the streets littered with potholes. My parents were very tired of this business of living from paycheck to paycheck. Me, I didn't really mind being poor since I didn't really think of myself that way. I had food, free time, friendship, uniforms that were only barely undersized. And since my mother and father were hardly ever home, Maria and I enjoyed an illusory and pointless kind of freedom. Illusory because my mother was just a half a mile down the way and pointless because we weren't very rebellious in the first place. Maria might have peered over the line to see what was available to her, but the worst she ever did was smoke a little weed, and even that she was reluctant to do. Maria's ambition outweighed any desire to ever overindulge. She envisioned the worst possible outcomes, at all times, and acted swiftly to avoid them. If she did drugs, she felt she would be arrested. If she got arrested, she wouldn't be eligible for financial aid and wouldn't be able to go away to college. If she didn't go away for college, she'd wind up marrying some nondescript man, tethered to an uninspired job, begrudgingly raising children who could never meet her expectations.

All the same, my mother's speech when she dropped by the apartment between her two jobs was always full of tedious warnings. That night was no different.

"If you sneak out or drink or do drugs, you'll wind up dead in a ditch. Remember that."

Then she said goodbye, gathered up her thermos full of coffee, and pulled the front door closed behind her. It was Friday night and we had no plans. In tenth grade pills and throwing up the food you ate were in vogue. So was talking about your top choice for college. Naturally Maria had strong opinions on all of these things.

"You can't trust any prescription drugs. They kill your liver..."

"Throwing up every once in a while's okay, it's when you do it every night..."

"You'll have to go to a school that has a good program for the arts. Somewhere far away from your parents. Mr. Fournier tells me I should go to Bard. His younger brother went there and now he's getting a PhD in philosophy at Fordham. Which is obviously very prestigious..."

Maria was spread out across the rug in my parents' living room, rattling off her designs on a college far away while I painted her toenails. She didn't want to go to Florida, she wanted to go to Cannes. Later I'd find Cannes on a map. She wanted to act, but only as a way into the industry. She wanted to be on the other side of the camera, and when she told me she wanted to be an auteur, I misunderstood and thought she'd said author. *Author of what?* I asked her. Maria also had a detailed plan as to how I'd become a painter. According to her, the drawings in my sketchbook were "good enough, definitely good enough." She spoke of studio art degrees and residencies, openings and things I'd frankly never heard of. No doubt she'd learned about this world from Mr. Fournier; with his theater world past and philosopher brother, he knew things we simply didn't, Maria explained.

"How much does a painter make? Enough to live?" I asked.

"More than enough!"

"More than a secretary?"

"They make *a fortune.*" She paused. "If they're any good."

That was almost reassuring. I'd have to be good, but if I was, I'd be rich. I'd be able to help my parents, give them the things they wanted.

"You won't have to worry about money in the beginning," Maria went on. "I'll help you with my money from the movies until your work starts to sell...Like a patron."

Riding Maria's coattails sounded like a perfectly viable path. I reached out for her other foot and shook the bottle of nail polish. We painted our toes since we couldn't have our hands painted at school. Private little rebellions that made no difference. Maria went quiet and opened up a magazine she'd smuggled out of her aunt's apartment. She read aloud from an article about women who were waiting until their mid-thirties to have children. Brave women, I thought, but why stop there? Why have the children at all?

My mother walked through the front door hours later than

usual with a checked-out expression on her face. She warmed up last night's dinner in the microwave.

"The man I look after fell and I had to stay until the paramedics came. He's dead." She sifted through the mail on the kitchen table. "There's dinner on the counter. Good night."

13

◇◇◇◇◇◇◇◇◇◇◇◇◇

I DECIDED I would go to art school because Maria said that was what we should do. Once I'd set my sights on that, Maria encouraged me to paint every day. She sat for me in a crooked wooden chair. My mother and father didn't discourage painting since it was a quiet, feminine activity. And it kept me in the house. So long as I kept my windows open while using oils, they didn't notice.

I made sketches of Maria and taped them to my wall. When I had cash, I bought canvases from the craft store in town and discreetly stole oil paints, one or two tubes at a time. I felt a little guilty taking things from the store, because the spacey retiree who owned it was so good-natured and undercharged me every time, but that didn't stop me. I could tell that she was one of those older white hippie types who came to the city for the art school and never left, the type who had strong, vague sympathies for Black people left over from the activity of their youth: protests, mission trips. When I really wanted to steal, I pretended the shop owner represented something colonial and nefarious, but in actuality, I knew as little about her as she knew about me. Maria told me I shouldn't lose any rest over stealing because no one opened an art supply store in a town like ours because they were hard up for cash.

Maria was a good model, surprisingly open to being told what to do. By the end of junior year, the corner of my bedroom was filled with portraits of her, impressionistic, muted half nudes of a girl whose face I'd seen so many times, from so many angles, and who still appeared novel and even alarming depending on the light of the hour. They were unambitious paintings, but allegiant to the model in front of me. They looked like Maria and that was success, as far as I knew. In the beginning it was almost possible to feel proud of my work, to feel a sense of completion.

On Fridays every week, young alumni, girls from East Coast colleges, came to Our Lady to hand out pamphlets and answer questions about majors and extracurriculars and study abroad programs to Italy or wherever. That particular week a girl from Bard came to give an informational session on the school. The girl's box-dyed hair was cut in a short pageboy bob and she wore thick eyeglasses. She told us that her name was Josephine, but that everyone called her Jo. Maria and I were the only girls who showed up to the meeting, besides a nervous girl named Kathy who had never spoken in all the years that I had known her. "Where's Bard again?" Maria asked.

"Annandale," the girl said.

"And whereabouts is Annandale?" Maria asked.

"Hudson Valley..." Josephine paused. "New York."

"New York, New York?" Maria asked.

"Not quite," Josephine said, handing Maria a flyer, handing me a flyer, handing quiet Kathy a flyer. Kathy whispered thank you and looked back down at the floor.

Josephine couldn't get through a complete sentence. She started talking about the size of the campus, forgot the number of acres, referenced her notes, did not find what she was looking for, got distracted, then started listing the majors. Anthropology, art history, art as in fine art, biology, chemistry, film, foreign languages, gender and sexuality, history, philosophy, photography, physics. *Sorry, did I say philosophy? Don't want to leave that out, I took a great class on continental philosophy last spring, all the big names, they certainly aren't teaching you Adorno here at Our Lady, and that's nothing against Our Lady, it's an okay place, but it's a bit limited is all I mean...Where was I? Okay, so...*She started over. *Anthropology...*

Then Kathy, who never spoke, raised her hand. She raised it even though it was just the four of us in the small, hot room above the chapel.

"Sorry," Kathy said. "I was just curious to know, if you don't mind, if it isn't too much trouble, I was sort of wondering, what the theater department is like? To be more specific, if it helps, disregard this if it's a stupid question, of course, but what sort of acting techniques are taught in the program?"

"Acting techniques? Acting...well, I'd have to get back to you on that. You're an actress?" Josephine asked, flipping through her notes, some of the loose-leaf sheets spilling gently to the floor.

"Yes," Kathy said meekly. "I'd like to be."

I looked at Maria, who was studying the pamphlet intently, holding it up close to her eyes.

"I took a wonderful class on Chaucer last fall, you know Chaucer, *Canterbury Tales*? And for our final, you know, our final project, we did a reenactment! Meaning, we put on a show with this student being the knight, that one being the friar, another playing the prioress, another playing the cook, so on and so forth. It was a lot of fun. I mean it was totally transformative. Each of us had to play five or six parts because there were only four students in the seminar, but it was really wonderful. That's a literature class, though, you were asking about theater, weren't you? Well, I don't have any information on theater here with me, but at the end of this meeting I'll give you all a phone number for the admissions office and you can give them a call anytime. Seriously, anytime. Between the hours of eight and four. Excluding weekends and holidays."

Josephine was visibly nervous as she looked down at her notes.

"Josephine? One question," Maria said.

"Ah yes, please, questions, I meant to leave time for questions. Do you all have any questions?"

"What's your major?"

"Economics," Josephine said.

Then the bell rang and it was as though it was ringing from inside our own minds, because we were so attuned to it. The shrill sound that ordered our lives. We gathered our book bags and lunch pails and stood up to leave for the next thing, physical education. Josephine followed us halfway out the door and handed us lanyards. Standing in the doorway, lit up by the white sunshine from the skylight with the tattered poster of Mother Teresa hanging over her shoulder, Josephine looked like some minor saint, the patron saint of crack-ups, the saint of nervous economists, of women.

In the locker room, stripped down to her underwear, her camisole, her tube socks, Maria put on her bleach-stained blue Our Lady sweatshirt and said, "How about Kathy?"

"I know," I said. "If this Bard is full of people like Kathy and Josephine, then I'm not so sure."

"To other people, we're like Kathy and Josephine."

"Crazy?" I asked.

"If this place is normal, then I fucking hope I'm not."

"Language!" Coach Deborah shouted from her desk, which was on the other side of a thin wall.

"What I'm saying is that I'd rather be counted with the Kathys and the Josephines of the world than with these maniacs who act like they're so put together and nothing matters except who's going to take them to homecoming, and when they go to Salve Regina, if they get in, will some fucking idiot marry them and give them a kid or two," said Maria.

"Language!" Coach Deborah shouted.

But I was normal, I thought. What would happen to me? I had had an ordinary childhood, ordinary parents. When Maria spoke of leaving home and forging a different life, apart from this one, was I part of the refuse she hoped to leave behind?

"Maria, if you get into Bard and I don't, would you go without me?" I asked.

"Of course," she said. "And if you get in and I don't, then you should go without me."

"I wouldn't leave you."

"You'd be stupid not to. You have to think of yourself. Always."

That spring, Coach Deborah gave Maria seven or eight detentions for cursing and cutting class, which she chose to serve in one three-and-a-half-hour marathon, which was her right to do. It was a rule she read somewhere. I sat with her throughout the detention, actually begging Coach Deborah to let me stay. We passed notes back and forth, crude drawings of our gym teacher with a thought bubble floating above her head that said, *I hate children and freedom*. I drew the picture and Maria wrote the caption, then added some details like short, dark hairs on her nose and chin with a rank smell wafting up from her front. Maria was often scolded for cursing, talking out of turn, and managing to disappear for long stretches of class, but the teachers couldn't help but praise her since she was so bright.

She wrote a short piece about her mother that the English teacher proofread before sending it out to a scholastic writing competition, one of those story contests for so-called gifted children. The same teacher said my essay on *Beowulf* showed a general lack of focus and failed to persuade. I got an A minus after rewriting the paper for extra credit. I spent hours on the first draft and just as much time on the revision. I couldn't get my ideas straight or put them in the proper order. Whenever I wrote I agonized over each word, tossing out page after page. Then, frustrated, I'd start to daydream and forget where I was. Then I would have to go back to the beginning and locate what I was getting at, at which point I would discover I wasn't getting at anything.

Maria said it wasn't so complicated. I should just write down whatever opinion I had, then find the relevant passages and plug them in. I shouldn't think too much and I didn't need to bother with revision. I knew she wasn't giving me bad advice to misdirect me because I'd seen her do exactly what she suggested, and when I read her paper about the symbolism of funerals in *Beowulf,* I thought it was very good. I felt again that in spite of, or maybe because of, Maria's original misfortune, she had gifts that I didn't. That she'd entered into some bargain that had made her beautiful and intelligent at the expense of having a mother and father.

For the first time, I was envious. But I would never have acted out on my jealousy then. I rarely gave in to my impulses; I was temperate, always temperate. For inspiration, I asked if I could read the personal essay she wrote about her mother, the one that went on to win first prize. She gave me a copy, saying it wasn't much. She admitted that she wrote it in only an hour. The essay was about the fact that the mental image she had conjured of her mother was based on disparate stories her aunt had told her. Because her aunt was erratic and often exaggerative, her picture of her mother was skewed, made up of many parts that did not match. Her hair was short because she had cut it in a fit of rage, but at the same time she was the envy of all the neighborhood girls for having such long, virgin hair. She was very tall, the tallest in the family, but was much shorter than Maria's father, who was apparently short for a man. She had a chipped tooth from a bicycle accident, but was known for her flawless smile, despite never seeing a dentist. Maria couldn't be sure what was true, so she created a maternal figure who adhered to the stories she preferred.

She wrote in her essay about finally discovering a photo album in her aunt's bureau and seeing pictures of her mother at many stages, right up until her death, and realizing she had pictured her all wrong. She wrote about mourning the person she had invented when confronted with the woman her mother had actually been. She concluded by saying she did not look at that photo album anymore, more content with her own invention. I wept when I finished the essay. I didn't know why, I just couldn't stop crying. It didn't help me with my *Beowulf* essay, but it did something else to me. It had an unsettling effect that made everything seem more strange and remote than before. I asked Maria if I could keep it so that I could read it again later. She shook her head no and took the stapled pages out of my hands and said they were nothing. She had never wanted to enter the competition but was encouraged by the nun who taught English Composition. She hadn't even given it much thought. In fact, the whole story was a lie. Her aunt had never offered these warring, vivid descriptions. She had just made it up, why not?

There wasn't anything left for me in school. The young nun who taught painting for senior girls said I had promise, but that I was better off pursuing something stable like nursing or education, finding someone to marry. You needed rich parents to study painting, she said. She also admitted that she found my still lifes warped and my portraits a little off, not all the way there. I dropped the painting class ultimately; it was an elective that offered me credits I didn't need. Homecoming came and Sofia Romano won homecoming queen with her boyfriend Bobby Something from the brother school, but poor Sofia never came back after Thanksgiving because, rumor was, she had gotten pregnant over the summer and had really started to show. A girl in our year died in a drunk driving accident and we all sang at the funeral mass. Maria got drunk on blueberry vodka before the somber service, but no one noticed. She still gave a wonderful performance. Everyone cried. We applied to Bard. The snow fell and was pissed on and driven over until there was no whiteness left, and when it seemed it couldn't absorb any more human waste, spring came and it melted into the gutters.

One day that last winter break at Our Lady, my father came home from work and parked on the street. He shouted as he walked up to the building. My mother, Maria, and I looked out the window. He was standing there with a brick in his hand. His latest job in construction depressed him and he had become tense, mercurial. He gestured as though he would throw a brick through the window of our apartment. He said as much. I'd never heard my father shout. We ran outside. He was there on his knees on the pavement. He told us how tired he was. How ungrateful we'd been. We'd taken him for granted and didn't know how hard it was to be a man in this country. *This country doesn't value men, it kicks them down,* he yelled. He was sick of paying off someone else's mortgage and working for scraps. He was an educated man in his country. Things to that effect. He was crying. The brick was still clasped loosely in his hand; his wrist was slack. The brick fell to the cement walkway. *I'll kill everyone before I let myself be killed,* he said. My mother, Maria, and I backed away slowly, and when inside the apartment, my mother called the police. She told them my father was having an episode and that he needed help. I sensed this was not the first time, but I'd never seen my mother afraid. We were cautious as we walked back outside behind my mother to stand at a distance from my dad. But we were curious, too, in the perverse way that everyone is curious about the distress of other people.

The cops arrived, two heavy Irish men. My mother told them everything was fine and said the call was a mistake.

"You dial 911 by accident?" the older cop asked, but they didn't insist. Maria and I were standing barefoot in the dead grass. My mother put her arm around my father and the two of them stood under the porch light like actors onstage, moving according to a script neither one believed in. The police car drove away. Maria and I watched from the lawn. Was that love? An unwillingness to incriminate the other person. We all went back inside and watched reruns. Sitting on the couch beside Maria, I held my breath because I didn't want the day to end, but I didn't want this life, either. I was eighteen. I had breasts and ideas. But next to her I still felt small and passive, childlike. The acceptances from Bard came and my mother and father agreed to cosign my loan. Maria got a full ride. She could have gone somewhere more prestigious but didn't apply. I thanked God they accepted me, too. I might have died if she went to New York and I had to stay there at home. I didn't think of our acceptances as equal. I took it as fact that what Maria had earned through hard work, I'd secured narrowly by chance, but I'd put the opportunity to good use however I got it because I so desperately did not want to be left behind here with the narrow possibilities that had so distressed my father and made him want to throw a brick through our window.

14

◇◇◇◇◇◇◇◇◇◇◇◇◇

MARIA PUT ON a white dress borrowed from my mother and pinned her graduation cap into her hair. I tried to stand tall next to her in the mirror as I put on my lipstick. She wore a gold braided cord that she got for being on the honor roll. We were the only Black girls sitting in the pews of the church during graduation; it was strange how I often forgot our marginality in that place or had failed to ever see myself as marginal. I saw Maria as a kind of epicenter, and standing nearby, I saw myself as central, too. The principal mispronounced my last name as I crossed the stage. As I passed from one side of the pulpit to the other, my childhood was over. No relief. Maria didn't smile as she walked across. They hired a photographer with a large camera to snap your photograph as you received your diploma: a camera roll of little white angels. I didn't say goodbye to anyone. Maria and I found my mother and father in the back row of the church. Her aunt was in the hospital. She was six months behind on her rent. A familiar story by then. My mother kissed Maria on the cheek and put her hand in mine. My father put his hand on my mother's back. We walked out in sync like a tight ensemble. My parents drove us to the Old Country Buffet. You could eat as much as you wanted for $6.99: fried chicken, mashed potatoes, creamed spinach, Jell-O. The restaurant had big Norman Rockwell reproductions on the wall. Glossy scenes of rosy-cheeked boys playing with long-haired dogs and pretty mothers around a candlelit dinner table. I could feel the coolness between my mother and father, but they put on a good front. *Do it for the children.* That night my mother gave us twenty dollars to spend at the movies. Maria decided we'd do acid in an empty football field instead. First we had to go procure it. We rode the bus to some girl's college apartment on Benefit Street, someone Maria had met downtown. I didn't trust it.

"What's this person's name, anyway?" I asked.

"Eden."

Eden had a pierced tongue and wore a black fishnet top. She was 5'11" and racially ambiguous. She had grown up in Jamaica Plain and wanted to be an artist. She didn't know why Maria and I weren't going to RISD instead of Bard.

"RISD's the best school in the country," she said. "For people like us."

Us? I thought. I didn't think Eden and I had anything in common. Her apartment smelled like the water poured out from a bong. She invited us in. Her roommates were in the back "recording an album." An overfull ashtray sat on the coffee table covered in black Sharpie drawings of sex. Sweet potato vines crept up the walls. Blank canvases were piled around the living room and a yellow poster hung above a futon that read: DO WOMEN HAVE TO BE NAKED TO GET INTO THE MET? I smelled piss from a black cat that was pacing the long hallway. I was scared to sit down. Eden asked if we wanted a beer. *Help yourselves to anything in the fridge,* she said. Maria sat on the couch next to her. Eden touched Maria's arm, they flirted. Maria took a hit of Eden's joint and sank into the couch. I stared out the window at the empty street lined with old trees.

I sensed Maria knew Eden better than she let on. It pained me to think of Maria leading a life that had nothing to do with me. The sun was setting, deep orange over the tops of the old colonial-style houses. Dusk called up all the dread I tried to push away during daylight hours and couldn't. I walked over to the fridge and took out a Stella. I sat down on a milk crate and watched Eden run her hand down Maria's thigh.

"Maria tells me you're a painter," said Eden.

"Just for fun," I said. I was tired of being there.

"If you don't give a fuck about it, no one will," said Eden. Maria nodded, stoned.

We never made it to the field. Maria was glued to the couch. Eden flipped through her records and settled on Tracy Chapman. We listened to her sad, piercing voice that was nearly drowned out by the sound of the boys playing in the back room. Eden reached into her denim bag and pulled out a sheet of paper. She ripped off a piece and put it in Maria's hand. She told her not to worry about the money. Maria broke me off a square and got up to get a beer. Eden looked me up and down, sizing me up. When Maria sat back down, she rested her head on Eden's shoulder. I put the tab of acid in my mouth, then spat it into my bottle of beer when the two of them started making out on the couch. I felt betrayed, but I couldn't leave her there in case she wasn't safe. I wanted to be lucid for wherever this night would go. Staring out the small window into the blue-black, I wished it were morning. Maria went into the kitchen for a drink and Eden looked at me again.

"You can sit here on the couch if you want," she said. I picked up my bottle and my purse and moved over toward her. I was still in the ill-fitting floral dress I had worn to graduation and my lipstick had faded. I was sure I looked terrible. Eden put her hand on the small of my back. Was this how people were in the world? I heard Maria break ice out of a tray and rummage through the fridge. Eden's hand hadn't moved and the record was still going, louder than before.

"Maria said you paint her nude."

I shrugged. I nervously took a sip of my beer.

"Could I paint you sometime?" Eden asked. She ran her finger over the strap of my dress, grazing my skin with her fingernails. They were reddened and bitten short. Up close Eden smelled like patchouli and turpentine. She'd colored her hair with box dye and it had stained the skin on her neck black. Eden heard Maria walk over and moved her hand away. She reached for the acid on the coffee table, offered Maria and me more. Thank God Maria said no. Eden did twice what she had given Maria and hit her bong, swaying to the music.

"They need to stop playing those drums," Eden said, sighing. "The fucking neighbors call the cops every night."

The idea of police coming didn't bother Eden. I wouldn't be surprised if she spent every night this way.

"Is it safe to mix alcohol with LSD?" I asked.

"We'll find out," Maria said, taking her spot back on the couch. I wanted to be able to get up and leave if we needed to. I needed to be clear, alert. Maria could overindulge if she wanted to. I'd take care of her. I saw a dark afterimage of Maria's face in profile after I turned away. I opened and closed my hands and they felt too long, like they were stretching away from me. The bottle in my hand was light. I held it like a prop. I looked at it and it was empty. Panic: I'd spat the tab of acid into my beer, then drank it. I put my head back on the couch and hoped it would wear off once I opened my eyes. I'd never so much as been drunk and now I was high on acid. My skin was crawling. What would I tell my mother? Maria and Eden were having a great time, holding hands. I felt sick, like I was going to throw up the spread from the buffet. The protest songs were starting to sound sinister and I wanted to go home.

"You alright?" Eden asked. I put my thumbs up and sat up

straight. I was paranoid about every detail—the way I was sitting, the look on my face, my thoughts that I was sure they could hear—but I played it off.

"Maybe Eden can be your mentor, Ruth. Teach you about the industry," Maria said, surprisingly lucid.

"Oh, I'll probably just be a secretary," I said. "Get married. Whatever."

They laughed.

"I worked as a receptionist at a vet's office in North Providence when I first dropped out," Eden said.

"Dropped out?" asked Maria.

"Yeah, like six years ago."

"How old are you?" Maria asked.

"I told you, twenty-six."

"But you said you lived in student housing."

"No, I said I was subletting from a grad student at Brown. Remember?"

I looked at Maria. She looked scared, but her hand was still in Eden's. My legs were shaking and I felt claustrophobic between the music and the smoke in the air.

"Do you two want another beer?" Eden asked. Maria looked at me. Her shoulders were tight. Against the sound of people telling Maria how tall she looked, how beautiful, it was hard to remember she was just a kid. She looked young underneath the fanned-out lashes, hard with mascara. I started to cry, though I didn't feel any sadness. I'd heard acid did that. It was unclear who I was crying for. I stood up.

"We have to go, thanks for your hospitality."

"So soon?"

"We have to be up early."

"Well, are you gonna pay me?" Neither of us said anything. "For the acid?"

Maria stood up and picked up her leather handbag, borrowed

from my mother. A tube of lipstick, some tampons, and a pair of costume gold earrings fell out. She bent down to pick them up and Eden walked over to the front door. If we were in danger, no one's responses reflected that possibility. Nothing seemed out of the ordinary. Even my crying appeared normal in that small apartment. Eden pulled a hammer out from the file cabinet by the door and walked back in our direction. She stood up on the futon and pulled four nails out of the drywall one by one. She stepped down from the futon and rolled up the yellow poster and handed it to me.

Maria was silent. I thanked Eden for the poster, my eyes darting from her to the door. We let ourselves out and ran down the stairs to the street. I looked around the intersection where Benefit met College Street and led us across the bridge over the Providence River. We walked fast toward the bus stop under the flickering streetlights. Some boys in a blue truck slowed down to shout "nice tits" through their windows. We waited and hoped another bus would come. Maria grabbed my hand for balance. She put it up to her lips and pressed them against my knuckle.

"Why do you let people treat you so badly?" I asked her.

"Why do you let me?" she asked, and then she got sick on my shoes.

She said that was how it was supposed to happen. She believed the vomit was cleansing, symbolic, Eastern. Maybe all the food from the buffet had spoiled her stomach, the shrimp cocktails and vanilla pudding. I didn't feel sick anymore, just glad to be going home. Glad to be getting far out of this place. I took my shoes off and got on the bus barefoot. The driver, a plump man with pink skin, took one look at us and told us not to worry about the fare. I didn't say a thing the whole way home. I had this odd idea that if I spoke, a policeman who was crouching somewhere hidden on the bus would spring up, zip-tie my wrists and ankles, and lock me in a jail cell. I also had a subtle feeling I was dying. The bus let us out by the cemetery. I shook Maria awake from her daydream or hallucination. I couldn't tell which it was. As we wandered home from the bus stop, Maria took my arm again. She faced me.

"When we go to school, we have to go our own way," Maria said. "We don't have to be together all the time. We can still be close and be...separate."

I pretended not to hear her. My mother was asleep on the couch by the time we got in. I prayed our footsteps wouldn't wake her, but if they did, what could she do? We were leaving for school so soon, likely never to come back to my parents' house, as my father had led me to believe. My days with my mother were numbered. Any power she'd had over me as a child was already spent. I swore I saw her sit up and watch us silently as we stumbled down the hall. I was startled by a baby picture hanging in a wooden frame by the bathroom. Maria and I brushed our teeth, our eyes bloodshot, and crawled into my bed. Before I switched off the lights, she opened the purse and pulled out a big plastic bag full of weed.

"Look," Maria said, grinning. "I stole it while she was looking for a hammer."

15

◇◇◇◇◇◇◇◇◇◇◇◇

MARIA HELPED ME pack up my childhood bedroom. All that she took from her aunt's apartment fit into a small duffel bag. My room was filled with talismanic, plastic garbage, and I didn't know what to do with anything I owned: cheap Christmas gifts, outgrown uniform cardigans with gold stripes on the sleeves. We went through the drawers systematically, throwing away nearly everything, not knowing what to save, not feeling particularly precious about our childhoods. Not knowing what a childhood really was. All that was left to sort through were the paintings we'd made together. As a subject, Maria felt as much a part of the making of these objects as I was. I felt they were more hers than mine. I asked her what she wanted to do with them.

"I want you to throw them in the garbage," she said.

"Are you joking?" I asked.

"You asked me what I wanted," she said. "I don't want those pictures of me in the world."

For the first time I wondered what would happen if I didn't comply. Maria had no physical power over me and still, her word was final. But girls and women know how unavailing physical power is, since we have very little. Maria knew that. Those paintings were the only work I had, I thought, but I could always make other paintings. There would be no paintings were it not for Maria. And she knew that, too. So we carried them out to the dumpster behind the apartment building. I had a hard time forgiving her for that.

Summer blew by without announcing itself. My father lifted our bags into the back seat of his Ford. He wanted to see us off to college. My mother had to work. She hadn't taken a day off in seventeen years. My mother was the busiest woman in the world. She would have you believe that. She was starting to moan, "I'm tired, I'm tired," the way Americans do apropos of nothing, a sign she was changing, could change. I was eager to run away from my parents; though they were not violent or neglectful, I felt I had a wound that was just the size of their mouths. The anxious sense of protection I felt over my parents, the need to stand by the void so as to stop them from falling in, had been supplanted by other feelings, curiosities about my sex, myself.

How to admit I didn't love them all that much? Especially to Maria, who longed for a mother and father, though she'd never say so. My father drove fast down I-90 and the car began to rattle. I felt my stomach lurch as the car careened down the road. When we got to the campus, my father carried our suitcases into our dorm room and said he needed to get something else from the car. I watched him smoking in the grass through the suicide-proof window that only opened a few inches. He came back inside and handed me a fifty-dollar bill and kissed me goodbye. I didn't notice how old he'd gotten until then. Had my father been a smoker all the while? Everything slipped past me. He looked like a sad, American version of Jesus Christ. Brown-skinned, with shoulder-length matted hair and threadbare jeans. My father's dreadlocks were another thing my mother hated. *Are you becoming a Rastafarian?* she asked him. He told her no, but that he just didn't see the point in cutting his hair anymore. He was just very tired of all of it. I sensed his tiredness. He stared at us for a while. I couldn't read the look on his face.

"You girls be good," he said and kissed Maria on the cheek. He hugged me. We were almost the same height and I saw echoes of his face in mine. When he left, we went down to the campus center for orientation. On the medical paperwork, Maria put my mother and father down as her emergency contacts. Despite Maria's warning about us going our own ways, she kept saying how glad she was that they'd assigned us a shared room. We unpacked immediately, too overcome by excitement to speak. Maria took out a portrait in a silver frame. She borrowed a hammer and a nail from two girls who lived across the hall, from Vermont and California, respectively. She put the picture up over her desk. A portrait of her and Mr. Fournier by the river downtown. Crooked, strange. She stared at the photograph, then straightened it out.

"He was always so generous with his time, his attention. I don't know what I would have done without him."

"I wouldn't give him so much credit," I said. "I mean, he was just a music teacher."

"He was brilliant. I mean, you couldn't tell, he was thwarted. He was stuck in a small town, in an unfulfilling job, but he cared so much about his work. About the world."

"Hm," I said. "Well, you would have been fine without him."

It was the first time I truly questioned Maria's judgment. She had always been bright. Did she think she was only in college because of a vaguely eccentric music teacher who encouraged her once or twice? He hadn't done anything for her. On the other hand, I had been devoted to her, protective of her always. I didn't see her hanging up any pictures of me. On my side of the room, I put the poster from Eden up on the wall: DO WOMEN HAVE TO BE NAKED TO GET INTO THE MET? I thought of my portraits of Maria, sitting in some New England landfill.

We went out walking across the campus. Maria was on a mission to stock up on alcohol, cigarettes, weed. She also wanted to find a camera. She still had the weed she had stolen from Eden, but that was *for emergencies only.* She went about as though she were preparing for a storm. The campus was idyllic in all the ways one might expect. It was true to the brochure: the manicured shrubs and immaculate stone walls and gardens for being contemplative in, the bicycle paths cut into the hills. Even the self-consciously dressed students, in secondhand clothes, projected vitality and openness despite their best efforts at coming across as cool and indifferent. A girl in pigtails Rollerbladed down the curved road; someone else walked barefoot down a grassy path. A boy read Kant and ate a green apple beneath the shade of a tall tree, but when we came closer we saw he was only on the first page. I adjusted quickly and I didn't miss my mother until she called. She didn't ask about my classes, which didn't offend me. I couldn't expect her to ask what I was doing in my philosophy class where I barely understood what I was doing. For fourteen years I'd come home from school and in the afternoons when my mother was home from work, she would ask me how it was. I'd say it was fine. She'd asked me what I'd learned and I'd say nothing. She would ask me what she was paying for if they taught me nothing. But they were teaching me how to be quiet and say *good* when someone asked how I was, how to write in perfect cursive so the shopping lists were neat, and how to do math well enough that I didn't overdraft my bank account. I was cynical about the lives of all those girls I went to school with because I had little hope for my own. Of course there were girls who might do something with their lives other than have children. Camila got into Harvard, but her father was the mayor. And I suspected she would just get married anyway and never use her degree. What my mother wanted to know when we spoke over the phone was whether or not I was keeping my legs closed. Everything was very straightforward with her.

"Remember," my mother said over the phone, "nobody's going to buy the cow if they can get the milk for free."

We read about the sexual revolution in my gender studies class, but it must have missed my mother. A woman was no different from a cow, as far as she cared. If she knew what Bard was, she never would have let me go. Sex was one of many ways of expressing oneself, and expressing oneself was paramount here, I was learning. Being who you were, even if your sense of self was in flux or in the process of drastic refashioning, was more important than getting along with others, being liked, being courteous, loving God, or honoring your parents. After so many years of the monotonous navy and white uniforms, suddenly there were people dressed not to project a sense of order, but to be transgressive and to signal they didn't care if their clothes were old, unironed, stained, or ugly. There was no one to discourage them. Quite the opposite. The clothes Maria and I brought from home were awfully plain compared to those worn by the kids from New York and Los Angeles, but we found we could cut our shirts and jeans up to better fit in. I was glad to have Maria there, as she would never admit to her disorientation. I embraced a uniform of black: black secondhand jeans, black T-shirt, black suede jacket, all bought from a senior selling clothes out on the lawn by the cafeteria. I spent all the pocket money my father had given me on those clothes. During my third week, I sold a pair of leather Mary Janes my mother had bought me especially for school and I used the money for rolling tobacco.

It was hot at night. Maria and I slept without clothes. We pushed our beds together in the middle of the room. The woods weren't quiet. The crickets drowned out our voices with their ambient cries.

"I can't sleep," I said.

"What's keeping you up?"

"Thinking about my parents. I hope they're alright without me."

"They're adults," she said. "They aren't your responsibility."

"Do you ever think about your aunt, whether she's doing any better?"

I looked over and Maria's eyes were closed. Without saying anything else, she fell asleep with her mouth wide open and her arms by her sides. She started to snore. I rolled over and stayed awake for two more hours, not thinking so much as playing out familiar scenarios. My father on the couch, asleep in his work clothes. My mother in front of her vanity, running a brush through her hair for the thousandth time. Maria's aunt, in and out of the hospital. In these long hours between putting my head down and rising up for oatmeal and black coffee, I felt an uncontrollable impulse to touch Maria. I turned to her and inched closer to the left side of her face. I brought my face as close to hers as I could without us touching. She twitched as she slept. I hadn't noticed that before. Something startled her in her sleep; she tossed her head to the side and saw me watching her.

"What are you doing?" she asked, half-awake, turning away.

The next morning we got dressed together. We shared clothes, books, everything. While we were looking over one another's outfits, she suggested we push our beds apart. I asked her why. She said she just would prefer it if we did. Again, I asked her why. She told me she didn't need to give me a reason, which was ultimately true. So we pulled our beds apart and didn't discuss it anymore. Before class we drank coffee together in the cafeteria. Calling it class would be painting a false picture. Our seminars felt more like book clubs and the few lectures I took were more like sermons, except I actually cared about what the person at the front of the room had to say. No more being told to pull down your skirt, no more being sent out to the hall because you couldn't afford to pay your fees, no more talk about sin. The real sin was what these corporations were doing to the planet, so on and so forth. I enjoyed school for the first time and found I wasn't as stupid as I'd been led to believe at Our Lady. I did well in my art history classes, even better in my studio art courses.

On a cool night in September, Maria and I met with some girls from our dorm on a field on the north end of campus. Some straight, others gay. One who had a boyfriend and was in something called an "open relationship." We spread out blankets and drank absinthe until all of our words slurred and our sentences started and trailed off into laughter and nods. We sprayed our ankles for ticks. Ticks seemed like our only problem then. There was a redhead in the group named Sheila with a camera. I noticed she was the girl from across the hall, the one from California who had loaned us the hammer. She showed Maria how to turn on the flash, load the film. For the first time, I saw Maria smile and laugh very freely, throwing her head back, looking unencumbered. I blacked out on the field and felt Maria would be fine, that she didn't need me to get us home safely. That evening in the tall grass was my happiest and I longed for it before it was over.

16

◇◇◇◇◇◇◇◇◇◇◇◇◇◇

MARIA WENT DOWN to Manhattan and did commercials a few times that year. Mr. Fournier helped her book these jobs somehow. I accepted that Maria had relationships that I didn't understand, friends I didn't know. That the overwhelming fixation I felt for her was not exclusive and could be replicated and enjoyed with others. She was in a Pepsi ad that paid her small residuals for a long time. Every so often her agent sent small checks that she spent frivolously. In a sort of "there's more where that came from" way.

This particular Saturday, I went with her for a job. We were early and had a bit of time to waste so we went to a flea market in Chelsea looking for nothing in particular. Maria got stuck by a booth where an old man with cherry red skin sold Americana, random ephemera he'd collected from wherever. I joined her, flipping through a box of postcards from the Grand Canyon with sweet nothings scrawled in the corners. One read *My love for you runs deep.* Maria stood beside me, rifling through a box of sepia nudes. Well-endowed women with manicured bushes. Blonde heart shapes and coarse triangles front and center. Maria had an appetite for dirty pictures and liked to include them in her short films.

"You like those?" the man asked.

"For an art project."

"Oh, you an artist? I just got these," the man said and placed a box of painted religious icons by the erotic 5 x 7s. Maria gave those a once-over, too. She spent thirty dollars, all in all. The best thing she found, according to her, was a set of playing cards printed on the back with scenes from pornos, orgiastic pictures of multiracial actors going at it. When we were leaving the vendor's booth, Maria asked him what time it was, and when he told her, she looked panicked and said we had to hurry.

"I have somewhere to be in fifteen minutes," she said.

"So soon?" I asked.

"I have to leave right now, actually," she said.

"To go where?" I asked.

"I'll explain later. But can you come with me?"

We stood on the edge of a congested intersection while Maria pored over a small map. She threw it back in her bag and we ran to make the light, her pulling me along. We were panting by the time we came to the diner for this meeting of hers. Before I could ask her to elaborate, we were sitting inside and Maria was staring out the window at the street. The expression on her face was one of fear.

"What's the matter, Maria?" I asked. She didn't say anything and looked up at the clock on the wall. Again, I asked her what we were doing there and she ignored me. So we watched the door together and I sat there with her because she had asked me to. A man came through the door with heavy boots, a dark, slick, full head of hair, and deep grooves on his otherwise young-seeming face. His hat to his chest, he scanned the room. I looked at Maria and her demeanor had changed. She grabbed my hand under the table. Her leg was shaking wildly. She hadn't taken her eyes off the man. He almost walked straight past us until Maria lifted the hand that wasn't holding mine and waved. He slid into the booth and then I understood. The long distance between his big, imploring eyes identical to Maria's, his top lip full like hers. I knew he was hers, her father. A childish simplification. Once, I lost my mother in a department store. As we searched for one another, I saw her before she saw me. I pointed to her and said, "That one's mine."

Maria and her father stared at each other without speaking. Our waitress came by to collect our orders and I waited for one of them to speak.

"Maria, do you want any coffee? I'll have a coffee with cream," I said. She stared back at me blankly and I put in an order for a second coffee for her. It was her father's turn, and he ordered without looking at the menu.

"Lumberjack," he said without a trace of an accent. He'd been here a long time. My parents hadn't been able to shake their accents, which was not to say they hadn't tried. It occurred to me that that might have been the first time Maria had heard her father's voice in her entire life.

"You girls aren't hungry?" he asked.

We shook our heads. He clocked us holding hands. He didn't seem hostile, but he wasn't pleased, either.

"Who are you?" he asked me.

"Ruth," I said. CARLOS was embroidered on his navy blue work shirt. All I knew was his name.

"I like this place," he said, looking around. "They don't skimp on the meat. Real bacon. Real fucking eggs. You don't know what the fuck you're eating in this city. Bite into a burger, come to find out it's horsemeat. Go home with a woman and find out she's a man." He winked.

We didn't laugh. Maria pulled her hand away from mine and took a sip of coffee. Her hand trembled and the light-colored coffee spilled on the linoleum tabletop. She put her mug down and took my hand again. Her palm was wet. I knew it was up to me to speak for her.

"What do you do for work?" I asked, looking at his uniform.

"Clean windows," he said, dumping sugar into his coffee.

"Do you like it?" I asked.

"Yeah, it's always been my dream. When I was a little boy I thought I'd come to America and clean bird shit off skyscrapers." He laughed. His humor skewed hostile. Eager to condescend, he sized me up, stealing glances at Maria.

I heard the door open with a chime. An attractive young woman stood at the counter with one baby in her arms and a toddler in a stroller. She pushed her tight curls away from her face and scanned the room as if she were searching for someone. Then she walked toward us, wrangling her bags and children, and took a seat beside Carlos. She rocked the baby impatiently and asked if he had already ordered. She was in her twenties, with soft, birdlike features and dark skin. She called the waitress over and demanded a high chair. Like Carlos, she seemed coarse, but once she was settled, she looked in our direction and smiled.

"My name's Anna," she said, extending her hand to Maria and to me. Carlos didn't broker any introductions but looked around impatiently for the waitress. His food was taking too long. He wasn't afraid to be impolite, balling his hands up on the table and just barely acknowledging the strange interaction he had occasioned. When the two plates finally came out bearing enough food for a family of three, he took one look at his butter and decided it was too cold. Could the waiter set the pancakes back under the heat lamp and bring them back out once the butter wasn't hard as a rock? Anna asked Maria if she wanted to hold her sister, and Maria shook her head. She couldn't speak and I didn't blame her. The baby in Anna's lap was like a doll, dressed in floral cotton overalls. There was a big, gaudy ring on Anna's hand. As Maria's father ate, his hands slick with syrup, I saw that there was a wedding band on his hand, too.

"How long have you two been married?" I asked.

"We're only engaged. We meant to have a wedding, then the babies came."

"You seeing anybody?" he asked, addressing Maria directly for the first time.

"I'm a lesbian," Maria said.

"You two together?" Carlos asked. "Plenty of your kind in this neighborhood."

"No, my girlfriend's up at Bard. She's white."

I sensed that she said this to antagonize him.

"Congratulations, kid." He bit into his sausage. "Bettering your race."

"Fuck you."

"You called me, remember that," Carlos said, pointing his butter knife toward Maria. He turned toward me and wiped the oil from his mouth. "I came to this city during the dictatorship. I left all my family behind in Panama City. They were all political, died right away. My younger brother was killed, my father was killed, and then my older brother, and my uncle…And I came here, I drove a cab and that was fine, but after Maria's mother hanged herself, I couldn't do it. She was always unhappy, but I didn't know… so I brought Maria to live with her aunt in Providence. I figured I was doing her a favor. I just couldn't do it. I was the same age you two are, I couldn't be a father. No."

"But you're doing it now," Maria said.

"I'm older now."

"I think I deserve an apology," Maria said.

"We all deserve an apology, don't hold your breath," Carlos said, moving on to the ham, swirling it around in maple syrup. I felt sick watching him eat. Anna looked at him with admiration, eating from his plate. She had probably heard the story of his dead relatives many times and had been moved by it.

"You should thank me. You're alive, you're in school," he said. "How's your aunt, by the way?"

"Still crazy," said Maria.

"Well, that runs in your mother's family."

We stayed until Carlos finished his plate. I downed my coffee and dug in my purse for some spare change. Carlos left cash on the table and stood up, pulling the brim of his baseball cap low over his face. With ease, he scooped his daughter from Anna's arms and took charge of the stroller.

"You know where to reach me," he said to Maria, then shook my hand. "Ruth, pleasure."

Maria didn't move but picked at the paper placemat on the table absentmindedly. I placed my hand on her back and rested her head on my shoulder. We didn't say anything. I didn't register how long we sat there that way, not saying anything, but the waitress came to refill our coffees and we stayed long enough to finish them. The waitress had a knowing look and asked us if we wanted blueberry pie on the house, which we didn't. I looked up at the clock and saw that it was nearly time for the next train, so I tried to rush Maria without seeming to rush her. The weather was mild and by all accounts it was a beautiful day. Cherry blossoms in full effect hung over the gray streets, goading us. The brown paper bag holding Maria's erotica ripped open and the pictures scattered on the ground. She bent down to collect them and held the fistfuls of naked pictures at her sides. She walked fast toward the subway, not saying a word. I struggled to keep up and didn't know why she was suddenly trying to get away from me.

"Maria," I called out. She walked on.

"What?" she asked, not turning back.

"We can just take the next train." I walked faster. I caught up with her, put my hand on her shoulder. Tried to console her. "We can go have a drink and talk."

"Talk about what?" she asked.

"That couldn't have been easy, seeing his new family."

"Oh, I'm fine," she said, outpacing me, turning left at the intersection, already in the street before I could catch up to her again.

We went back to school like two ex-believers after a long, arduous pilgrimage, our feet sore from walking, totally disillusioned. I was exhausted and couldn't remember eating anything in the past twenty-four hours, only drinking coffee. But I put on a good face for Maria, smiling over at her and leading the way onto the train so she didn't have to think for a while. Before she tracked him down, Maria's father must have been a wide-open, looming possibility. Now he was just a man, not the demigod she had hoped for. I wished it had been a happy reunion, too. That might have been a better story.

I remembered when Maria disappeared when we were children, how I had never seen it snow that much before or after. She had been looking for her father. Now she'd found him, but of course only on television did these things go as desired. The Bible, television, the movies, were full of prodigal sons coming home, full of seamless repair, resurrection, outlandish reunions at the last minute, but in life you were lucky if even one person said sorry and meant it. If someone walked out of your life and humbly came back, you were lucky and surprised. Maria looked out the window at the setting sun over the river, the storybook scenes left in the wake of the Poughkeepsie-bound Metro-North that would become familiar in later years. Like coming out of a trance the morning after a hard night, she turned to me and sighed, her body slight in the wide maroon seat.

"I didn't have much use for a father anyway," she decided. "If he'd stuck around, where would I have put him? There wasn't enough room for him and me both."

"You know it's okay if you are disappointed. Anybody would be. You have every right," I said.

At that, Maria put her head on her knees and wept. She was loud enough for the conductor and the old woman across the aisle to take interest. The three of us—the old woman, the conductor, and I—couldn't console her, so we let her be.

17

◇◇◇◇◇◇◇◇◇◇◇◇◇◇

SENIOR YEAR, EVERYONE talked of dropping out and moving to New York City, though who knew if it was true or just a pose. Everyone wished to seem rebellious, but at their core their wish for order and approval was paramount, I knew. Not finishing college became the thing to do. I didn't want to leave; I wanted to stay and paint and go to the pub. Even Maria talked of leaving school, which didn't make any sense because she was doing so well and she loved her job as a projectionist. She held a screening each week showing her own work and the work of other students. The theater was full of people each Friday. All of them coming just for her. Sheila was one of the many women who never missed Maria's screenings and always sat in the first row. It was difficult to watch her fall in love with Maria so quickly, to learn of the letters she sent through campus mail, long pseudo-reviews praising *Maria's truly innovative, truly idiosyncratic, nonlinear, post-this or post-that short films.* Sheila came to the screenings with wine and beer for everyone. She had red hair down to her waist, faint brown spots on her face, and sharp, untrustworthy features. I thought Sheila was an opportunist. I told Maria so.

"But what could she possibly use me for?" Maria asked.

"Social cachet. With your screenings and all," I said.

"Yeah, I wouldn't want anyone riding my coattails," Maria said, rolling her eyes. "She brings free drinks. And she's nice. Not bad-looking, either."

"I guess that's cool, if that's all you care about," I said, picking up my things and leaving for my studio. What right did I have to be jealous? After that, I never said a bad word about Sheila again. Sheila came to the United States from Cuba and was orphaned by her mother. So they had that in common. Sheila was adopted as an infant by a married pair of psychiatrists from Los Angeles who organized their practices such that they saw each of their clients simultaneously, for only two hours per day, so as not to miss out on any time with one another. They were very independently wealthy and didn't need to work, but they were called to psychiatry. I was really dubious of that. Maria told me all of this and I nodded along, trying to be happy for her. Sheila's parents overnighted granola and dried fruits to her each month at the college. It wasn't only the granola that they sent. Apparently, Sheila's father sewed two ounces of weed into the lining of a suede jacket and put it in the mail from California. I had also heard that in Venice, Sheila drove a white Mustang, on top of the Jeep she drove here in the Hudson Valley. Not to mention, when she turned twenty-five, she'd have access to a small fortune, passed down from a wealthy grandparent. A film producer.

She never ate on campus. She made coffee, sent from California, in her dorm for breakfast and ate Japanese food in town every night for dinner. She had a Man Ray hanging in her bedroom at home and she had a small "priceless" drawing hanging in her dorm at school, a little Picasso her mother and father bought at auction in New York. I'd never seen it, since she was very private about her room, very paranoid apparently. Everybody had heard the story. So, at twenty-two, she was already a collector. And a patron, evidently, always bringing a case of alcohol to Maria's happenings. I knew all of this because my botany lab partner, Sabrina, told me everything there was to know about Sheila. How Sabrina knew, I didn't ask. I knew that if I questioned Sabrina, she'd cut me off from this wellspring of information she had as the campus gossip. I was one of the only people who had no reason to dislike Sabrina for the rumors she spread, since I was a minor figure as far as life at the college went. There wasn't any gossip about me. I looked forward to sitting by Sabrina and talking about Sheila's charmed upbringing and speculating about just who she thought she was.

The conclusion I came to was that Sheila already had so much love in her life, and as though it weren't enough, she was constantly trying to seduce Maria, offering her dinners in town and free drugs. As a gift, Sheila bought Maria several rolls of Super 8 film and stayed up all night helping her edit her 16-millimeter final, a twelve-minute silent film that explored the history of ascetics by depicting quiet, starvation, self-abnegation, and prayer. A tiny first-year played a bright, pious nun, Sheila played the ethnographer. Maria hardly ever left her studio. I saw Sheila, red hair and swimmer's body, more than I saw her. Almost every day, Sheila came into our dorm looking for a book or magazine or article of clothing that Maria needed.

"You don't happen to know where I can find her copy of *The History of Sexuality,* do you?"

"It's on the nightstand," I said.

"And a black cardigan?"

"In the top-left drawer under the bed," I said.

"Thanks, Ruth, you're the best," Sheila said.

I rolled my eyes and mocked her when she left. I played out a one-sided argument with Sheila. I figured Maria had had a hard life. A truly difficult life, with her mother's suicide and her dad not being in the picture, the money troubles. Sheila couldn't empathize with that. Where had Sheila been when Maria's aunt couldn't pay her meager school fees and where had Sheila been when Maria was sticking a finger down her throat and throwing up dinner and where had she been when we sat in the diner and watched her father piss on her fantasies? Sheila was a rich girl from Venice who thought the world was peaches and cream and dinner parties. I thought Maria was a Marxist. I guess I was wrong.

18

◇◇◇◇◇◇◇◇◇◇◇◇◇◇

JAMES SAT NEXT to me in art class but wouldn't talk to me. Wouldn't acknowledge I was there, only a few inches away from his easel, even though I knew him from an American literature class we had been in together. In the seminar we had been assigned *Three Lives* by Gertrude Stein. The book had an unsettling effect on me, and I remembered feeling riveted and afraid when I read it. I had never heard of Gertrude Stein before and was interested to learn she had lived in Paris, slept with women, and repeated herself a great deal. That sounded like an interesting life and indeed the book had been interesting, more than interesting. During our discussion in class, everyone knew just what to say, raising compelling questions and making striking connections, but I sat silently, taking simple, short notes in my binder, hardly looking up. The way I behaved during class couldn't have been more different from how I had felt while reading. I was particularly taken by the section of the book that followed Melanctha, a bright, curious, biracial woman, on her bids for freedom from her father and, by extension, her home. In addition to her being defiant and strong-willed, I was drawn to Melanctha because I could imagine her, flesh and blood, walking through the world I lived in as a child. I read the line "Boys had never meant much to Melanctha" and I understood. I followed this character on her search for wisdom and felt I had actually taken part in her endeavors in the way dreaming of falling is like falling. At sixteen, when Melanctha met the older, charismatic, and seductive Jane, I felt I was meeting her, too. When Melanctha said that she learned wisdom not from the men she knew but from Jane, I understood.

Perched on the edge of my bed, I read about the long hours Melanctha spent with Jane in her room, sitting at her feet and listening to her stories, and feeling her strength and the power of her affection, and slowly beginning to see clearly before her a *sure path to wisdom*. And I understood what it meant to sit at Jane's feet and how quickly those long hours spent kneeling at her feet must've passed because I understood devotion. So much so that I quickly shut the book and threw it at my desk, my hands trembling. I was shaking for a long time as I lay in bed and waited for Maria to come home. I did not leave the room until the following afternoon, and when I slipped into my usual back corner of the classroom I added nothing to their lively discussion of the book that had been nothing short of rapture for me. If I spoke, I risked saying not only to others, but to myself, what I had denied without even knowing I had denied it. At the end of that class, I stood outside alone smoking under a tree with weeping branches. I watched students trail after our professor and carry on the conversation they had been having inside. James approached me and having noticed my silence, he said he had hated the book, too. He called it precious, flimsy, and trite. Then he asked me if he could bum one of my cigarettes. I held out the pack to him and before I could clarify what my silence had meant, that it hadn't been disapproving, he walked off without thanking me.

So James was notoriously rude, and because of that, not in spite of it, girls liked him a lot. But James didn't love us because, like keeping a job, art history, and alcohol, sex was beneath James. I admit I thought about our short interaction a lot after it happened and when I found out we were in the same painting class, that he was a painter, too, I was curious to know more about him. He didn't sleep with anyone the first three years at Bard, at least no one I knew. He just read his Gramsci and his Stuart Hall, dressed us down during crits, and wore his handsome outfits, which he stressed were all bought secondhand.

James was Black British and extremely good-looking. Extremely. Worse, he was talented and our professor's clear favorite. James knew it and exploited that fact. Our painting professor, Moser, had us each go through these hour-long critiques that were painful. According to Moser, an hour was cutting it short. If it were up to him, each crit would last two hours, but time didn't allow for that. There was no hiding during these long stretches of time when every possible question in a painting was probed and every technical flaw pointed out and rehashed, with the professor encouraging everyone to chime in and explain *just how* a piece had failed, was failing. This was how an artist grew, through a calculated kind of degradation. I thought I hated school before. When I sat on the uneven stool in the middle of the classroom, not allowed to say a word in defense of my paintings, which really always did look horrible from that silent point of view, I felt a tenderness for Our Lady. Its punishments suddenly felt fair in comparison. People always deferred to the first form of punishment they knew. A girl who lived down the hall in my dorm told Maria and me that she liked to be beaten until she bled during sex, but boys at school never let her have it. Her mother was a Russian ballerina. Maria found that very interesting, and as the girl spoke about her proclivities, I noticed Maria writing in her journal. She would look up with great concentration, ask the girl to elaborate, and then take down more notes. Later, when I asked Maria why she had been writing while our dormmate told us that awful story about her asking men to hit her, Maria looked at me with confusion and said she was going to put it in a movie.

That Wednesday, it was my turn to be critiqued and before class James looked particularly invested in the slender copy of *Every Cook Can Govern* he was reading. Later I would make a note to find it in the campus bookstore and read it right away, but then I just hoped for the hour to pass quickly. Sometimes, when I looked at him in class, I felt wet between the legs, but I didn't like him and found him standoffish, so I really didn't understand. I looked away from him as I gathered my three paintings from the corner and put them in the center of the classroom. At the start, the student being critiqued had a chance to speak, but after that, she kept quiet and listened to what her peers had to say. I started to explain my interest in twins and the choice to situate the doubled subjects in the peripheries of the canvas as a nod to the marginalization of darker subjects in the Western canon and so on. I went on and on, losing faith in my ideas, wishing I had never been born, etc. Until James interrupted me.

"It's a bit whitewashed, isn't it?" he asked. My ears started to ring. My face was hot.

"Say more, James," Professor Moser said.

"Well, I just mean I understand what Ruth is trying to do here—I think we *all* understand what she's trying to do—since it's been done so many times before. I just think it's a bit simple, nascent...undeveloped. Besides, I don't see what the twins have to do with the bits about colonization. I think, really, these are six paintings, not three paintings, like you have here. The way you have them here feels unfinished and the choices, they feel arbitrary. Then there's the trouble of mining the archetypes of Western culture to critique Western culture, but maybe that's another topic entirely."

I nodded slowly, my legs shaking. Not visibly, I hoped. Our

professor furrowed his brow in fake deliberation, since he always agreed with James in the end, and then cleared his throat.

"All good points," he said. "All excellent points." The room was silent. The class stared at me. I stared up at the clock.

Sabrina raised her hand.

"I like the work," she said, smiling. "I'm not totally sure I understand it, but it seems really...yeah, I don't know."

I didn't like Sabrina's paintings and it was discouraging to hear her approval, but it was kind of her to step in and defend me. That was how I saw us in the classroom: being defended, being attacked. My classmate Alex looked up from the notebook in her lap and said she found the use of color in the paintings evocative and someone else disagreed. *I actually found it flat.* Sabrina said it was like Alice Neel, Alex asked how. James rolled his eyes as the girls spoke. I tried to think of anything but where I was. I thought of James, admittedly. I thought of moving to Manhattan. I thought of living with Maria in a modest but stylish apartment. I thought of the paintings I would go on to make, which would be both beyond the understanding of my peers and totally inspiring to them, paintings that would be impossible to put down except by hopelessly jealous people or, I supposed, conservatives. In the moments when my insecurity was most apparent, I had these deluded flashes of grandeur, an overcorrection to the very real possibility of jumping out the window from shame.

I thought of the futility of critique, how it stifled students, pitted us against each other, made us desperate to sound savvy and intelligent. Every so often, I nodded or turned my head in surprise. I thanked God I couldn't blush. I thought of my mother and father, total philistines, but my parents all the same, part of my past and inevitably part of my future. I thought, *I'll forgive my parents, but only once I've made enough money and earned enough status to fully insulate myself from them.* But by the time I had those things, since I wanted to be an artist, my parents would likely be long dead. Then the hour was over. Amen. After class Professor Moser asked if he could have a word with me.

Christ, I thought.

The room cleared out and I stood a few feet away from Moser, who sat on a stool with his legs spread open, seemingly comfortable with himself, or uncomfortable and trying to fake it.

"Everything okay, Ruth?" he asked.

"Everything's really great, yeah. I love this class," I said.

"Alright," he replied. "Fine. Very good. I have a job for you, if you want it, that is. During the winter break. I'd pay for housing and food, and a stipend. There's a car you can use."

I was so broke. Every afternoon I sat around and thought, *Shit, I need a job.* From my lips to God's ears.

"I'll take it." I nodded.

"I haven't even told you what it is," Moser said, smiling. "I need an assistant to work in my studio, underpainting, stretching canvases, organizing, things like that. It'd be for a few weeks while I'm in Texas. The studio's attached to my house, so my ex-wife may be in and out, but she'll stay out of your way. She's very antisocial, so she won't bother you or anything like that. I'll pay you seven hundred dollars for the month. If you're interested, you can come to my office sometime and I'll give you the keys and address."

"Okay," I said. "I'll come by. Thanks."

"Fine. Very good. Very good. If you don't mind, please don't tell the others."

"Of course," I said, zipping my lips childishly. I waved goodbye and left the room awkwardly, catching my large portfolio in the door frame and apologizing and thanking him again.

In the dim hallway, someone tapped me on the shoulder. I startled. I turned and saw that it was James, holding a pouch of tobacco in one hand and a leather bag in the other.

"Sorry," I said, then, "Hey."

"I didn't mean to be rude, in class," he said, uncharacteristic of him. Then, rolling up his cigarette, he kept talking. "But some-one had to say it. I mean, we were all thinking it. It wasn't your best work, but it's a phase every painter has to go through, the bad social commentary. But you're a *decent* painter, Ruth, you've got potential at least, more than I can say for the..."

The brief exchange with Professor Moser made me arrogant. I didn't feel like I had to stand there and listen to James. I mean, Moser could've asked James, but he'd asked me. Although it was possible he'd already asked James and James had said no. He prob-ably didn't need the money. In fact, it was possible that Moser had asked all six seniors in the class, and everyone had said no, leaving me as his last choice, but then he wouldn't have asked me to keep it a secret. Suddenly, I felt better than James. At the end of winter break, I'd be seven hundred dollars richer; I'd have a place to work alone. It was strange how tenuous status was, that the person you were so painfully jealous of could be suddenly made to feel jealous of you and then just as quickly, there could be a total reversal. I walked down the hall. James followed me.

"Where are you off to?" he asked.

"The library."

"Then we can walk and talk. I have some reading to do, too."

"I have to stop by my dorm," I said, "and make a phone call."

"I live up that way. I'll give you a hand with your portfolio."

"I'm meeting a friend."

"That girl you always hang out with. Maria. Lesbian until graduation, isn't it?"

"What'd you say?" I asked. I didn't understand what he meant.

James handed me a cigarette and pulled a lighter from the pocket in his flannel.

We pushed the doors open to the early darkness, the frigid air of December in the valley. James sat down on a large rock outside. He gestured at the space beside him. I sat down. He struck a match and held it up to my face.

"Maria's dating the girl with the red hair?" he asked.

"Maybe, maybe not."

"And you, who are you with?"

"I don't know what you mean?"

"I mean sex. What do you think I mean?"

I shook my head and shrugged.

"So you just spend all your time alone in this desolate shithole?"

"I like it here; I think it's nice."

"Where'd you grow up?"

"Rhode Island."

"Near the ocean?"

"It isn't actually an island," I said. I put the cigarette out on the sole of my shoe.

"Yes, I know what Rhode Island is; my mom went to Brown. Is your family still there?"

I pictured my mother and father. I pictured the idea of a mother and father James probably had, upright, loving, the kind of parents who would send their son to a school in another country to study art, strong, reliable, good-humored forces to be rebelled against, then embraced.

"Why are you talking to me?" I asked.

"Why?" he asked.

"Yes, why? You're rude...to everyone. So I'm wondering why you're now talking to me."

"This might sound ridiculous," he began.

I waited.

"Well, I dreamt I was leaning over a stove in a one-room house, stirring a wooden spoon in a huge cauldron, throwing in carrots and salt and all that. Then a baby started to cry, so I looked around the room, trying to find the baby, the source of the noise, since it sounded so loud and excruciating. I looked under the table and the baby wasn't there. I looked in the cabinets and the baby wasn't there. I lifted up the floorboards and looked under the floorboards and I couldn't find the baby. I tore the entire house apart and found nothing. So, I got up on a stool and looked into the pot and, finally, I saw where the crying was coming from. It wasn't a baby, it was you. With the peas and carrots and tomatoes, whatever. You were *in* there, crying, simmering away," James said.

The red light from the cigarette's ember refracted against James's eyelids, his nose, his shaved head. He looked and sounded truly insane, even more so because he was so beautiful. Deceptively so, I thought. I heard the footfall of deer somewhere behind the trees. Devils came as everything you wanted. I squinted at him. It was darker then.

"Do you understand," he asked, "what I mean?"

"No, I don't." I looked over his shoulder. Was it a prank?

"It's when I realized I was fond of you. I was meant to know you," he said, searching for approval in my expression. "And I understood this dream as a sign that you might feel the same. Or at least I understood that I should tell you how I feel. I know it's out of the blue."

I didn't know whether to laugh at James or embrace him. He took himself so seriously. He took himself as seriously as I hoped to take myself.

"I wrote down the dream and it was all right there. First, I'm in a one-room cabin, poorly lit, seemingly alone, which of course represents the college, tucked away in a valley, almost culturally homogeneous, alienating—obvious, right? Then I hear someone crying, but I don't know the source of the sound, but that's because I'm ignoring the reality of the situation. I've put you in the pot, *I've* turned on the fire, *I've* made you cry. I knew when I first saw you but I sublimated those feelings by being competitive, by being, sometimes, overly critical of your work. I looked down on you as I, finally, looked down from the height of the step stool into the pot. I talked about it with my mum over the phone. She's an analyst. It's all really obvious; once I explained it to her, she agreed. It's clear as day."

I looked down at my shoes. I thought of Sheila.

"Is everyone at this school the child of therapists? Is that why everyone's so...?"

"Well, my dad works for Deutsche Bank, so I don't think so."

I laughed.

Professor Moser came out from the building carrying a backpack and a hammer. His silhouette grew larger and larger, and then he stopped before us.

"Hi," James said.

"Young love," he said, looking down at us, sighing.

"We're not..." I said.

James put his hand on my knee and smiled, seeming even crazier than before.

"Have a good night," Professor Moser said. Then he turned, swinging the hammer as his silhouette disappeared into the dark asphalt and the dense mist beyond the parking lot.

James turned to me, his hand still resting on my leg.

"Can I just talk to you? Can I explain? Come to my room, I'll call my mother, we can all talk about it."

"I don't want to talk to your mother. I don't want to talk to anyone's mother."

"Then talk to me," he said.

"This feels strange," I said.

"It's fully normal. Epiphanies, change. Look, let's get out of the cold," James said.

He took my hand and stood up. Despite my reservations, I wanted to go with him. Suddenly, it was all I wanted, to be led away from normalcy and ushered into the fringes so that I would know that I was actually young, actually living as opposed to feigning a performance of vitality. I knew it was cliche to think a woman needed a man for that, but I didn't have anything better to do, had nothing to occupy my time apart from schoolwork and vague dinner plans. We cut through the dead grass up the hill, unable to see more than a foot or two ahead of us. The bright eyes of a pair of small deer blinked in the distance, then the animals were gone, startled by the bicycle rolling up the steep incline behind us. We stood outside the heavy doors of a stone building I'd only seen in passing as James searched for his keys. He held the door open for me and we climbed two sets of narrow stairs. It was hot and difficult to breathe in the halls. The walls in his room were lined with dull red bricks. Stacks and stacks of books with frayed and missing spines obscured the floor. It smelled dizzyingly of weed and ash.

I remembered that I was meant to meet Maria and Sheila for dinner at the Japanese restaurant in town. It was one of two places Sheila frequented and she always paid, so we never complained. I felt wrong blowing them off to be with this boy. Worse, I didn't know what I was doing with James or what James was doing with me. I went along passively. James put a pile of books on the floor and pulled out a chair for me to sit on. He flipped on an electric kettle and turned to me.

"Beef or chicken?" he asked. "Instant noodles."

"Whichever," I said.

The kettle whistled. James handed me a Styrofoam cup of soup and a pair of child-sized plastic chopsticks. They were short and awkward in my hands. We ate in silence, listening to the depressing sounds of Wilco and loud sex that bled through the adjoining wall. James's bed was covered in a white and blue quilt, old and pristine. He sat on it, eating intently. He threw his cup into the garbage can below him and lit a stick of incense, then he lay down.

"What are you doing during the winter break?" he asked.

"Not sure yet."

"You should come to London."

"I'll be working."

"For Moser. Assisting him, right? I was listening through the door."

"Then why'd you ask?"

"Congratulations, anyway. You deserve it, after all."

"Are you making fun of me?" I asked.

"No."

"You must have expected to get the job. He loves you."

"Me? No, I'm no painter. I'll probably just work in a gallery or cut out the middleman and go work at the bank."

"I thought you were a Marxist," I said.

I wasn't joking. I'd said it in earnest but James laughed with his eyes shut as if he was struggling to force out the sound. The backdrop of the quilt, the shadows against his face, made him look like his eyes were closed forever, like he was sleeping in a coffin. Like he was laughing while asleep, while dead.

"I've gotta go. My friends are waiting for me."

"Maria and that girl with the red hair?" he asked. I nodded.

Then James explained to me that wherever Maria and Sheila were going, they had already gone. They weren't waiting for me. They'd probably forgotten completely that I'd been a part of the plan because they were in love and couldn't be interested in anyone but each other. I could kiss my friend goodbye, James explained, but I shouldn't rule her out entirely, because soon enough, just give it time, they'd have some nasty, idiotic breakup and then Maria would need me and she'd be back, but until then, don't bother.

"Come lay down with me, Ruth. I've done some acid and it's kicking in. I just keep seeing you like you were in my dream, boiling, crying. It's so messed up, but beautiful. You really are beautiful, the more I look at you."

I rolled my eyes, but at the same time I didn't see why I shouldn't at least stay and hear what he had to say. At twenty-two, I'd never been in a relationship, never even been kissed, and soon I'd be past the point of expiry, so I had to act quickly. I got into the cramped twin-XL bed beside James, trying to leave an inch or two between us, which proved impossible.

"That's so nice," he said.

After some time, I fell asleep. I woke up early in the morning and James was gone. When I walked back to my room, I could still smell the incense in my braids. The next day in botany, Sabrina sat next to me, but she seemed cold, not striking up any conversation. Sabrina liked James, too. Everyone did. Even I was beginning to like him, in spite of myself. As our professor went through his slides in the dark classroom, Sabrina turned to me and gave me a self-satisfied smile.

"My friend said she saw you and James walking into Stone Row. She didn't see you *leave* until the next morning."

"So?" I asked.

"So...you don't live in Stone Row," Sabrina said, no longer smiling, copying down the notes from the slides in purple ink. "Fun night?" she asked.

"I don't know what you're talking about," I said, and tried to catch up with the slides: *Kingdoms are divided into groups called phyla, phyla are divided into groups called classes, classes are divided into groups called orders, orders are divided into groups called families.* I didn't get the rest. I figured it didn't matter; the class had no homework, no final exam, and was graded Pass or Fail. No one ever failed.

After class, I found James was waiting for me on a nearby bench, smoking, staring intently into a heavy hardcover, looking totally dejected. He saw me and smiled. I waved goodbye to Sabrina and she rolled her eyes and walked on toward the library.

"How did you know where I'd be?" I asked.

"I'm following you," he said.

"You know some women would be put off by that."

"You'd be surprised," James said. He stood up and didn't tell me what was in the large bag he was carrying.

He led me around the edge of campus through the small unassuming graveyard where a philosopher's bones slowly shifted from the movement of the roots and mycelia that shared the soil, past a small man-made pond where orange koi swam in unison, past a daycare where professors' children learned to deal with one another as their parents dealt with ideas.

"Where are we walking to?" I asked James.

"Here," he said, setting his bag down in the middle of the empty field.

He pulled a small blanket, a tray of watercolors, a blue glass bottle, a camera, and a sketchbook out of his bag, among other things. In the tall grass, James spread out the blanket and instructed me to sit down facing him. He moved my arms and lifted my chin, turning and positioning me as though I were inanimate, as I'd done so many times to Maria, in my bedroom. It never occurred to me how vulnerable it must have been to sit in her place. To be propped and used as a reference and not know if you were coming across beautifully. When he was satisfied, he pulled out a small, thin wooden easel and started to paint, stopping every so often to light a cigarette. I watched him from the corner of my eye as he sketched, presumably, my face in profile, my hands, the square of white cotton situated in the grass. It was cold and I had to brace myself to keep from shaking in the wind. It was almost silent there, aside from the perpetual noise of small animals moving through the woods. James seemed to work quickly, but I didn't know what he had in mind. It was unclear how long he planned to have me sit there. Even as I wanted to be seen by him, I disliked being on this side of the arrangement, being the one who had to sit still and wait it out. The suspense, too, of not knowing what he saw made me impatient.

When Maria had asked me to throw away all of the paintings of her, I'd been offended and secretly harbored a grudge, feeling it was just another example of her trying to construct her identity at my expense. They were my paintings. Some of the only things I had.

I didn't feel that, as a subject, she had any right to the objects she'd inspired. I didn't think that a representation of something and the thing itself were inextricably tied in a way that would ever necessitate discarding the representation at the request of the one who had influenced it. Did Maria own the images of her that I'd made? I didn't think so. I hadn't said these things at the time. I simply complied. Maria had frequently encouraged me to paint and gladly sat for said paintings, complimenting the progress I made and the license taken in this or that portrait, then she had a change of heart. Now, on the other side of the situation, I understood Maria's entitlement. I hoped that James would "get it right." Maybe what Maria feared was incrimination, the exposure of the distance between how a person wanted to be seen and how they really looked. It was inevitable that I would seek out someone to do to me what I had done to Maria. I was tired then. I wanted to stand up, to feel the blood circulate through my limbs. Whatever feelings of romance the gesture was meant to elicit in me were overshadowed by the sensation of my numb hands and strained neck. I turned and broke my pose.

"Perfect timing," James said. I rose and stretched my legs. I shook my hands and put them in my coat pockets to warm them. James walked up to me and lifted my hands and held them in his. He guided me back down into the soft patch of yellow grass, a foot away from where I had been sitting a moment before. I looked at the easel; it was firmly planted in the ground. He kissed my neck and unbuttoned my coat. I wanted to see myself. I didn't have the same hang-ups about being a subject that Maria had had with me. I wanted to see what he had painted. Looking up from under James, I saw the canvas. I was a dark, angular smudge against a fading yellow backdrop. It could not have been more accurate.

At the Chinese restaurant in town, I watched James eat fried shrimp, shrimp fried rice, and crab rangoon. Shellfish made my skin break out in hives and my throat narrow; it wouldn't kill me to eat it, but the reaction was extreme enough to keep me vigilant.

I wasn't hungry anyway. The nicotine and the thrill of just being around him were enough and I didn't find myself wanting food. Plus, I was cautious about spending the little money I had. Maybe James would pay for whatever I ordered, but I didn't want to be presumptuous and ruin the romance so soon. Drinking his second Coca-Cola, James wiped his fingers on an oily napkin and placed his hand on my knee. He leaned in and I told him a kiss would make me sick after what he'd just eaten.

"Good?" I asked.

"Delicious, and I've *been* to China."

"Where haven't you been?" I asked.

I looked down at the plate of discarded pink tails. On the other side of the foggy window, pairs of kids from the college walked back and forth from the gas station, leaving with boxes of cheap American beer.

"I've been all over. Every place is basically the same. I'm getting out of this death cult after graduation, that's all I know," he said.

"Meaning America?" I asked.

"I'm going East."

"Back to London?" I asked.

James laughed. "Are you coming with me?"

"Maria and I have plans to live together," I said.

"Forget Maria," he replied. "Maria isn't a serious artist. She isn't a good influence. All these rich kids she hangs out with. So-called filmmakers. They'll never actually make anything. None of them will actually be successful, you know that, right?"

"You're a rich kid. Are you a so-called painter?" I asked.

"Maybe," James said. "But at least I'm honest about what I am."

Everything he wanted, more or less, had been available to James all his life, from his mother's attention to his father's money, so it was easy for him to make sporadic plans and keep and abandon them as he felt inclined. From close up, I saw that what I had mistaken for meanness in James was a genuine conviction in his moral superiority and his transcendence of silly things like relationship to country and peers. Either way, it would be too tedious and too unsexy to explain to James that the reason he could act like he didn't need people was because he didn't need people. Mom and Dad would bankroll his loneliness, and if that generosity ever ran out, which, based on the way he swiped his Amex, was not likely to happen, James was beautiful, unquestionably so, and young and a painter of not inconsiderable talent. He could always try his luck in New York. James phoned for a taxi back to campus. The doggy bag of shrimp sat between us in the back seat.

In bed James closed his book and said he needed to tell me something. I didn't know what to expect. Had he slept with someone else? He started to explain that he had gone to a talk given by a Canadian poet who had said something that had changed his life. The scales had fallen from his eyes. I didn't expect this kind of enthusiasm from anyone I went to college with, let alone James, who had seemed so uncharitable and sophisticated before.

"What she said, basically, is that all pain is bearable. Like the pain of rejection a person has to tolerate when sending out work that will be inevitably disregarded, or the pain of unsupportive parents, the pain of unrequited love and the attendant physical pains of being alive or whatever. She said that the pain, you know, of aging and decaying could be coped with and assimilated, surprisingly easily, into our elastic and, you know, resilient human understandings: childbirth, bad falls, heartbreaks, scrapes, all of it. It's incredible, really, because we, Westerners especially, live in such a pleasure-seeking, hedonistic, consequence-averse society, where hardship is something to avoid. I found it so refreshing for someone to embrace pain, you know, look at it as a welcome fixture of life, that doesn't even necessarily require treatment or fixation."

James spoke slowly, so I wouldn't miss anything. His eyes looked wet like he was moved all over again. He was actually crying. I sat and nodded, until he finally calmed down.

"It sucks you missed it; I just couldn't stop sobbing walking back to my dorm," he said.

I wasn't convinced and I wasn't moved. I was inured to big feelings of epiphany, which James seemed to be seeking in everything. Maybe that was why he read so compulsively, at all hours of the day and night, looking for some sort of shaman to offer direction. Why did it surprise James that human beings could withstand unthinkable pain? That was Christ's whole thing. James needed the guidance of those poets and all of his secular ideologies. My elementary, middle, and high school education had done so much to inculcate an all-encapsulating Christian worldview in me so that I would be able to scrutinize the secular world and not be seduced or corrupted by it.

James, on the other hand, had gone to Waldorf school until he was taken out and homeschooled because of what he called "intense racist bullying." Terrified, his mother homeschooled him alone, all the way through high school. He didn't really learn to read until age ten. He had never been to any church and he was totally without religion, although he often described his mother as a *spiritual woman.* I had no idea what that meant and he couldn't really explain it, either, something to do with crystals, with incense, with Reiki, with Jung. What was Reiki, I asked him. He couldn't really sum it up. It was hard to know which of us was better off.

19

◇◇◇◇◇◇◇◇◇◇◇◇◇

I DIDN'T SEE Maria again until her next screening. She'd cut off all her hair; she was practically bald. It suited her, but it was still jarring. We had come from a background so full of salons and chemical straightening, of hair as a first impression, and now she looked like a stranger. She pierced her nose, too, and had on this dark purple lipstick. Yet another role for her to play. She wore a white men's dress shirt, a short skirt, and motorcycle boots. Sheila had on a similar outfit and had cut her hair shorter, too, but it was less drastic.

"Wow," I said.

"Do you hate it?" Maria asked.

"No, it's...interesting."

"Sheila did it."

"I figured."

James came in holding a jar of olives and a handle of whiskey and added it to the spread of drinks on the folding table. He waved hello to Maria and me. I introduced them. It was a stupid formality, because we clearly all knew one another; the school was small and there were only so many Black students. No more than ten in our year. Maria and James pretended to figure out where they had met before: a party, a talk, a class.

James held my hand and Maria looked down at it, puzzled.

"Oh, you two are...that makes sense," she said, then she walked up to the front of the room and quieted everyone down. Maria introduced the first short, telling us the director's name and reading off a short bio: *This is Marianne from St. Louis; she is interested in poetry, photography, and feminism.* The lights dimmed and the film began. It was a tense reenactment of a breakup. A tape recording of a heated argument played over a loop of a girl in our year sitting on a stool using makeup and wigs to present herself first as the woman in the relationship and then as the man. The man in the recording really upbraided the woman, telling her how worthless and frivolous she was, how sorry she felt for herself. The woman held her own, but struggled to shout back through tears, and as you listened you began to be persuaded, in spite of yourself, by the man's insults, since the woman did sound weak and frivolous and self-pitying, crying that way while his voice remained measured and clear. It had this strange effect of making you side with the stronger, more aggressive party even as you knew they were behaving cruelly. When it was over, the girl who made the short film grinned as we applauded and I realized those must have been recordings from her own life and she must have been smiling because she finally felt vindicated for having refashioned that humiliation and shame, turning them into something that others could enjoy. As a child, I'd understood suffering as preparatory, as something that prepared us for death, glory, and eternal life. Now, I saw it as useful in a new way, as something that could be made into art.

Someone else showed a fifteen-minute Claymation piece that depicted the creation of two people from a mound of clay. In the background was a terrible vaudeville song that gradually became quieter and quieter the more developed the clay man got, until he looked not lifelike but fully formed, with two legs, two arms, and all the rest. That film I didn't understand. After that, a quiet girl with box-dyed red hair stood up and said, "If you're squeamish about blood or mice, then you should step outside for a smoke now. Thank you."

No one left. The video opened with a cage full of mice, ten or fifteen, let out into a dark room. It was so dark that the figures in the short were scarcely visible. But you could hear shouting and stomping feet, as well as the chorus of small mice running around, united in some common goal. After a minute or two, traps started to go off. I wasn't sure if that was allowed, but animal rights activists had more expensive targets than the informal film society of a small liberal arts college.

With all the mice dead and the screen black, the program was over. Maria stood up and announced that the sign-ups were in the back of the room for next week. We clapped again half-heartedly. A handful of boys rushed to the back of the room to jot down their names. We drank the sweet white wine that Sheila supplied and the whiskey that James brought, plus the customary cheap American beers, lukewarm. The audience migrated outside and chain-smoked in front of the film building, planning their evenings. Maria hovered beside James but didn't say anything. I had the feeling that she'd be the deciding vote on the course of our relationship. That she had more say than James or me in the matter.

"Hope we didn't bore you, James," said Maria.

"Oh, I just feel lucky to have been invited."

"But you weren't," Maria said. I could hear the gavel falling. James looked at me and laughed. But I couldn't do anything.

"I'm only joking. Any friend of Ruth's is a friend of mine," Maria said. A group of girls came over and told Maria how great the "programming" was and Sheila eyed them suspiciously. They told Maria they had signed up for the following week and hoped they were chosen. She explained that she chose names through a lottery so that no one felt privileged over anyone else. It wasn't true, I'd seen her pick the names herself, but I was impressed by Maria's ability to play the power broker, but still come off as benevolent and fair. They told Maria that they really, really hoped their names were chosen, playfully brushing her arm and tossing their hair behind their ears. Sheila prodded me with her elbow and nodded in Maria's direction.

"Talking to her groupies," Sheila said.

"You have nothing to worry about," I said.

"What are you two talking about?" Maria said, pulling herself away from her fans.

"Just that there's a party in town," said Sheila.

We had missed the shuttle during the screening and the only other way to get to the party was to walk several miles or get in a car with someone who had been drinking, and we weren't going to walk. People broke off in small groups and walked to their respective cars. It was only a short drive, just a straight shot down the road. You could basically drive there with your eyes closed. It was common to drive drunk and none of us cared. Our classmate Paulette offered us a ride. I always felt a wistful feeling when I heard Paulette's name because she shared it with the nun who taught me as a child, though they couldn't have been more different. Sheila, Maria, James, and I followed her to her yellow Volvo. Paulette had gotten a DUI last year, but only because she had been stupid enough to drive way under the speed limit when she was wasted. They pulled her over for how slow she was going and there was a beer in her center console. Paulette became more cautious and now drove at a normal speed when drinking. She was back behind the wheel of her Volvo like nothing had ever happened. The president of our school told us we were only protected from police within the boundaries of the college's thousand acres. Beyond that, we were on our own. But for whatever reason, we didn't care about the police and were more concerned with being stuck on campus, with feeling confined. Maybe it was the immunity to authority I saw in my rich, white classmates that made me feel inured to authority. Nothing seemed consequential at all. The party was at this boy Ben's house. And he had had two roommates, but one had dropped out and gone to the city to model and the other got addicted to heroin and left without saying anything at all, so Ben had this big house all to himself.

"Yeah, she's this big model now, apparently," Paulette said, speeding down the road.

"Idiotic. Why would you quit school to model? She isn't going to be young forever," said Sheila.

Sheila said that modeling was stupid and trivial, though Maria still modeled and did commercials for money here and there. I had never seen Maria defer to anyone so easily before. If I had said the same thing, she would have told me I didn't know what I was talking about and didn't understand the world. But with Sheila, she was permissive. I figured that was love. We were all squeezed into the back of Paulette's sedan that smelled like weed and heavy air freshener. She said we had to save the front seat for her boyfriend. Maria sat beside Sheila. I sat on James's lap. The wind in my face made me feel unmoored. Then I felt the weight of the car speeding through the one-lane highway and I was brought down again. Paulette wouldn't say who this boyfriend of hers was. She just pulled over at a small, run-down-looking ranch tucked behind a grassy lot and idled the car. A man in basketball shorts and a ratty white T-shirt stepped out and Paulette leaned over and opened the door for him. She gave him an overlong, sensual kiss, like we weren't there, and when he turned around to say hello, I saw that I recognized him. He had a handsome, classic face aside from all the little red cuts on his cheeks. I had seen him at parties before. He sold weed and coke. Sometimes he sold acid and was known for fair prices, particularly if he was sleeping with one of your friends. Paulette was happy to have him there and she sang along to a pop song on the radio, sort of performing for him.

"Babe, are you drunk?" he asked. She put her finger over his lips, playfully quieting him. Paulette wasn't worried about the fact that she was over the limit or that the man to her right had drugs in his bag or that she was carrying too many people in her back seat. She often said that if things didn't work out for her in school, she'd just go back to Vegas. Her father developed property on the Strip. She was the only person I knew from Nevada, a "nowhere place," as she called it. If Vegas was nowhere, what was Rhode Island? Paulette studied human rights. What did you do with a human rights degree in Vegas? Did they have many violations of human rights in Vegas? What I should have been asking was, *What will I do with my art degree?* I partied too much. I didn't work hard enough. I told myself not to drink too much at the party. I couldn't afford to be hungover in the morning. I needed to work. James squeezed my waist and pulled me out of my thoughts.

"I think she'll crash the car. Should we tell her to stop?" James asked. He looked afraid.

"Oh, relax," Sheila said. "Paulette isn't going to crash. Paulette is an *excellent* drunk driver."

We got to the long unpaved driveway just fine. The music blared through the drowsy street. Paulette made us cough up a couple of dollars for gas. James gave her a ten-dollar bill for all of us. It felt good to stand beside him and watch him take money out of his wallet. I had many fantasies; who knew that was one of them? It certainly wasn't the main one. Maria walked inside. We followed her up the rotting porch steps. The party was crowded with the usual suspects. Maria and Sheila split with Paulette and the coke dealer. I lost James in the pack and searched the refrigerator for a beer to steal. There was no such thing as having bad manners here. There was nothing shameful about going to a party empty-handed. Living this way, I wished my mother could see me. What would she say? *This isn't how I raised you.* Doing anything illicit, I thought of my mother's recriminations: heathen, sinner,

Godless, forsaken. My mother: a woman from the generation that put baby powder between their legs and wore scented panty liners each day and never swore and never broke down. Upright, upright women, unimpeachable. I was sick of feeling guilty. What had I done to anyone to feel so guilty?

The box of beers in the back of the fridge was empty. I remembered the bottle of wine I had snuck out from the screening. I pulled it out from my bag, twisted off the top, and drank and drank. Every weekend, I remembered how easy it was to annihilate myself. How there only seemed to be a moment between the first drink and the dulling, yawning last. I found that drinking was a balm for the guilt, right up until the morning when you also felt guilty for the drinking.

I spotted Maria across the room making out with Sheila. I felt a chill. I watched Sheila run her hands over Maria's cropped hair. I wondered where James was but didn't care to find him right then. I wanted to stand there and watch, possibly understand. Maria opened her eyes and behind Sheila's silhouette, she glanced at me. She pulled Sheila closer and I looked away. I didn't want her to think I was staring, even if I was. There was a band playing upstairs and people were jumping, dancing hard so that the floorboards shook above us. The houses rented to students were old and poorly kept; it wouldn't be inconceivable for the ceiling to cave in.

Maria pulled away from Sheila. Her pale face was covered in plum lipstick. She wiped it away with her sleeve and scanned the room, looking for something. I ducked behind a tall boy I didn't know and tried to join his rambling conversation. A card game was starting or ending, I couldn't tell the difference. I turned away and wandered off alone to the back porch past a game of beer pong. The vinyl table was covered with small yellow pools that looked like urine and everyone cheered. There was a small yard outside and a fire burning unattended in a pit fenced by broken bricks. Beyond the yard were the woods. I sat on a log by the waning fire. I could hear the music still. I watched the party from the outside as Maria climbed down the steps and came over like she had something on her mind. She sat down next to me, drunk, not wearing any shoes.

"I was looking for you."

I threw a scrap of cardboard from an empty six-pack into the fire. It didn't do much. Rarely was it just Maria and me together anymore, and I was glad she had sought me out. We watched embers leap out from the fire and land in the dark soil.

"Why aren't you inside with your boyfriend?" she asked.

"He isn't my boyfriend," I said. "We just hang out and talk about painting."

"You talk about painting?"

"Yes," I said, "we talk about painting."

"Well, be careful. Something's off with him. I get a weird feeling."

"A weird feeling?"

"I don't trust him. I mean, the whole British nice guy, offering-to-pay-for-gas thing. I don't know what his deal is. I mean, it seems like you're rushing into…"

"Isn't that a bit hypocritical? I mean, you rushed into things with Sheila. And Sheila always pays."

"But I *know* Sheila. I don't know James. Do you?"

"You met Sheila just like I met James. You only know what she tells you."

"But Sheila's a woman. James is a man, a man that you don't know."

"Oh," I said. "I see."

"I'm only looking out for you."

"Look out for yourself and I'll look out for myself," I said.

We heard footsteps approaching. Sheila floated down the steps. Her hair was neon under the cool porch lights. She stood between us and the fire and didn't ask any questions at first. Just sat down. Maria and I turned away from each other.

"What's going on here?" Sheila asked.

"Jealous?" Maria asked Sheila, smiling. Maria's whole demeanor was different. Her body language was friendly and open.

"Should I be?" Sheila laughed, looking at us.

Maria shot up and said she needed to pee. She left Sheila and me sitting alone. When Maria was out of earshot, Sheila spread her hands out over the fire.

"Cold night," she said. I nodded.

"Can I have a sip of your wine?" she asked.

"Of course, it's yours. From the screening." Sheila thanked me anyway.

"I have to ask," she said.

"What?" I asked. Sheila pointed her head toward the trees and back toward me.

"Are you two...?"

"Maria and I?" I asked. "No."

"No?" she asked.

"She's like a sister," I said. "I'm straight."

"That's what everyone says. Give it five years," Sheila said, handing me back the bottle of wine. Sheila squinted at me like she was really trying to get a good look.

"Because if you did go after her," Sheila said, "I'd be hurt. Or maybe angry. But I wouldn't stand in your way."

A branch broke and Maria climbed out from the brush. I stood up and knew then how drunk I was. I wouldn't be painting in the morning. I needed to find James and go back to campus. Maria sat back down. She sighed and rested her head on Sheila's shoulder. Maria and Sheila held hands and were beautiful in the shifting light of the flames. They carried out their own conversation, speaking in sweet, hushed tones, but wanting to be heard. The way couples were, always pretending to be private, then putting their privacy on display. As I walked inside, I felt tart, watery vomit in my throat. I swallowed it and looked around the living room for James. He was huddled close to the dealer and Paulette by the record player downstairs. Paulette was cutting up lines on the face of a tattered album and James was talking about the opioid crisis.

"What's the opioid crisis?" Paulette asked James.

"Don't worry about it, Paulette," James said.

I sat down on a milk crate and tried not to be sick. I did a line. Thought about my mother's judgment, leaned against James.

"What's the matter?" he asked. "Don't look so down. Want another line?"

I fell asleep on the couch and woke up hours later in James's room, with last night's dress still on. I sat up in his bed while he leaned over his desk, smoking a cigarette and reading under a green and gold lamp.

"You passed out last night. I carried you back here," said James.

I went back to sleep and dreamt of an orphan swimming in a dirty fountain, stuffing her pockets with coins.

"Get out of that water," I told the orphan. "It's dirty."

"But there's money in here," she shouted back in another language that I somehow understood. I wondered when I'd start to dream of love the way James had. I looked at him and wasn't sure if I could trust him. Him, myself, anybody. He said that when I was up we would go for a walk.

"What if I don't want to go for a walk?" I asked him. "I don't need you to tell me what to do."

He glanced at me, laughed, and turned back to his book.

20

SOME DAYS LATER, at the end of the term, I called my parents in Rhode Island from a pay phone in the library lobby. I returned a book of sonnets I hadn't even cracked open. My father answered. I told him I got a job and wouldn't be home until January.

"They're *paying* you to paint?"

"Yeah." I told him how much.

"This country. So much money, they don't know what to do with it."

I walked across a frozen lawn toward the arts building to get the key from Moser's office. The door was locked and the lights were off. There was an envelope taped to the door with my name on it. Inside the envelope there was a key, seven hundred dollars, and a list of directions to his home written in terrible penmanship. In the cafeteria I ate a salad: lettuce, tomato, two boiled eggs, all covered in Thousand Island. It took all my strength to keep it down. I felt very nauseous and had been feeling a bit sick for days. Maybe I'd eaten something bad. James met me in the cafeteria and I told him I wasn't feeling well.

"I'm sure it's nothing," he said. "Drinking, probably."

"But I didn't drink last night," I said impatiently.

"Okay, sorry for suggesting it."

James asked me to come to his studio to look at the paintings he was working on. We had these little booths in the arts building that we could use to paint our senior projects and up until that point, he had been very private about his. It was a big step in our relationship, him asking for my feedback, since he had always come across as very critical of and unreceptive to others' opinions.

The more I came to know him, the more I saw it as a facade and understood that he pretended to be indifferent only because he knew just how impressionable he was. I told James that before we went to the studio, I had to go back to my room because I didn't want to carry my money around and he walked with me. He waited outside and smoked while I placed the money in my dresser. I hid it underneath my socks and underwear. It was an unnecessary precaution since it was unlikely anyone would ever break into my room. It was really a way of safeguarding the money from myself, so that I didn't spend it all right away or misplace it.

Maria hadn't been around in weeks, and her absence began to seem deliberate, not mere busyness or absorption in new love but a punishment directed at me. I didn't think she had any right to be upset. I was the one being condescended to and treated as though I didn't know anything. It was my judgment that was being called into question. She found one steady girlfriend and suddenly she had become an authority on love. I felt she needed to mind her own yard. Still, I was leaving that night and if I didn't see her today, it would be a long time until I saw her again. She was going to Los Angeles during the holiday to visit Sheila's parents and three weeks was the longest time I had ever spent away from Maria since I met her.

I figured I should just go by Sheila's room and say goodbye. I had far less pride than Maria. I didn't mind admitting that. James was waiting for me in the grass, bundled in his flannel coat. The collar was rolled up around his face. He lit up when he saw me and asked where we were off to next. He told me how excited he was to spend time alone with me in Moser's home and that it would be like we were really living and working together. It was my idea to have him join me. I figured it would be lonely in the woods, surrounded by snow for weeks over the holidays. He was postponing his flight to London to keep me company and I didn't know why Maria, seeing all of this, couldn't understand what a decent man he was. Still, I wasn't going to parade him in front of Maria. I'd go alone to say goodbye and then meet up with him later on. I squeezed his hand and told him so.

"I thought you'd come visit my studio," he said.

"We can go later," I said.

"Why can't I come with you?" he asked. "Then we can go to the studios straight after."

"I just think it's better if I go alone," I said.

"Because Maria doesn't like me?" he asked.

"No, she really likes you. I just haven't really talked to her in a couple of weeks and I want to say goodbye before I go."

"She doesn't seem to make you a priority in the way you prioritize her," James said.

"What are you talking about? It isn't about being anybody's priority. It's about saying goodbye to my friend before I leave for three weeks. And I don't need to be attached at the hip with you every second of the day."

"Fine, fine," he said. "But when you end up alone because you've let Maria come before everyone else, blame yourself."

"That's ridiculous," I said, but he was already walking off.

When I knocked on her door, Sheila said *one minute* and I heard some moving around before she finally answered, looking happy and dazed. The room smelled like sex. Maria was in bed, under the covers, pretending to read. I asked how they were doing and Maria looked up like it took a really great effort to rip herself away from her book. She smiled, then looked back down, turning the page. I felt like an apparition, seeing and hearing, but unseen and unheard.

Sheila stood by the foot of the bed awkwardly with her arms crossed and asked me how James was and how my thesis was going. *Really good,* I said, *fine.* Sheila's eyes were bloodshot and she smelled like powdery perfume, like she was trying to conceal something.

"I just came to say bye," I said. It didn't come across as I'd imagined it, with Sheila there as an interloper, everything passing through her. I'd expected my goodbye to be calm, yet tragic, full of feeling, but it just sounded like I had mucus in my throat and no real reason to be there. Maria nodded.

"Maria's exhausted, she's been very busy with her editing," Sheila said.

"Well, can't Maria tell me that?" I asked. Maria stared back at me with this wooden look. I rolled my eyes. "Can't Maria talk?"

"I think it's best if you go, Ruth," Sheila said. "It's a very busy time and we're getting ready to travel, so I don't think you'll get what you're looking for right now."

Sheila smiled and opened the door. The weird, sunny, tranquil disposition from Venice that she couldn't shake. She led me out the door gently, as though it were my idea to leave, a real keeper of peace.

"Maria and I are very proud of you. This job is a big deal," Sheila said.

She kissed me on the cheek. Maria nodded up from her book as if to say goodbye. The two of them had become a single unit, acting as one, speaking on one another's behalf. The door closed and I was out in the hall alone. I walked across campus to James's room, but found it empty. So I went to the studio and waited. I waited for almost an hour and he never showed. I went back to my room, thinking he might be waiting for me there as he occasionally was. Again, it was empty. I started to feel uneasy. To make matters worse, my stomach was still killing me. I figured I would go into town and get some antacids since I had Moser's car. I went in my underwear drawer and rummaged through my socks and bras, feeling for the envelope, but it wasn't there. I emptied the drawer, tossing its contents on my bed. I sifted through the bundle of cotton and lace, telling myself to remain calm, to look calmly. I pulled the drawer off its tracks to check if it had fallen into the back of the dresser. It hadn't. I emptied all my drawers, every drawer in the room. I pushed the dresser away from the wall and all I saw there was dust and an old art magazine.

Seven hundred dollars, I said over and over. How could I lose seven hundred dollars in such a short time? I checked my coat, my jeans, my bag. As I sat with all my belongings strewn across the room, I knew it was gone. I fell asleep hyperventilating and woke up in a pile of blouses. I started to look again, though I knew it wouldn't yield anything. It was already late and I wanted to head out before the coming storm. I straightened up the room and gathered my things. Then I walked across campus to James's dorm and went up to wake him. I hoped he would loan me a little bit of money until I figured out what happened to my envelope. I was sure he wouldn't mind since he could always just ask his parents to wire him more from England. We had agreed to leave that night and even if he was hurt by my failure to visit his studio, I was sure he wouldn't back out of our plans. I would apologize for blowing him off and that would be that. James wasn't a vindictive person. He wasn't a cruel person the way he had seemed to me at first in our critiques. I knocked on his door gently, then more forcefully, and no one answered. I let myself in and found his room neat and bright, but empty. Outside, the snow fell down quickly and stuck. I would have to make my way to Moser's and email James when I got to a computer. I couldn't wait and get caught in the snow.

I found Moser's car in a parking lot by the north end of campus and threw my bag in the back seat. He drove a white van, the kind of ominously nondescript car people lure children into. But he needed the extra space since his paintings were so tall. I drove up 9G, stopping twice for crossing deer. It was a road that appeared straight and direct but wound in directions that were dangerous in the snow, dangerous in the event of passing animals. A mile past the Shell gas station, as it was in Moser's directions, there was a condemned blue house and a narrow road. I took a left there and drove what seemed like a quarter mile until I reached a yellow mailbox. I took a left there. I drove a mile up a private road scattered with small sheds and woodpiles and came to a house with glass on all sides. That was his house. *It will be like a greenhouse,* he'd written, and it was.

I pulled my bag from the back seat of Moser's van and sat on a stump to smoke. I wasn't even a smoker, not really, but all that time spent with James had given me this habit I didn't want. Suddenly, I missed James terribly. His quirks that had irritated me before seemed lovable now. His way of just showing up where he knew I would be, bearing strange gifts like cans of anchovies or political pamphlets, then leaving just as abruptly to get back to his books. How he rarely slept. How the nights after our senior painting class would turn into long marathons of eating nonperishable foods, smoking through a slit in the window, and listening to him read aloud from dense Marxist tomes. How if I felt one of my paintings was incomplete and didn't know how to fix it, he would know just what was missing and sometimes even make the addition himself. I hoped this time at Moser's together would bring us even closer. His stoic, cryptic way of coming off was really starting to mean something to me. Sex wasn't really part of it.

In the time since he'd told me about the dream, we'd had sex only once, in the field, after he made the portrait. I didn't know if it signaled that there was something wrong with me or something wrong with him, or something wrong with the both of us, but I really couldn't afford to scrutinize any of it too much. I was afraid that relationships could be ruined just by being thought about. But then again, what did it say about the quality of a relationship if it fell apart under the mildest scrutiny? I went inside, a bit damp from the snow. Moser's painting shed had a loft overlooking the studio, with a daybed, a microwave, and a small refrigerator. There was a makeshift bathroom with a toilet, sink, and cramped shower. The walls were littered with photographs of various coasts and fauna. Moser mostly painted landscapes, but there were portraits hanging crookedly on the wall, too.

I started working right away, stretching canvases and consolidating all the tubes of paint in Moser's drawers, moving through the to-do list. When I checked the time again it was eight o'clock and still no James. I didn't know why I held out hope that he would come. It would be impossible to call a taxi in this weather and that was if he even remembered the address. I heard a knock on the door. Then another.

"Hello," a woman's voice said. "Hellooo."

I picked up a heavy book and went to the door. Through the peephole, I saw a frail, dark-haired woman with blue eyes and a long, silver down coat.

"I brought some dinner. Some soup. I'm Daniel's wife. Are you the intern?"

I opened the door. The woman shook the snow off her shoes and smiled.

"Oh," she said. "You look pretty. He doesn't waste any time."

"He mentioned you would be here. I'm—"

The woman set down a large thermos and two heavy blankets, then took off her shoes and plopped herself down on the floor, sitting crisscrossed. I couldn't tell what she was, certainly not an American.

"I'm Hildy," she said.

"Ruth," I said, shaking her hand, which she had extended to me.

Hildy gestured at the thermos.

"I figured you were a vegetarian, seems that everyone at the college is. It's barley and split peas."

"Thank you," I said.

Hildy took off her coat. She was wearing a green fisherman's sweater. I sat down on a stool opposite her and waited for her to speak or, better, leave, but I could tell she wouldn't.

"I hope he's paying you a decent wage," she said, looking around. "It's a mess in here. He's always trying to outsource his work. Lazy."

"Are you a painter?" I asked her.

"Mmm, no. I'm a photographer. I do something called e-commerce—have you ever heard of it? It's new."

"That's cool," I said, trying to be polite.

"No, it really isn't." She laughed. Her laughter made me want to laugh, too. She tossed back her head and brushed her hair back. Her diamond ring was very large and caught the light in a distracting way. Hildy stood up and opened the old furnace, moving pieces of wood into it intently. She struck a match and pulled her hair back from her face, fanning the fire. Kneeling back down, she took off her sweater and adjusted the small red children's T-shirt she was wearing. A cartoonish brown bear was printed on it and below the bear it said CALIFORNIA.

"We're separated, you know."

"Yeah, he mentioned that," I said, looking at the clock.

"I'm sure he didn't tell you why."

I shook my head.

"It's because he's addicted to seeing prostitutes," she said, her blue eyes frigid.

I said nothing.

"I'm joking! Sort of," Hildy said, laughing, though there was pain in her laughter. "But there were other women. I was never very attracted to him. I got married very young. Your age. Big mistake."

"I'm sorry to hear that."

"Don't be…I don't regret it; he gave me a lot of freedom from my family. I'm from Norway and he brought me here to New York where I could explore…Anyway, has he paid you? Do you need money?"

"I'm okay. Thanks for the food," I said. I looked up at the clock again.

"Of course. No trouble at all. You can come into the main house whenever you want to, you know. There's TV and books and movies. I have, you know, board games. Scrabble. It's very lonely here during the winter, so… if you want someone to talk to."

"Thanks," I said.

"I see you keep checking the time—are you expecting someone?"

"No…no. I'll stay out of your way, I don't want to intrude."

"Oh, but it wouldn't be intruding. I'm staying here this winter because I'm trying to dry out, you know. I don't want to go to New York and start thinking about my life and drinking. I'm just here trying to take it easy. It would be good to have some company. When you aren't working."

It was hot that close to the fire. I took off the scarf I was wearing and moved to the couch across from the furnace.

"How old are you?" she asked.

"Twenty-two."

"So young, so young," she said. "You remind me of myself then—my parents were very Christian and I was very shy, very self-conscious. Was your family that way?"

"In a way," I said.

"I can tell! You can always tell."

Hildy got up and sat on the couch beside me.

"Whoever you're waiting for isn't coming, so you may as well take your mind off it," Hildy said. "My friend sent me a copy of this movie. I've heard it's really great. It's about these twentysomethings by this Chinese auteur. Not my usual thing, but it sounds pretty interesting."

For whatever reason, I said okay. I picked up the thermos of soup and followed Hildy through the door to the other part of the house. The wide hallway opened to a large open-concept kitchen and living room. There was another fireplace in the room where the television was. Around the TV were enough sofas, ottomans, armchairs, and floor pillows to sit twenty or thirty people. The walls were filled with a similar excess: decorative plates, paintings in heavy wooden frames, primitive masks.

Hildy explained that she collected antiques: shaker furniture, folk art, quilts.

"To sell?" I asked.

"No. To keep around. I just like old things," she said.

Some of Moser's paintings hung on the wall: large, desolate, kind of ironic landscapes with purple skies and white sand, clear horizons and virgin forests. There was something very sad about them and when I saw them, my chest started to pain me.

"Sit anywhere you like," Hildy said, pushing the tape into the player.

I sat down on a brown mohair couch and she sat down next to me, toying with the remote. From the first scene, the movie was washed in green light. The actors and actresses were all thin and impossibly tall. The point was, they were all attractive, brooding, and sexually entangled with one another. After about twenty minutes, Hildy got up and went into the kitchen.

"Don't pause it, just let me know if I miss anything," she said.

I heard glasses move around and ice fall onto the counter. She was mixing a cocktail. I stared at the screen, enjoying the ambient, moving scenes of the city, but it was hard to not be distracted by the walls. Hildy came back into the room holding two highball glasses filled with dark liquor and ice. On top of each drink were identical, curled orange peels.

She handed me one and sat down.

"This movie's great, isn't it?" she asked. "I love Hong Kong."

"I've never been," I said.

"You'll go one day, if you want," she said. "With a face like yours, you'll go anywhere you want."

The drink was mostly whiskey. Too strong, but I drank it all the same. Hildy got up quietly and made us both another. I felt myself sinking into the couch, feeling comfortable, forgetting the original arrangement that had brought me into Moser's home. I worried that what I was doing would get back to him somehow and reflect poorly on me as a student, but I wasn't doing anything wrong, just watching a movie by a Chinese auteur with his ex-wife, Hildy, and having a drink that was supposed to be an old-fashioned but was really just whiskey diluted with melting ice.

I reclined farther into the couch and put my feet up on the ottoman. I considered all the places James could be and I hoped he was alright. I also considered the fact that to James, it did not matter whether or not I was alright. The second consideration didn't take anything away from the first.

The movie played on. Someone died, someone else made a phone call. Without comment, Hildy put her hand on my thigh and left it there. I looked down at Hildy's hand, the wedding band bright on her finger. She wore all these bangles and her hand made a shining, faint sound whenever she moved it. She rested her head on my shoulder. Gradually, as the movie progressed, Hildy moved her hand farther and farther up my leg and undid my jeans. I didn't feel particularly overpowered, and while I knew that at any point I could have stood up, ending the whole thing, it occurred to me that I didn't want to.

Hildy moved her right hand absentmindedly and I felt the coolness of her jewelry against my skin. I sensed that for her, this had everything to do with pain her husband had inflicted on her and nothing to do with me. Hildy made stifled noises and kissed me. The credits rolled down the screen. Neither of us stood up. Hildy kept entertaining herself, moving her hand around in my jeans. It didn't feel bad, actually. It felt okay, good even. I felt so much sympathy for Hildy then. Not to mention Hildy was such an unfortunate name, so awkward. She had to carry that name around with her, all day, every day, as long as she lived. And her husband was so disinterested in her that he paid for sex. And it had demoralized her to the point that she admitted it openly, to me, a stranger. I thought about what it must have felt like to be her and I was moved. In our exchange I could see the five-year-old girl, the sixteen-year-old teenager, the twenty-year-old lady, and the forty-year-old woman contained in Hildy like a set of nesting dolls. I was Hildy and Hildy was me. It was easy to forget how we all belonged to one another. We all wanted the same thing, more or less: acceptance into a loving group that would embrace us to the point of dissolution, eradicating all loneliness and ending our searches for meaning. Or at least that was the general idea. We never gave one another what we needed. But Hildy gave me my first orgasm. Silently, I thanked her. The screen of the large television went black and Hildy stood up, cleared the glasses away, wiped the coffee table down, and kissed me good night on the forehead.

"I'd appreciate it if you didn't mention this to Daniel," she said. "Things between us are very complicated, as you can imagine."

I buttoned my pants and went back to the studio. I shut the furnace door, spread out a flannel sheet, and slept on the rug. None of it felt real until my body touched the floor and I remembered I was myself. Before the sun rose, I heard another loud knock on the door, then the door opened.

Moser stood on the threshold, shaking off his boots and setting down his luggage. I asked him if he needed any help. He saw me waking up and told me it was alright, to go back to sleep. Hildy heard the noise and came in from the house, to see what had happened.

"Back so soon?" she asked him.

"My residency's been canceled."

"So, what, you think you're going to stay here?" Hildy asked.

"I'll have to."

"Absolutely not," Hildy said.

Moser gestured at me and told Hildy to be quiet, as in, *Not in front of the guest.*

"I can go," I said.

"Darling, you can't drive in this weather," said Hildy.

"You two have met?" he asked.

"We watched a movie together last night, actually. It's just nice to have someone around who appreciates a quiet night in. Someone to talk with about films and art, not always just gossip and vulgar, sycophantic conversation. Someone *kind,* who actually shows an interest…" Hildy trailed off.

Moser ignored her. I gathered my things and started to put on my shoes. I could go to my parents' house and maybe beat the storm if I left right away. I figured the van would be fine in the snow if Moser would let me take it. Going home required accepting that James would never come.

"I think I'll go if that's okay with you," I said.

"At least stay for breakfast," Moser said.

"Thanks, but that's okay," I said, several times, until finally they stopped asking. Moser let me use his desktop to print out directions. He said I could borrow the car for the remainder of the winter break and I couldn't reconcile his generosity with the portrait of the selfish man that Hildy had described. Moser handed me forty dollars for food and gas. He couldn't have known how badly I needed it. When I got on the road, it occurred to me that I should call my mother and father, in case they had made other plans. I decided against it, though, since I had a key, and knowing my parents, my mother hadn't made any plans, never took any trips, had given up on the fantasy of travel. I stopped at a Stewart's for coffee. I paid for the coffee and a blueberry muffin and had thirty-seven dollars left over. I didn't stop again until I hit I-95 and turned into Cranston for a can of air freshener to spray on my clothes, which smelled like liquor and smoke. At ten in the morning, I pulled into the driveway of my parents' apartment. I lifted my bags out of the car and walked across the cement, over the snow, which was still falling.

When I knocked on the door, I heard my mother ask herself, "Who could that possibly be?"

She was wearing a robe and had her hair up in purple rollers. I was tired from the drive, from the night before. I dropped my things in the hall. She put her cup of tea down to help me. On the small television in the kitchen, a weatherman ran his hands over the East Coast of America and snowflakes materialized on the surface of New Hampshire, Massachusetts, Maine, and Rhode Island.

"I'm clearing out your bedroom and I was hoping you'd help me sort through it for a donation pile. We're renovating. We're buying this building from the landlady," my mother said, helping me out of my coat. Hearing my mother go on about renovating sounded like talking to a person at the end of their life who insisted that when they got well, they'd travel to this or that country.

I spent the long hours of winter break drawing portraits in charcoal in the corner of my empty bedroom. The walls were still painted this terrible shade of blue that made me feel like I was in an institution. My mother had given my bed frame, desk, and all of my remaining clothing to a women's shelter in the next town. She'd kept the mattress, though. We'd cleaned it over the years, but the urine stains, the blood stains, and the general discoloration from all of that sleep had made it unsightly. The doctor's office had cut my mother's hours, which I didn't know, because I never called. She had gotten another receptionist job, which would start after Christmas. In the meantime, she was watching over another elderly couple who lived nearby. They paid my mother okay, under the table, but it was a short-term gig, because the couple's adult daughter was moving back to Rhode Island. My father had hurt his knee when he fell on black ice and was in bed on a painkiller. Finally horizontal, bedridden as I'd always imagined him. My mother was more the patriarch. She sat down across from me on my bedroom floor and sorted a box of my belongings into two piles: garbage and things to take with me. She sounded calm and indifferent to her problems.

Then she said, "Enough about me. I'm glad to see you, Ruth. You look really skinny. Did you go vegetarian or something? I've been hearing all about vegetarians..."

I smiled at her politely, foreclosing conversation. That was as affectionate as my mother got, asking about my weight. I knew she didn't mean any harm. Again, I felt extremely worried about my parents growing older here by themselves, and these jobs they worked, which seemed precarious and, all in all, like dead ends. I realized thinking about the dullness of a job was a luxury, one I wouldn't be able to afford, either. What exactly did I think I'd do with a fine arts degree, except maybe get another fine arts degree?

"Where's Maria?" my mother asked. "I saw her aunt at the Stop & Shop a couple of weeks ago, buying a pound cake. She looked miserable as ever."

"Maria's in Los Angeles, with a friend."

"Oh," my mother said. "She was always such a free spirit."

"I'm a free spirit, too," I said. It came out childish.

"No, I wouldn't say that," my mother said. "You always followed suit. You always followed Maria."

In the evening, my mother braided my hair and we watched *Jeopardy!* After dinner, I told her I was going to the library.

"Can you get some eggs? You can grab five dollars out of my purse."

Outside, I brushed the snow off the windshield with my sleeve. As I neared the library, the Christmas decorations lining the lawns became louder, more elaborate. I logged into one of the computers by the adult fiction section on the first floor. A man who maybe had a home, or maybe didn't, played Pac-Man on the monitor to my left.

I checked my email. James had written me:

> Ruth,
>
> I'm writing to tell you I'm going back to London. I'm dropping out. None of this is easy to write. I think you're brilliant and, as you know, I'm crazy about you. However, I can't be in America anymore. It's a sick and atomized culture, unconducive to making any decent art or staying afloat in general. It turns out that poet was wrong. Some pains are too much. I put a book in campus mail for you. A Gorky monograph. Gorky was someone who could really suffer. You're more like him than I am. You're a lot more solid, which comes as quite a surprise.
>
> I don't want to burden you with any bad news, but I made an attempt on my life and now I think it's best I go home, be closer to my mother and resume therapy, before I wind up actually killing myself. I ask that you don't write me. It's better we don't speak, it would only make me more upset.
>
> As ever,
> James

Naturally, the first thing I did was type up a response. The librarian called out, "Fifteen minutes," from behind her circulation desk. They were closing soon.

The man at the computer next to me slammed his fist down on the table. He'd lost his last life in the game. I started the email out on a sympathetic note. I wanted to find a way to agree with James, while also convincing him against his plans. I told James that first and foremost, I was sorry to hear he tried to take his life and that I was relieved he'd been unsuccessful. My hands shook as I typed. Yes, American life is atomized but not so much so that it's impossible for us to be in love here. As for the poet, I wrote, firing off truisms was easy, whereas living was hard. I realized that was just another truism, but I didn't have much time. I told James that he should see a doctor, talk to his mother, then come back to Annandale and get his degree. That was logical thinking. I signed the email, yours truly. Then I sent it off. I wasn't much of a writer, but I thought the letter had good bones. A moment later, I refreshed my email and got an error message. It was undeliverable. James had deleted his email or blocked me or he was dead and someone else had deleted his email or blocked me. The man at the neighboring computer slammed his hand down against the table again and I startled.

The librarian got up and flicked the lights on and off. I zipped up my bomber jacket and went back out into the cold. I cleared the snow off Moser's white van and stopped at a Cumberland Farms for a pack of Marlboro Golds. I felt sick as I stood outside in the fluorescent white light of the gas station sign. My stomach was still killing me. I walked inside to buy a dozen brown eggs, contemplated the cigarettes, and left without them. What did a young woman do at a juncture like this? Get very drunk and listen to music.

I remembered the English teacher I'd had in my junior year, Ms. Bowles, a single woman in her sixties, who told us that we would all have to try alcohol and decide for ourselves whether it suited us or not. Her only advice was that alcohol made promises that it couldn't keep. Small pieces of advice from my school days came back to me and it was hard to say whether it was worth anything, all that moralizing. I was twenty-two and I could go to the liquor store nearby and drink myself to a point of total apathy, forgetting James, forgetting Maria, but in the morning, the liquor would leave my blood and I'd still be there, having to deal with myself. Maybe

I'd just sit in the car and say a prayer, then go home and watch a Turner Classic with my mother and assimilate with the pain, like the poet had told James.

After Christmas, Professor Moser emailed me and asked if I'd like to go back to the studio. If so, he'd left a key. I'd be alone, since he and Hildy were going to New Mexico together, to work on their marriage. The morning before I left, I finished the drawing of my mother and father that I'd been working on absentmindedly. My mother put it in a frame from the Salvation Army and hung it in a dark corner of the living room where no one ever sat. My father, sluggish from the medication, didn't come down to see me off. I went into my mother's bedroom and found him passed out on the full-sized bed, too small for the two of them. I brushed his hair aside and kissed his face. He muttered a short goodbye, turned over, and fell back asleep. I always envisioned him going this way. He'll live forever and die slowly. I didn't know why, but the thought crossed my mind many times. As she handed me my bag and walked me out, my mother held my face in her hands.

"You know, I had a dream you were pregnant, last week. In fact, every night last week I dreamt you were holding a newborn."

I brushed her off and said goodbye. As I pulled out of the snow-lined driveway, I felt like a changeling, like I had nothing at all to do with my parents or this place where I'd lived. How to explain my new life to them, the things I'd learned? That the powerful were evil while the weak were good, that a few evenings before, I'd had sex with a woman my mother's age and enjoyed it. Did my mother know that women were no different than men and that race was a social construct? There wasn't much room for my parents in the future I hazily envisioned. Family was also a social construct.

21

◇◇◇◇◇◇◇◇◇◇◇◇◇

I EXPECTED TO see James on campus, with his head down, look-ing a little too focused on a political pamphlet, like a younger, darker version of *The Thinker,* but I never did. The first weeks back, I believed I would turn a corner and find him there, but that never came to pass. What scared me was that if he had killed him-self, I'd have no way of knowing. Maybe I'd feel it in some indirect way, like an invisible light going out inside of me, but I doubted it. I assumed something like that had to be bidirectional, a pull between two believers. James didn't believe in anything except for his mother and Marx.

That I was meant to wake up in the morning and dress and go about my day colored the world as cruel and indifferent. That he had been there, then was gone, while everything continued as it had before, registered as an injustice. To stand under the weak drip of the communal showers, to sit in the dining hall and feed myself, to walk to botany and sit in my usual seat, felt too ridiculous to justify.

"I heard that movers came to James's room and packed up all his books and left, in the middle of the afternoon," said Sabrina.

She arrived to class early that day, already settled into her place, eager to gossip with me, but to me, it wasn't gossip.

"Did they say anything?" I asked Sabrina.

"No," Sabrina said. "Have you heard from him?"

I nodded and told her about the email.

"Oh, Ruth, I can't imagine what you're dealing with. Guys are the worst."

Sabrina put her hand over mine, curling her pink fingernails in a tight, placating grasp. The slide on the projector flashed to a photo of the oldest tree in the country, an unremarkable pine somewhere in California.

I had gotten so used to the stomach pain that I could pretend it wasn't there. Then I would feel a sharp pang and double over. Just as quickly, I could ignore it again. I decided I wouldn't sulk or feel sorry for myself and that the best way to get over the pain was to distract myself. Otherwise, I'd spend all day pacing my room, ruminating on James and the email, like I had been doing for weeks. I had already squandered the day, so I stood in my room and rifled through my closet for something revealing to wear. I put on a white dress and fixed yesterday's eyeliner so that it was even. There was a party. I drank a glass of tepid white wine alone and tried to coax myself into putting on a pair of shoes, going outside. There was a half-finished painting on my desk. A small piece I'd set aside because it was off in some way, imbalanced, a bore. I wanted to ask James what he thought. I missed him. I turned it over and looked at its wooden frame, its white underside. Someone was at the door. I opened it to see Maria in a nightgown, our old uniform cardigan, and a pair of rubber flip-flops. She was alone, which was unusual these days. I looked behind her to be sure.

"Are you going to let me in?" she asked.

I stepped aside and she sat on the chair at my desk. She turned the painting around and suspended it in the air in front of her and put it back down.

"Drinking alone?" she asked.

"I was off to that party," I said. "I was just picking out a pair of shoes."

I opened my closet.

"I'm not here to say I told you so," Maria said.

"Why are you here?" I asked.

"To see how you're doing. I heard about the email he sent. He's totally insane."

"Who told you about the email?"

"Sabrina, who else?" Maria said. "I hate James's type. He thinks he's so fucking tortured. He really shouldn't flatter himself."

"He had a difficult life," I explained. "His father was never around, always working, at the bank, and his mother…"

"James was a spoiled, antisocial crank who couldn't paint his way out of a paper bag. And I don't believe that was his real accent."

"Thank you, Maria. That really makes me feel better."

"Sorry," Maria said. "But it's true. And I warned you."

"Someone I cared about might be dead and you're gloating because you saw it coming?"

"He isn't dead. He's probably somewhere in New York as we speak, doing the same number to another girl. He bashes your paintings, tells you he loves you, gets weird about sex, sends a stupid email about wanting to kill himself, then steps out of the way."

"Do you really think he's in New York?" I asked, perking up. Maria sighed and rolled her eyes, a little vexed by the fact that she wasn't getting through to me.

"What if he really *is* dead?" I asked.

"James is too self-absorbed to ever kill himself. He's alive, and I promise you'll see him again. But the question is, will you have enough self-respect and good sense to ignore him?"

"No," I said.

Maria shook her head and took a sip of wine.

"Let's get out of this room," she said. "It's stale."

The sun moved low in the sky beyond campus. We watched it through the window as we watched each other. Maria finished the bottle of wine and pulled out a flask of vodka. She suggested we go swimming in the waterfall. Drunk and low from confronting the fact that James had done the obvious, I was impressionable enough to do anything she said. We packed a small bag with a towel, citronella oil for the mosquitoes, a pack of matches, and a flashlight for the dark walk back from the creek. We should have been afraid of the woods, afraid of the rocky, steep decline we would have to go down in the night, but we didn't particularly care what could happen to us. There were rumors of murders, but nothing confirmed, not that we read local news, or any news for that matter. The more I looked at Maria's hair, the more I liked the clean, dark look against her soft round features, which weren't round at all anymore, had not been for a long while, but were jaunt and angular. We held one another for support as we faltered down the unkept path through the dense brush.

"Is this safe?" I asked.

"Definitely not," Maria said and took my hand.

We peeled off most of our clothes and got into the water. First Maria, then me. We set the flashlight down by our belongings. You could only see about a foot ahead of you in either direction. Maria went out a bit farther and held on to a branch for balance.

"Come here," she said, extending her arm. I swam out in the dark water, but I didn't need to swim. I was tall enough to walk through it. The waves moved past us gently, falling down into the stream. Maria let go of the branch and put her arms around me. Our chests and legs pressed up against one another; I felt naked, though I wasn't. I let go of the branch I had been holding and held on to her. She kissed my face and then my neck and moved her hand down my back. I stood still. Then she let me go and went beneath the water.

She swam a foot or two back to our pile of clothes and got out, lit up partially by the fluorescent white of the flashlight, mosquitoes buzzing around it. Her body was long and slow-moving, casting dull shadows on the graffitied rocks behind her. What had made her so endearing to me as a child—her voice, her innocence—was in direct opposition to what made her alluring now: her sex, her silence. I got out and sat beside her, our knees brushing against one another's. She pulled at my spandex shorts. Her hand moved searchingly down my leg. When she kissed me, I wondered if it wasn't a consolation for James. We touched each other instinctively and it felt suddenly like an inevitable progression of what we'd started in the third grade. I felt, drunkenly, that the tides in my life were shifting. That I had found love. That I was brave and would confess everything to Sheila and forge a life with Maria.

Maria unclasped my bra. Something shook in the trees across the dark channel, an animal or a breeze. Footsteps broke through the brush. Then a stream of light and taunting laughter shot out across the water. We took our things and ran, barefoot, half-naked, a quarter mile uphill. When we stopped, I was panting. We stood by the lot in front of the film building. From her bag, Maria pulled out a key ring. She held it up to me to suggest we could go inside and dry off. We crept into a small, red velvet–lined theater. Maria gave me the towel and we sat in the front row, drying our hair. Without speaking, we started to caress one another, grabbing indiscriminately wherever, all over. Then, without any preliminaries, Maria's head was nearly in my lap and she was pushing my legs apart. I looked down at her and around at the plush room. I stroked her thick hair and ran a finger around her ear. I didn't think of what I did, I was just enjoying myself and hoping things would continue like this, all evening, in the movie theater. Then I felt a terrible pain and I shot up. Maria pressed her palm to her eye; I'd jabbed it with my knee. I held my stomach and there was a whole stream of blood rushing down my leg. I cried out in pain and she tried to get me to describe it. In a moment we were in the clinic. Me in my blood-soaked white dress, Maria in her Our Lady cardigan and her still-damp nightgown. The nurse was a matronly, unfazed woman who you could be sure had seen it all before. She handed me a cup of water and told me to take a deep breath. Maria sat on the vinyl hospital bed beside me and squeezed my hand. The nurse asked me a few questions about my periods and my sexual activity, then gave me a knowing, nonjudgmental look.

"I'm going to give you a test," the nurse said.

"A test for what?" Maria asked on my behalf.

"For pregnancy, dear."

She pulled a clear cup from a cavernous drawer and told me to go to the toilet. I shouldn't be shy, she said, she needed a decent sample. Maria walked me down the hall and back. I peed with great effort. My urine was murky and speckled with red globs that wouldn't quite settle or mix. I handed the nurse my sample and we waited.

"Bleeding is normal in the beginning. Perfectly normal. But you bled quite a bit."

"The beginning of what?" I asked.

"Pregnancy, dear," the nurse said.

The results of the test weren't legible yet, and while she couldn't confirm until they were, she was very confident I was pregnant. We waited in silence, Maria hanging her head and wringing her hands. She knew what a hindrance it would be for me to be saddled with a child. Of all people, she knew. But we weren't talking about a child, just a bit of blood on my leg and some pain in my stomach, nothing at all. The nurse picked up the test strip and held it to the light. She handed me a pale pink pamphlet on pregnancy and told me I had options, to keep it in mind, that I had options.

"Well, she's going to get an abortion, obviously," Maria said.

"Maria," I said. "Please let me speak for myself."

I took many shallow breaths and scratched my head. I looked down at the shiny floors; many dark drops of my blood had fallen there, but the bleeding had slowed considerably. I didn't feel any more pain, or maybe because I knew the source of my pain, it was less troubling.

"Can you do it here?" I asked.

"Abortions?" the nurse asked. "No, I don't do abortions here, hon. That would be more convenient, though."

She gave us the address for a clinic in town. Maria and I walked out of the building, shaken by the night in more ways than one. Maria suggested we get changed and call a cab right away. She instantly went into a directorial role, telling me what we should do and how. She said I could expect to spend a couple hundred dollars at least. I could use the money from Moser, she said. I hadn't told her I'd lost the money because we hadn't been speaking. I looked at her and tried to conceal my embarrassment about it all.

"You spent all the money?" she asked.

"No, I lost it."

"Lost it where? When?"

"Before break. In my room. It was there and then it wasn't."

"So someone stole it. When something's there and then it isn't, it's because someone stole it."

"No one knew I had the money, except—"

"James," she said. My shoulders sank. "Ruth, how could you be so fucking clueless?"

I stood in the middle of the road on campus holding my wet towel. There was toilet paper wadded up in my underwear and my breasts were sore. Maria said she would get the money from Sheila. Sheila said yes without any questions. As she always said yes to Maria without any questions. So, I had Sheila to thank for my abortion. I didn't sleep and early in the morning Maria and I were the first at the clinic. I begged her not to bring Sheila with us and she understood.

There were protestors encircling the clinic who reminded us we would burn in hell for what we were doing. We walked through them like parted waters and didn't care since it wasn't the first time we had heard about hell and burning. Before going forward, the woman doctor told me she had to show me an ultrasound and I looked at it without seeing it. I glanced at the curving, bluish-gray lines that were supposed to be a picture of life. It could have been a painting or a postcard; I felt it had nothing to do with me. The procedure was quick, all in all. The doctor made it seem like a nonevent, as ordinary as getting your blood pressure checked, and I was grateful to her for being so casual. In the taxi back to campus Maria looked at me and feigned a smile.

"All better now," she said.

On Monday, I went back to botany. I went back to my studio. I went back to my life. James was not there and neither was the fetus.

At the end of May, we collected our degrees. Maria had offered me a spare room in Sheila's family apartment, and whatever happened by the waterfall hadn't changed that. Maria might make me regret accepting her kindness, but she wouldn't rescind something she had already given. School was over, we were meant to go out into the world now. We had bachelor's degrees; it was unclear what one did with those. We loaded up a rented van haphazardly for New York, though I had no sense what I'd do there. I called my parents before I left Bard. Their voices still filled me with strange panic and always would.

"What will you do there?" my mother asked.

"How does a person make a living as an artist?"

My father had finished his certification to work as an electrician and now he was doing alright. His knee had healed okay, but it hurt when it rained. He had bought a good, new pickup truck and bought my mother a little red Honda. He'd become very pragmatic, eager to give advice.

"I've heard the new thing is IT. Women can do it, too, apparently," he said.

"Where will you live? Is Maria there? Can we say hello to her?" my mother asked.

"I'm sure you'll be fine if you're moving with Maria. Maria's got a good head on her shoulders," my father said.

"Yes, very hardworking," said my mother. "Oh, maybe you can get a job teaching at a Catholic school. It doesn't hurt to drop off a resume."

"She's young, she has time," my father said, the bleeding heart chiming in.

"Americans always say, *You're young, you're young. You have time.* Twenty-two isn't young. When I was twenty-two, my life was over."

"Because you had a child," my father said. "Ruth won't have a child."

"And why not?"

"Because *artists* don't have children," my father said with so much authority I almost believed him. In university, he'd done well on his English exams and since then, he felt he understood life and beauty more than my mother did.

"You're the one who gave her the colored pencils. Now she's spoiled for motherhood," my mother said.

I answered my parents' questions politely, then I hung up the phone. I walked out of my dorm for the last time and got in the front seat between Maria and Sheila. I would miss the college. Coming here was like coming to another country, learning a different language in order to speak to these rich children from California. It certainly didn't prepare me to make a living, but I wouldn't have survived in my parents' home, and here I was in one piece. James was the only casualty, and he probably wasn't even dead, according to Maria. In college I learned how to have sex with a woman, I found a boyfriend and then lost him, I learned to paint shadows and then found I didn't need to. You couldn't say it was a waste. Looking out over the dashboard, I saw that everything was green again: The lush moss and tall grasses would be here to welcome other young people. I put away my resentment for Sheila for a moment and thought that at least I'd been able to be with Maria that one evening. The evening could last a long time in my memory. We drove down the winding Taconic with Sheila playing with the radio dial the entire time, not satisfied by what was playing on any station.

"It's all so mainstream," Sheila complained.

"That's the point of the radio," said Maria.

I said nothing. Maria chain-smoked as she drove, in spite of the sticker on the driver's side window that said smoking resulted in a two-hundred-dollar fee. Maria didn't care. Sheila had put the rental on her parents' credit card. Sheila let Maria do whatever she wanted.

Sheila's family apartment was old and hadn't been refurbished but conveyed, all the same, the status of her aunt and uncle who owned it and the two units below it, which they rented to artists. Sheila insisted they got it cheap. It was a loft split into two bedrooms by thin walls that made having a truly personal life impossible. Sheila and Maria took the larger room on the left side of the apartment, and I took the smaller room to the right. Because the walls were thin, I often heard Sheila and Maria having sex or arguing, both of which they did with equal disregard for whoever was listening. Maria was happy to stay home and work, subsisting on cheap fast food. Sheila, on the other hand, wanted to go out to bars and restaurants. Back in the world and away from the enclosure of school, it became apparent how different their upbringings were. Just when I thought this would put a fatal strain on their relationship, I would hear them having sex again and assume they had come to an understanding. Then the arguments would start up again. Since I was unemployed with very little to do, I spent a lot of time eavesdropping. Occasionally, their voices would fall to a whisper, which gave me the sense I was the subject of their conversation.

One afternoon, I had the window open, and I was finishing two small oil paintings I thought I'd take to the flea market for some cash. There was a vendor I often saw selling art that looked like it was made by students, and I was sure he could sell my paintings, too. I heard Maria and Sheila shuffling around in the next room. Then Sheila started to speak in a tense, low voice. I closed the window to better hear her, not caring about the fumes.

"You take advantage of me," Sheila said. "I think that once you're successful you'll leave me. You're using me."

"You want me to be dependent on you," Maria said. "You offer these things, then get angry when I accept."

"Whenever we go out, I pay."

"That's because *you're* the one who wants to go out. I'll stay home and eat burgers; it's all the same to me."

"That's the problem, you don't care. You're dismissive. You're ungrateful."

"Ungrateful?" Maria asked. "I don't have time to argue with you. I need to work. I have an interview tomorrow. Anytime something important happens for me, you start an argument."

"You're paranoid. You think I'm out to get you. I'm the only one who seems to care about you. I'm the one giving you a place to live. I'm the one paying for your film and paying to develop your work. And you don't even thank me!"

Something crashed to the floor loudly and I heard a glass breaking. I heard the door swing open. There were aggressive whispers and I heard the sound of books falling.

"Go talk to Ruth and complain about how I'm so needy and oppressive," Sheila yelled. Maria called her a bitch, which I had never heard her call Sheila before, then she slammed the door closed and before I could move my ear from the adjoining wall she was in my room with a stack of photographs in her hand.

"I have to get out of here," Maria said. So we did. We walked a few blocks to a restaurant that sold pizza, burgers, and wings. In fact, it might have been called Pizza, Burgers, and Wings. We ordered a cheap special that gave you a bit of everything and sat by the windows where the light reflected on our food, making it look just as it did in the posters. I waited for Maria to broach the subject of her argument with Sheila. I took a sip of my Diet Coke and looked at the passersby with great curiosity since the allure of New York had not yet worn off on me.

"I don't know what you heard," Maria said.

"Barely anything," I said.

"But you have to understand Sheila's a very angry person. There was no room for anger in her home."

"Sure," I said.

"I think because her adoptive parents were so attentive and they were analysts, she thinks she sees everything very clearly and in this levelheaded way, but it's just the opposite."

"I heard something breaking, I think—glass?"

"That was just an accident. I had a frame on the edge of my desk and she moves her hands a lot when she talks and I rushed to move it out of the way, so it fell."

"Right," I said, patting the oil off my slice of pizza.

"The bottom line is that I think I need to get a job...and maybe break up with her."

"Do you think?" I asked.

"She doesn't know about us...getting together at school or anything, but I think she feels like I have a wandering eye. Or maybe she thinks I only care about my work or I only care about her money. Either way, I just can't take the accusations anymore. I don't want to feel like I'm a bad person."

"You? You aren't a bad person."

"Do you think I should end things?" Maria asked.

"I don't know if my advice is any good."

"And she says I'm a mess because of my mother. How could she say that? I don't talk to anyone about my mother, and she just throws it in my face."

"I don't think you should leave her until you have money and a place to live," I said. "I mean, maybe just do what she asks until then."

Maria looked at me curiously and ate one slider, then her fries, then what was left of the onion rings. She seemed to take comfort in the bad food and the silence. Maybe she was considering my advice. Of course, it was at least, in part, self-interested. I didn't have a job, either. I had nowhere to go except back to my parents'. We walked back to the apartment arm in arm, as we sometimes had when we were children. I hadn't felt so close to her in ages, and I wondered if there was a way to safeguard this intimacy, a way to encase it and ensure it wouldn't go away again. As we stood behind the front door, Maria quietly thanked me for my advice. We found Sheila in the kitchen drinking wine out of the bottle and stirring pasta on the stove. I went back to my room and opened the window and began a new painting, not thinking about what I was doing, just making marks on the cloth. It was something to do. Over the sound of the radio in the kitchen, I heard Maria apologize to Sheila. "I'm very sorry for how ungrateful I've been," she said. "And I love you." The night was peaceful and we ate together at the table, with a pillar candle in the center, melting into itself. Sheila served me a lot of food, though I wasn't hungry.

22

◇◇◇◇◇◇◇◇◇◇◇◇◇◇◇◇

MARIA TOOK A job assisting a photographer who was an acquaintance of Sheila's parents. At home, she rarely spoke about the work they did together, hoping to keep it as separate as was possible under the circumstances, not wanting to feel any more indebted than she already was. Now that she had a regular income and time away from Sheila, I figured breaking up and moving out on her own would reemerge as preoccupations, but she never mentioned anything to that effect again. Late into the night, I still heard Maria and Sheila having sex and I noticed that their arguments were fewer. In fact, they seemed happier than before. Through them I learned something about the elasticity of relationships, how they could appear strained, nearly ruptured, then just as quickly resume their previous, harmonious form. I saw that a partnership could withstand much more battery than I would've expected and that just because someone said they wanted to leave, it didn't mean they actually would. But of course there were aberrations like James, who left without saying anything. I'd just been unlucky, I guessed.

While Maria was at work, I sat at home highlighting jobs in

83

the paper that I felt I was overqualified for. Then it occurred to me that I wasn't overqualified for anything. I was finishing a phone call with another restaurant offering minimum wage when Sheila interrupted me and told me she knew of a job opening. Was I interested? I said yes and Sheila eagerly set me up as a personal assistant to a friend of her parents who lived on the Upper East Side. Sheila told me to show up the following morning and make sure my clothes were ironed.

The woman's name was Dorinda, and she hired me without so much as a ten-minute interview. She told me that I came highly recommended and she expressed her interest in collecting Black art. I told her I didn't know much about Black art and she laughed. Dorinda worked as an art consultant, connecting clients with emerging artists so that they could invest early. Despite the occasional verbal abuse, which I could make allowances for once I heard the way her husband spoke to her, the job was fine, sometimes good even. Dorinda reminded me of my mother in small ways, picking lint off my clothes and telling me to stand up straight. She seemed to belong to an older world where it was fine to scold any child who acted badly and console anyone who was upset in public.

Some weeks into the job, I accompanied Dorinda out on a night that a handful of openings were taking place. We walked from gallery to gallery and she encouraged me to drink all the wine I was offered. She knew what it was like to be young and broke. She knew better than anyone. Her youth had been hard and she liked to mention this in a way I was coming to see was common with upwardly mobile people in New York. Once they were rich, they loved to reminisce on what it was to be poor. I could appreciate that Dorinda didn't pretend the world and money didn't exist as we looked at art together. It was so unsettling how no one ever spoke about money or how they were making it; somehow it was seen as unsophisticated to admit that you couldn't afford to live. Dorinda didn't care about that. She was open about everything: the size of her husband's bonus, the cost of her second home, how much she had spent on a private investigator when she found out her sister's husband had a lover in San Diego. We breezed past most of the art and we hardly discussed it, talking about anything but the art, until we came to a particular painting, vague Cy Twombly–esque white scribbles against a black background. The sort of thing that wouldn't look out of place in a bank lobby.

"Jesus Christ, why the fuck am I even here?" Dorinda asked loudly. She was drunk and she hadn't intended for anyone to hear her, but we all heard. I led Dorinda out the door, and we shared a cigarette in the alley, passing it back and forth like lovebirds. The gray roots protruding from her hairline made her almost beautiful.

"I have very little to show for all of this pointless socializing, this running around," Dorinda said.

"Well, you seem pretty successful to me," I said.

Feeling benevolent, Dorinda asked to visit my studio, but I had no studio, which made me feel ashamed. That was the last night I ever saw her—I just stopped answering her calls. I found work as a hostess in an Italian restaurant where all my tips were stolen away. When Sheila asked me why I did this, I told her that I was sick of art and had no future in it.

I'd been working at the Italian restaurant for a few weeks and getting the hang of it. Before my shift, I put on the long black polyester dress that I had bought from a by-the-pound Goodwill and rummaged through my closet for a pair of black stockings without any holes. The bike that my mother and my father wired me money to buy when I graduated from Bard had been stolen in Gramercy, so I rode the train to the Italian restaurant. Those days when I stood on the platform and watched the subway blow by, I fantasized about jumping, because how could one not?

My manager, Frankie, never touched me or shouted, though his demeanor suggested it was not beyond him. He was just shy of six feet tall and incredibly muscular, so much so that he couldn't rest his ripped, red arms flat at his sides. They always sort of hung several inches from the rest of his body, like an aura. His one request was that I put on makeup for my shift. *You look sick, sweetheart,* he would say to me during our family meal. I didn't think it had anything to do with sex or power; I think he was just genuinely concerned. I looked into the compact mirror of the blush left at the stand by the last hostess. I did look sick, fatigued. A bustling group of twentysomethings walked toward the hostess stand and toward the back were Maria and Sheila, arms locked.

Sheila spoke first. "Hey, Ruth, you look great. Table for five."

They were with two clean-cut gay men, one plain, the other very striking, and a mousy girl wearing transition glasses. She peeked out from the blue lenses with a friendly air. They were all drunk, talkative.

"Yeah, right this way," I said, walking them toward a red velvet booth far away from me. I glanced back at Maria from the corner of my eye. I'd been dying to see her, I realized then. She was hardly ever at the apartment when I was. The group filed into the booth and ordered a pitcher of house wine without looking at the menu. Sheila was especially taken by the pair of boys at the table, and they giggled covertly at an apparently hysterical private joke.

Maria stood up from the table and tapped my shoulder.

"Ruth," she said.

"Yeah?"

"Where's the bathroom?"

I pointed down the hall. She walked away without a word, her oversized trousers brushing against the carpet as she went.

"Friends of yours?" Frankie asked as I stood at the hostess stand, my chin in my hands.

"Sort of," I said. I wouldn't call Frankie homophobic, but he wasn't a champion of gay rights. Money was money, as far as he was concerned.

I read *Sula* discreetly under the stack of menus as patrons ambled out the door toward taxis and bars. Every so often, I looked over at Maria's table. Dressed plainly, she was even more beautiful. And she was clearly the guest of honor at the table, Sheila's hand on her back as she spoke with the others hanging on her every word. I brought Maria and Sheila and their friends a free dessert, a heavy plate of cannoli. I thought it was the kind thing to do, but I immediately regretted it as I walked over to the table and heard the conversation fall to a whisper. How ridiculous I must have looked trying to balance the tray. Maria looked at me as though she didn't know me as I set out the small plates and new napkins for the five of them. Sheila overcompensated as she always did, grinning, acting as though it was some impossible act of generosity: the day-old cannoli.

"Thanks, Ruth," said Maria. The humiliation was enough to kill me. "We're all going to a party later. If you want to come once you're off."

"Yeah, I sometimes go out with the back of house, but I'll stop by after," I said, wishing I hadn't.

Sheila handed me two hundred-dollar bills for the meal and told me to keep the change.

Maria sifted through her wallet and pretended to reach for the check.

"It's fine," Sheila said.

"I'll get it next time," Maria said.

"Right, next time," Sheila said coolly. The discord between them made up for the earlier embarrassment.

Their other friends smiled blankly and sat on their hands. I never got their names or the address to the party.

At the end of my shift, Frankie doled out the cash tips, which were smaller than expected for a Friday, but Sheila's tip was enough to hold me over for the weekend. I had pocketed it and told Frankie they didn't leave anything.

"These fucking people," he said, sucking his teeth. I shrugged and asked if I could slip out a bit early for a party, leaving my side work for the following day.

"I'm glad you're going out, hon. It's good for the depression."

I rode the train back to the apartment and found a note on the refrigerator in Maria's handwriting. It was an address. Beneath the address she had written *party* in her straight, serious penmanship. I put the piece of paper in my purse and pulled a can of Genesee out of the refrigerator. I went into Sheila and Maria's bedroom. It was always so clean. The maid still came by once a week. Someone was paying her, but it wasn't me. I didn't let her into my room, though, because that felt like a break in the order of things. Sheila and Maria's California king was made up in baby blue linen sheets. They were like an endless dress shirt, crisp at every corner.

On the wall across from the bed, there was a framed photo of Sheila and her parents. They were dressed in white and microscopic against the vast blue ocean behind them. I assumed they were on an island. Everything behind them was turquoise, white, and green. Above the bed, there was a photo of Sheila and Maria sitting on a picnic blanket in the grass in the middle of the old campus. The contrast in their coloring made the photograph appear staged, as though it were torn out of a brochure, a diversity ad for the school. Sadder, though, was that they looked so in love. The weight of the secret that lingered between Maria and me didn't do much in the way of empowering me or supplying me the upper hand. Anyway, I didn't want the upper hand against Maria. To end her relationship with Sheila would be to render Maria homeless and to subject Sheila to pain she didn't, if I was being truthful, deserve.

I opened the top drawer of Sheila's long teak desk and took a pack of Parliaments out of a box of duty-free cigarettes. I felt around the inside of my purse for a match and shut off the light in her bedroom. While I smoked in the kitchen, I opened another beer. I thought about putting on some music, but I decided against it. I couldn't get the terrible barbershop quartet songs that played in the restaurant out of my head. I took a third beer into my bedroom. It was a small room with only enough space for a dresser, a twin bed, and a stool. I didn't want to get to the party too early, so I figured I'd just hang around for a while. I sat on the stool and took a box of watercolors out of my top drawer. I ripped a sheet of paper from the sketchbook in my purse and set it on top of the dresser. I submerged my paintbrush in the old glass of water sitting on my dresser and began to paint the edge of the island in Sheila's family photograph, but it turned into something nonrepresentational. A frothy blue blanketed the page. I populated one small corner with a green island. They bled together and became inscrutable. I finished the beer and flattened the can onto my desk.

I shut my bedroom window. Suddenly, it was cold in New York. Summer's long days were over. I took off my stockings, took off my dress, and put on a pair of jeans and a white wool turtleneck. I tried on a wool-lined leather baseball jacket that was my father's and a hand-knit scarf that was also my father's. I thought I looked okay. I put all but ten dollars of my cash deep in my underwear drawer and headed out for the address Maria had left me. I didn't check the time. I was sort of drunk, but I didn't see how else I'd make it out to another party. Not once in my life had I been invited to a party and thought, *That seems like a nice uplifting time in a welcoming place to meet good people and have intelligent conversation.* Or *That seems like an opportunity to have fun and leave feeling better about myself,* but you inevitably longed for the warmth of people packed into a cramped room. You did occasionally crave conversation with intoxicated strangers. That was what got me out of the apartment that particular evening. That and Maria had invited me.

I walked farther downtown, but when I got to the building, it looked uninhabited. *Would Maria really give me the wrong address? Why go through the trouble?* I looked down at the sheet of paper. The number that had looked like a one earlier appeared more like a seven under the streetlamp. I walked down farther and heard music and saw red lights. The stairs were steep and run-down. The door that the music rang through was unlocked, so I let myself in. It was dense inside, packed with faces I didn't know. Some people danced, but very few. Mostly pairs or groups of three nodded and shouted in each other's ears over the music. I smiled at a girl who waved to me, but when she came closer, she said, "Sorry, I thought you were my friend from school." I didn't know anyone there and I didn't see Maria. I didn't see Sheila either and that meant neither of them were there. I went out to the fire escape for another smoke, but a boy with empty eyes came out and started talking to me about his dissertation on the representation of childhood in Kafka's stories, so I pretended to drop the cigarette and went back inside through the window to get away from him.

I didn't leave the party. I had come all this way. I figured Maria and Sheila would get there eventually. I made myself a vodka soda in the kitchen. The light from the fridge was a putrid yellow. It shone on me. I drank a bit in the light of the open door and then I topped off my glass. I saw people smoking inside, so I did the same. I felt happier then and started to dance to the music. It wasn't very good. It must have been made by a friend of the kids there. While I danced, I saw the time on the oven and realized it was nearly two in the morning. Had I painted that long or had I been drinking for hours? Lately I didn't like my life and there were hours I couldn't account for. I thought of the lazy blue and green watercolor. It was the cartography of my life. I topped off my drink and felt sadder then. I sipped the vodka soda and a painful hunger shot up from my stomach. I cast it aside and threw myself all over a boy with long limbs, dark features, and an unenthusiastic smile.

He told me that he was a writer, and that he had just come back from a city I can't remember the name of, from a reading in a small bookstore whose audience was eager and geriatric. He came back to Manhattan to write another book, then another and another. I didn't follow what he said when I asked him about the novel he was writing. I don't know what ever became of that novel. He must have gone into stunning detail because I watched his mouth move for a long time and his hands move in tandem with his speech, for effect. I became so invested in his hands, watching them narrate whatever it was he was going on about. All the while, though, I thought of Maria, that she'd stood me up. The city felt large then. Large and hostile with me alone in a party full of people I didn't know.

"Are you alright?" he asked me, taking the drink from my hand. I was spilling it on the floor.

"Yeah, I'm good, why?"

"You're crying," he said.

"I know," I said.

"My car's parked across the street. Do you want a ride home?"

I stared at his hands, then I looked at my own. They were the same in a way, almost clenched. I looked at the young people in the room, so lost, so talkative. I nodded.

"My name's Ed, by the way. Do you go to school with these guys?"

"I'm Ruth. I don't do anything," I said. He laughed at this. Then we walked down the claustrophobic stairwell.

Maria and Sheila and the hangers-on from the restaurant were coming up the stairs while Ed and I were going down.

"Who's this?" Maria asked.

"I'm Ed."

"Where are you taking her?" Maria asked.

"Wherever she wants to go," Ed said. He was calm, not defensive.

"She's drunk. You aren't going home with her," Maria said.

"I'm fine," I said. "What do you care?"

Maria grabbed my arm and walked me back up the stairs. I pulled away from her and we struggled in the dim light of the narrow staircase. She didn't care about making a scene. Sheila watched for a moment, thinking of what to do, and stepped in to de-escalate, drunk herself.

"Why don't we all just go upstairs and have a drink. Ed? I'm Sheila. We're all old friends. Maria just wants to make sure Ruth's safe. Make sure you don't have a bunch of women locked up in your basement."

"Of course," Ed said.

Sheila smiled. I was grateful. Generally, I found Sheila patronizing—her overtherapized, peacemaking disposition, her perpetual claim to a moral high ground—but in the stairwell, I finally saw her as well-meaning. We went upstairs and joined the party, which was becoming more uninhibited and openly sexual: people making out in corners, a girl stumbling to the bathroom, holding the wall for support. I wound up in the bathroom with Maria and Sheila. Sheila took out a crisp bill and portioned out a line atop a defunct art magazine on the counter.

Sheila gestured toward the magazine, tried to hand me the bill.

"I'm fine, thanks," I said.

"Who's that guy?" Maria asked tersely, inspecting her nose closely in the mirror.

"A writer."

"Yeah? So is everyone in this apartment," she said, rolling her eyes. "*Sheila's* a writer."

"He's kinda cute," Sheila replied.

"He looks like a pervert," said Maria. "He's old."

"He isn't so old," I said.

"Are you gonna go home with him? I mean, he's old enough to be your father," Maria said.

"I might," I said.

"Maria, he can't be older than thirty. I think Ruth should go for it," Sheila said.

"I don't think you should go home with the first pervert you pick out of a crowd!" Maria meant for it to come across as a joke, but I wasn't so sure. Still, we all laughed. Sheila laughed. I laughed, too.

The mood in the bathroom was more lighthearted as Sheila brushed the coke off the magazine and placed it back in the rack. I knew that Maria didn't approve of my prospect and would make her disapproval apparent once we were alone. What did she have against this man she didn't know and why was she so comfortable disparaging someone I had expressed interest in, particularly after the way things had ended so badly with James and I had been so alone all summer? Why didn't she want me to have the sort of romantic companionship she had? It wasn't as though I wanted to marry the man, only that as a young woman it was nice to have someone be drawn to you for a change, and say so. Maria knew I cared a great deal about what she thought, and I didn't know why she chose to wield that authority to make me doubt my own judgment.

"I'm gonna grab a drink. I'll find you two out there, then?" Sheila said, leaving us behind in the bathroom.

"You don't have to invest everything in the first person who pays attention to you," Maria said, rubbing her finger across her gums. "And you wonder why people like James prey on you."

"Why are you so angry with me?"

"Why would I be angry? It doesn't matter to me one way or another. I'm just not sure if you're attracted to him or just scared of the alternative." Maria spoke over me. "Still worried about getting into heaven?"

"What are you talking about?"

"Just be honest with yourself, at least."

"Is this about what happened at school?" I asked.

"What happened...is that you had sex with a woman."

"With you...it's different."

"I'm a woman," Maria said. "You're so repressed, Ruth, I feel sorry for you. Everyone can tell you aren't attracted to men."

"It's you I feel sorry for," I said.

"What?" Maria asked.

"I said, I feel sorry for you. I'm the only person who has ever been a friend to you and you hate me for it. When no one else wanted you, I cared for you and this is how you treat me. My family and I took you in and you treat me like I've done something awful to you."

"Do you want an award for your charity?" Maria said. "What's this with you and Sheila about me being ungrateful? I don't owe you anything."

"No, Maria, you don't owe anyone anything."

I stood up from the edge of the bathtub and straightened myself out in the bathroom mirror before heading back out.

"Wait, Ruth, I'm sorry."

"I think I'm going to start looking for another place to live," I said, then I shut the door behind me. I found Ed in the corner, talking to the grad student from before. He was still explaining his dissertation. Ed looked relieved to see me.

"Ready to go?" I asked. I took his hand and he led me down the stairs. I stumbled behind him, and he propped me up as we crossed the street to his red sedan, cautious of the black ice.

Ed helped me into the passenger seat and pulled the seat belt across my chest. We sat together as the car warmed up and watched the frosted glass grow transparent. I couldn't remember the last time I'd been driven anywhere.

"Your friend seems like a real people person."

"I don't want to talk about her," I said, turning the dials on the radio, searching for something good. Ed asked what my address was and I told him I wasn't going home. He told me that he lived uptown. I said that was fine and we drove onto the highway, where I watched the lights ripple over the water. We went up to his apartment, which was clean and well appointed for a single man. A bowl of fruit sat on the counter, uniform curtains hung in every window, the shoes were lined up by the door. There were flowers:

short white tulips in a green glass pitcher. "From my mentor," he explained. *Who used the word* mentor? I asked myself. Ed cut up a carrot, a sweet yellow pepper, a handful of green beans, and a head of cauliflower. All of it went into a pot with a pouch of orange spices. He boiled rice. I sat at the counter and watched him move about the kitchen and trusted him right away, which I understood as nothing but a testament to my own stupidity. I felt unhappy, but I was glad for his company, for the hot food, for the kindness. We sat in front of his television, but talked over the sound of the tense Western that was playing on AMC.

"I don't know what you're expecting, but I'm not gonna sleep with you."

"I don't wanna sleep with you," he said. My brows went up. Ed laughed. It sounded a bit rehearsed. I nodded. Ed set a plate in front of me. I swallowed a spoonful of rice, then another. It was the best meal I'd had in years. I knew this wouldn't last, so I enjoyed it while it did. People were unreliable, they couldn't be depended on, that I knew. I tried to eat as much as I could, but suddenly I was exhausted. I could barely lift my spoon up to my mouth. I felt like I'd taken a long, long walk in a desert and finally found a place to sit down. I could have collapsed there and then in the middle of the kitchen. I put my plate down.

"You're tired," Ed said. "You can take the bed."

I woke up alone to birdsong in his bed, under the heavy comforter, still wearing my jeans and turtleneck. There was a glass of water and an aspirin on the nightstand. I swallowed the pill and washed it down. When I went out to the living room, I saw the makeshift bed Ed had set up on the couch. The kitchen was straightened out and there was coffee on the table. It was quiet for a while, and I thought I was alone until I heard a wooden chair scrape against the tile floor. He stood up with a pen in one hand and a sheet of notebook paper in the other. I wasn't going to trust him or be as naive as I had been with James. I just needed a bit of a vacation from Maria and my own life. I had every intention of being guarded and elusive, but as we drank coffee and spoke, I found I couldn't withhold anything from him, that I didn't want to. I told him I'd had an abortion in college, which prompted several questions about what that meant to me. I told him a lot about my parents and about God in order to contextualize the abortion and all that had led up to it. Maria came up many times, and finally he interrupted me.

"You and your friend must have really done a number on each other," he said.

I pulled back, said less then. I doubted that in telling the story of her life, Maria would allow me to dominate her narrative to the extent I had allowed her to loom large in mine. Ed noticed that I had gone quiet, and to engender trust or because he wanted to, he told me that he felt his parents never approved of his writing. Even as he made a decent living, wrote books that sold well, and was devoted to his mother and father, they never seemed pleased. There was a lot of Black art hanging on Ed's walls. Things I recognized from working with Dorinda briefly, expensive things. I asked him where it had all come from and he told me his parents had given it to him, they hadn't had room for it all. He said that he came from a very prominent Black family. I laughed when he said the word *prominent*. Strange way to describe a family. I told him that I came from a very obscure family, very unknown. I felt I could tell him anything. We continued to exchange confessions that way, and before I knew it, I was telling him that my maternal grandmother had drowned and that it had always made my mother seem distrustful of the world. I didn't leave that day or the next. We didn't discuss the arrangement, but I just continued to stay. I called out of the three shifts I had that week at the restaurant and told my boss I was sick. He told me to get all the rest I needed. *I can tell you aren't doing too good, sweetie.*

Every day at Ed's went on the same, more or less: His alarm

rang, he woke up and ran. During the early hours, he sat at his desk making fervent edits. There was a time in the morning when he did nothing but open mail and respond to letters, grade papers. He had a stack of large monographs in the corner of the living room. I pored over them and really wrote for the first time since my junior year. I wrote the first two pages of a story about a girl dying from the fumes of her oil paints. I sat on the lid of the toilet and read it to Ed as he spread out in the bath, and when I folded up the paper and said, "That's it," he applauded. An earnest applause. It was theatrical, but true. His medicine cabinet was lined with orange bottles. *Of course he has insurance,* I thought. *Wait until Maria hears about this.* His fridge was full of food. When he did not cook, we went out for dinner and drinks. There was no expectation that I would pay. It took a while to see myself in the other patrons. Spiritually, I identified more with the busboys. On the third day we had sex. It lasted longer than I had ever known it to last: forty or fifty minutes at least. He looked at me all the while. Each time that I opened my eyes, his eyes were on me. I did not know what to make of that information. On the fifth night, he took something and we finished a liter of wine quickly and he became sloppy and incoherent. He wasn't cruel or erratic, but he slurred his words badly and broke a wineglass and a small ceramic dish for salt. I tried to play music and light a candle and open the window for fresh air, but nothing made him more lucid.

"Oh, God," he said over and over, as though he had just heard something astounding or had heard a bad joke.

"I'm making a fool of myself, aren't I?" he asked.

That night, as I got him into bed and listened to him mutter, high and incoherent, I realized that I cared for him quite a lot. This signaled big trouble in my mind and I did not want to go along with it. I did not want to live a life organized by passion. Grade school had been full of warnings about following temptations and impulses, that much I remembered. That night, after he fell asleep,

I phoned the apartment for Maria, but there was no answer. I left a message. It was as though I was calling Maria to ask permission to go back. It seemed that in her silent and cryptic way, she had asked me to leave. The next morning while Ed was out on a run, Maria called me back to tell me she was going on a trip to Miami with Sheila's family and that we could talk once she was back. I told her that was fine and didn't push. Then I called my father and asked if I could come visit for a while.

"We're so busy with the renovation now, Ruth. Wouldn't it be better to wait until Christmas? Your mother and I are very busy."

"Sure," I said, "Christmas."

In the afternoon, I called my parents' house again. My mother answered after the first ring, but before I could tell her the situation I was in, she cut me off.

"I'm so tired, Ruth. Do you think I should leave your father? I always dreamt of leaving. He keeps talking about this renovation, but I don't know. I don't believe in divorce, but maybe I'll just move into the apartment downstairs. I can't take it anymore. Anyway, how's Maria? How are you?"

"I'm good, Mom," I said.

I hung up the phone. Ed came in and showered. It did not seem like the man from the previous night and the man before me that afternoon could be contained in one. He blended fruit and yogurt and made espresso on the stove. We had sex on the living room floor on a carpet that looked like a dark Mondrian. When I finished, he got up and asked me if he could see my paintings, if I would take him to them. I told him that they were all in storage, in a shoebox of a unit. I drank more coffee and pretended to use the bathroom, but instead I let the faucet run and looked through his pill cabinet again.

On the seventh day, Ed took me to my storage unit in Midtown. A small echelon of white birds flew overhead as we drove up. When I got there, the man in the lobby told me that a pipe had burst in the building. Some of my canvases were damaged, so they refunded me two months of rent. He made out a check to me. I thanked God for the flood. I needed the cash. There was one trash bag full of clothes from college that was salvageable and one that wasn't. Ed helped me carry it all down to his car. I leaned against the hood of his sedan, in the narrow street, and smoked a cigarette. He took a camera out of his glove box and took a photo of me. I hid the cigarette behind my back in case I stopped smoking one day and didn't want to remember this year by it. Before we drove off, we stood together staring at the crowded street and Ed told me that when he considered all the pain that was passing over a given city block, he just didn't know what to do, or how to keep the dread from encroaching on all sides. And there I was thinking he was so chipper and even.

"I love you," I said. I wasn't sure if he heard me over the traffic.

When we got back to Ed's apartment, I laid out the paintings and tore off their plastic wrapping so that he could see them. He stood over the pieces for a while and then he pushed aside the bureau on the far side of the room and opened the low, heavy door behind it. It was something between a large closet and a small bedroom, big enough for a child. Aside from a cheap vinyl folding chair, the room was empty. He had planned to furnish it minimally and rent it out for money. I didn't understand why he needed the extra money. He seemed to be doing alright.

"You can paint here, if you want; there's a spare room, it's really only the size of a closet," he said. "We can put a mattress in here, too. Maybe you'd be happier here than you are living with Maria."

"I can't pay a lot," I said.

"We don't have to discuss money now," he said.

He handed me a key and left me alone at the threshold. He was holding a small painting in his hands. It was a portrait of Maria and me, dressed in matching navy blue, the color of our childhoods. Our ages in the painting were intentionally ambiguous; all of our sexual features were cropped out, and only our faces, vaguely sketched, were visible. They hung somewhere between the space of girlhood and adolescence.

"You two look a lot alike," he said.

"Thanks," I said.

I moved my paintings into the small room. He went into his cupboard and brought me a hammer and a handful of long nails. It was hard to accept Ed as purely benevolent. Was he a cloaked villain or a kind benefactor? I resented being of a culture that led me to this cheap kind of understanding, that it was one or the other, but really I wondered if he wasn't trying to ensnare me, control the conditions under which my art was made. That would be an easy way of trapping me, keeping me dependent. I barely had any money and I was full of a not-unearned mistrust. *The devil comes to you as everything you've ever wanted,* my mother had told me offhandedly when I asked to enter a TV sweepstakes, but where was my mother now that I needed her? I decided to stay with Ed anyway. His friend had a spare queen mattress and we moved it into the spare room, but I never slept on it once.

The weeks elapsed. Wasn't it always a fugue state, stripped of lucidity, falling in love? I did not register the gradual shifts of the seasons. For me, winter ended several days after the first tree bloomed. I went outside less and less. I became obsessed with the color field painters, poring over art books on Ed's couch. I looked at the most nondescript objects with a magnifying glass, looking for color everywhere. Everything became significant. Ed's black shoe, my red knit hat, the brown wood floors. Everything was animated with life. Everything could be used. The whole world became material.

Just as everything that happened reminded me of this new relationship with Ed, everything I saw reminded me of the possibilities of color. I hadn't been so motivated to paint in months. I called the apartment and left Maria a message. I wished we could just talk to one another straight. Her pride got in the way. I wanted to tell her about Ed and also just to see her and see how she was faring. I invited her to a gallery on the Upper East Side that was exhibiting the paintings of an outsider artist I'd read about in the paper. He was from Mississippi. Decades before we were born, he came to New York, but never had a solo show, never had much recognition at all. His education was not formal, but the educations of the friends he made in this city were. The artist was sick. He would die soon, in Mississippi. That exhibition was, or was meant to be, a final and long-awaited celebration of him. It was advertised in the art newspaper I read in the library as the discovery of an unknown genius from the outside world.

I made my way to the show without hearing back from Maria. In one corner of the gallery, under a cool, blue-toned spotlight, a foreboding, tall, erect cross was carved out of a piece of corroded scrap plywood. Nailed to the cross was a small taxidermic bird, its wings pierced with two rusted nails. The cross was covered in the man's abstract signs, formless black marks, inscrutable writings. In the other corner was a small assembly of dilapidated miniature shacks propped up on white pedestals. I assumed, without having read the press release, that the compact broken houses were meant to look like whatever town the artist was born in. I stood alone at the threshold, watching the clean, vacant street, looking to the left and to the right of me for Maria. I knew she wouldn't show, but I looked anyway. I walked back in, looked at the crooked cross, then looked through the windows back at the street, then I looked at the cross again and left to hail a cab back to Ed's apartment, where I cried on the battered leather sofa until the end of the afternoon. Ed brought out lemon tea and offered me a pill, some weed. I said no. He sat beneath me on the rug with his legs folded, like a schoolchild, as he marked the pages of my story of the girl and the fumes with red ink.

Then it was February and all my friends (Maria and Sheila) had been supplanted by Ed's.

Phil, Rodney, Barbara, Cecil, Art, and the others, all employed in strange ways: in bands, tailor shops, Montessori schools, mural painting, selling upscale knives door-to-door, selling ecstasy. Ed mostly only used when his friends were around. I came to associate his friends with the drugs and drinking, though I couldn't be sure of the timeline. I didn't know which came first: Did the friends produce the drugs or did the drugs produce the friends? I sat at the margins while they talked until two or three in the morning about how terrible literature had become, about how the movies were ruined and music would never be the same after Miles Davis went and died and took it with him. I liked to hear them talk, I did. What I feared was that at the end of the night I would be let out and sent home like all the other houseguests, that somewhere in those conversations, sobriety would come and it would be revealed that I was a visitor who had stayed too long.

I was grateful for the space Ed had given me to live and work, but couldn't fully enjoy it for fear of it being taken away. It was the first time that I had enough room to paint at a large scale, but rather than expand, I worked in smaller and smaller dimensions. The walls of the room were sparsely hung with miniature portraits. I tried to paint myself, tried to paint Black people I saw on the street or on the trains, tried to paint Black people I saw in old nature magazines, in old movies, but I didn't find the work I was making very compelling. And worse, I knew that the motivations behind these paintings were impure. I painted figuratively, in part, because I knew that would be easier to sell than anything abstract. With recognition, I felt I might be able to move on to other kinds of work, less overt, more personally gratifying.

But as it stood, I was a young, unknown woman dependent on the generosity of her boyfriend, and I needed someone, anyone, to buy my paintings. I had to admit that those days, my idea of security was churning out paintings of unnamed Black subjects for heiresses to hang in Fifth Avenue apartments they would never dare invite me into. The trouble was that I never could complete these portraits. Hanging unfinished on the wall, the subjects antagonized me. They were full of hostility, reproaching me in unison. The paintings said: *You're driven only by money, we don't mean anything to you and you don't know, or care, about us...*Their reproaches were not untrue.

I thought of a Black American painter who said that in America he could only make portraits, but in France, he was able to find a way to go on in abstraction. He stayed in France until he died and never came back to his New York studio, abandoning his early paintings there, which were never found. Abandoning his early self, as it were. Maybe what I needed was to leave the country, find another way to live. The change that painter had needed was geographical. Was mine? Just as I was sitting and thinking about this artist and his flight from America and whether or not I should flee, Ed called me over and asked if I would help him blow up some balloons.

We were throwing a big party for Ed. Cecil was bringing a case of wine and I had stolen candles from the drugstore and brought home an angel food cake from the restaurant. He made a large pot of lentils for the guests and I started to tell him a story about my mother and lentils, how she cooked large batches of them to save money, but I stopped myself. No one wanted any memories on their birthday except their own.

I heard the voices of Ed's friends spilling into the apartment and I rushed off, shutting the studio door. They were elated. I couldn't relate. I was tired of going to parties. I didn't want to drink any more wine or have any more conversations. Ed called my name from the next room and I ignored him. *"Ruth!"* he called again.

"Come out, Ruth, everyone's excited to see you," Ed said, standing by the door in an apron.

"I can't go out there. I'm sorry."

"Why not?" he asked.

"I don't want to impose. I don't feel well."

"But you felt fine an hour ago. Come on, it's my birthday. Everyone's here. Phil and Rodney, Barbara, Cecil, Simone and Pat and Art. They want to see you."

"I don't like Phil and I don't like Rodney and I don't like Barbara or Cecil. I hate Simone and I hate Pat and I hate Art." I turned away. But I did like his friends. I respected them, at least. Underemployed or not, his friends were real people with real lives, interesting, bright, well-traveled. I suppose I felt territorial.

Ed laughed and shook his head. "These are *good people*. These people like you."

"They don't take me seriously," I said. "They talk about your work, they don't talk about mine."

"Ruth, you can't make a crisis out of everything. You just can't. They're just people, it's just dinner, these are just paintings, it's just work. Like flipping burgers or any other job. Who cares if they talk about it or don't?"

"I feel self-conscious."

"Do you want me to give you something for that? A Valium?"

"Do you think that'll help?" I asked him.

He walked over and leaned up against the wall where I was. I took the wine from his hand.

"I love you. I'd never do anything to hurt you," he said. He kissed my hand; I drank from the plastic cup. From his pocket, he took out a loose blue pill. He gave it to me and I washed it down with the wine.

"I'll give Maria a call," I said. "Maybe she'll come by with Sheila?" I shrugged.

"That sounds great," Ed said, helping me down from the windowsill. Ed left the room and came back with an orange halter-neck dress for me to wear. He'd pulled it out of the trash bag from the storage locker, washed it, and ironed it. When he blew out his candles, we locked eyes and smiled. I didn't remember the rest of the night, aside from the fact that it never truly got dark. The moon seemed uncommonly bright, but that must have been the Valium. I blacked out, couldn't recall anything after the candles. The next morning, sitting on the fire escape, Ed told me that I'd had a lot of fun.

"Oh, God, what did I do?"

"What do you remember?" he asked. "I'm not even sure what I remember."

"I remember you trying to cheer me up, then I remember you giving me a Valium. We sang you 'Happy Birthday,' you blew out the candles. Then...nothing."

"You and Art got into a big argument."

"An argument about what?"

"Art said that your paintings aren't African. He said he didn't believe them. He said that we were, um, a sensual people, and that we've lost our sensuality, particularly our women. I didn't really follow."

"He said that? He said 'our women'?"

"Yeah," said Ed. "That as a young African woman in her sexual prime, you can bring back some of that eroticism, some of that good humor and beauty, but instead you choose to be an ascetic, self-serious prude. His words. Art said that when he was twenty-five, he slept with a different woman every night. He was never bored; he didn't care about having a career or making money. That's what made his work so good. He said you paint like you've never been fucked right. He said young Africans are all so Victorian. Repressed. Boring."

"That doesn't sound like much of a debate. I mean, don't you find it sexist?"

"I find everything he says sexist. He hates women, he'll tell you himself," Ed said.

"And you didn't think to stand up for me?" I asked.

"You stood up for yourself," Ed said. "I don't think you need defending the way you think you do."

"Well, I don't remember anything."

"You told him, 'First you'll die, Art, then every last woman will die, then what we know as Africa will cease to exist, and America, too, and I'll still be painting, because I'm going to outlive all of this. I'm going to live forever because I'm not beholden to any of these illusions and I don't care what an old, washed-up critic thinks…' or something like that. Everyone loved it.

"Do you really not remember? You looked really pleased with yourself…" Ed said.

"That doesn't sound like me," I said. "I must have read that somewhere."

"I guess it worked because Art wants to buy one of your paintings."

What I'd allegedly said the night before had been spoken from a newer part of me, an inebriated and self-certain part that diverged from my old way of keeping quiet, keeping my head down. Ed had enabled me to live as I pleased, do what I wanted. Behave badly if I wanted to. Was it Ed who had that effect on me or New York? I sat in Ed's apartment alone. I called Maria while Ed got lunch with a friend, a stage actor, in Midtown. Ed was a fixture of my life and I wanted him and Maria to get to know one another. But she wouldn't return any of my calls. I left a voicemail. I called again. My pride was gone. There was no answer. I called again later that night and a subletter answered, a sculptor visiting from Cape Town. She absentmindedly explained that Maria was away, traveling with Sheila, seeing relatives. I didn't hear from Maria for a month. I figured she was still angry with me. Then, out of the blue, on a Monday, she called from a number I didn't recognize.

There's an opening for this show, I have a couple of videos in it. You should come if you're in town on Thursday night. That was all Maria said on the phone, before reading off the address and saying goodbye.

I took it as her trying to seem cool and indifferent, trying to act like she just flew in and, *God, I'm so busy, and you must be, too, right?* Where else would I be, if not in town on a Thursday? *Some of us had obligations,* I'd wanted to remind her, but mostly I missed her. I tried to be understanding. I knew, even then, what it was like when you grow up and have nothing—never any new clothes, never any restaurants or cable—then an opportunity comes for all the excess you never knew, and you take it without looking too closely. I didn't fault her for that. But I blamed Sheila for corrupting her. This was a time when I believed in the simplicity of corruption, that it went in one direction, with one person rubbing off badly on another. Maria wasn't doing anything she didn't want to do.

It was hot on Thursday and I changed four times before settling on a black shift dress and a pair of leather sandals. I asked Ed to come along with me. By then we went nearly everywhere together.

"So glad I get to finally see the muse," he said, "in broad daylight."

"She isn't my muse, we're just old friends."

"But you two were close, weren't you?"

"Not really," I said.

"Didn't you meet in the fourth grade?"

"It's not a big deal. I'm just going to be nice, since she went through all the trouble of inviting me. I don't want to be impolite. And we met in the third grade."

"The more you try to act as if you don't care, the more invested you seem," Ed said. "Which isn't a bad thing. It isn't a crime to care about someone."

I resolved right then to start an argument with him the moment the opportunity presented itself. We stopped for cocktails before the show at a dive bar that had a buy-one-get-one happy hour special and I had one, two, three, four cosmopolitans for the price of two. Though the price didn't matter, since Ed would pay. Ed asked me to slow down on the drinks and I was glad for the opening.

"You're one to talk," I said loudly enough for the bartender to hear, but he didn't. Ed said nothing, which was smart.

"At least I don't polish off a bottle of wine with my Ambien every night. I mean, really, it's incredible that you can even hold your head up in the morning," I said.

It was only six and the sun had not set. Beside us sat an old drunk with his head down on the counter. Other than him, we were the only people in the bar. I launched into a tirade about how many nights Ed would stumble into bed in a stupor after holding court with his idiotic friends and the time he wet himself from getting too drunk and passing out on the sofa. The more I spoke, the worse I felt, but it was impossible to stop. I told him he wasn't acting his age. I told him that the days of alcoholic writers were long gone, that he was behaving like a caricature. I told him that while he might be able to hide his depravity from the people who liked the image he projected, he couldn't hide it from me.

"You're embarrassing yourself," Ed said. Our first argument. Ed and I walked to the gallery in silence, doing what couples do, masking the presence of their perpetual disagreements, saving face. When we got there, there was a circle of tall young men smoking outside and some girls stood beside them, dressed in well-fitting clothes. Inside, people wearing over-ear headphones stared at small televisions propped up on pedestals.

I saw Maria standing in the middle of the gallery, talking to an old woman with gray hair and dark eyeliner. Maria wore black trousers and a gray mohair sweater with a collared shirt beneath it. She had started to dress like a man. Her hair was long again but she tucked it all away in a bun at the nape of her neck. Sheila stood a few feet away, nodding as Maria spoke, beaming, like a proud parent. I found it really creepy, to tell the truth. But maybe I was just drunk, maybe it was a projection that Sheila's expression betrayed something evil. It certainly would have been easier to just write Sheila off as opportunistic and cruel. When Maria saw me, she pointed her chin at me to call me over. She shook the woman's hand and then walked away. Maria feigned a smile, but there was something in her eyes that looked unsettled, something beady and faraway.

I reached out my hand to her.

"Don't shake my hand," she said. She opened her arms. I hugged her politely, but she held me close. She patted my back and I did the same to her. I felt how much weight she had lost; she was gaunt underneath her breezy clothing. I pulled away. "It's been a while," she said.

"This is Ed," I told her. "You maybe met at the party. I mentioned him on the phone."

"I know, we were so surprised," Maria said, looking at Sheila, who nodded along. "I thought maybe you were gonna become a nun or something."

"After everything with James," Sheila added. "You just waited such a long time before dating anyone new."

Ed, Sheila, and Maria laughed. Ed hugged Maria. I wasn't laughing.

"I've heard great things about you. Ruth talks about you nonstop," Ed said.

"She does?" Maria asked.

"Yeah. I'm starting to get jealous."

"Don't be. I bought one of your books, you know." Maria cleared her throat and smiled. "Do you always write about prostitutes?"

"Lilian isn't a prostitute, she's an actress."

"Then why does she have sex for money?" Maria asked.

"That's one of many interpretations. I would argue that her boyfriend loved her and he wanted to support her career. It was complex. It wasn't just transactional."

"Like you and Ruth?" Maria asked.

"Well," Ed began. Sheila interrupted.

"I thought your book was lots of fun," she said. "I read it when we were in Panama City. They were selling it at the airport in Miami."

"You were in Panama?" I asked. Too quick, desperate. Maria hadn't been since her grandmother died and she'd insisted over the years that she'd never go back. I had questions but didn't want to let on.

"Yeah, that's where all this footage is from." Sheila gestured at the screens. There were more people standing around them than before.

"I have an unfinished longer video," Maria said. "I shot half of it in Miami, the other half in my family's old house. Do you remember when I went there as a girl? It's condemned now. No family left. I'd love it if you came to do a studio visit, Ruth." Maria's voice cracked. We were all quiet.

"Have you been painting?" Sheila asked, looking at my shoes. I looked at Maria. Ed answered.

"She spends *all* her time in the studio," he said. "She's been writing, too."

"Not really," I said. I felt sick, maybe from the cosmos. It was claustrophobic in the crowded gallery. It smelled like sweet white wine.

"You know, I always pegged you as more of a writer than an artist. You're just *so* well-spoken," Sheila said, holding her elbow in her hand. There were dull red marks on the soft fold of her arm.

Maria rolled her eyes. She put her hand on my shoulder and led me through the exhibit. We left Ed and Sheila standing in the middle of the room. Before he was out of earshot, I heard him ask Sheila, "So what do you do?" Sheila paused and squinted in concentration, and said it was a long story.

I walked past the customary photographs of Maria's vagina and breasts—all the more "shocking" work. Really boring stuff, I had to admit. She didn't push herself. Maria had the thing of precocious children. The sense of being predestined and not needing to work very hard. But I was under her spell, too, and while part of me looked down my nose at the photographs, another part of me was drawn to them, impressed, threatened. The more obvious sexual gravitation aside, I cared about whatever she had to say by taking pictures up her own skirt. A few weeks ago, over the phone, my parents asked if Maria and I would send some of our art over for their renovation. They were redesigning their sitting room. I said yes, but I knew we never would. I don't know what they expected, something quaint, something to be proud of. I doubted they'd hang the close-up of Maria's breasts over the mantel. Nothing I painted would do much for them.

I followed Maria toward the far end of the gallery. No one was really looking at the art and people were hitting the open bar hard, so it was as though we were alone back there. Alone for the first time in a long while.

"I wanted to show you this sooner," Maria said.

The monitor was low to the ground. There was a blue milk crate in front of it. Maria gestured for me to sit down.

"Don't listen to Sheila. She's off the wagon. And I don't even know if it's worth begging her to stop. She hasn't got anything better to do. I love her, but God, it's like dating a toddler."

"I'm surprised you two've lasted so long," I said.

Maria ignored me. She moved my hair away from my face and placed a pair of headphones over my ears. I felt Maria's gaze as I stared at the still black screen. After a few moments, an image began to emerge from the darkness. It was me. I was leaning against a weather-beaten tree. I was hardly wearing any clothing. It was summer. It was night. I recognized the outskirts of our campus. The image of my younger self began to speak. My mouth moved, but my speech was barely audible. Over my voice was the sound of dogs howling. The faint drone of crickets grew louder over the sound of the dogs. The screen cut rapidly to an image of feral dogs fighting over a scrap of meat on an empty sandy road. Then my younger voice returned, louder. The camera moved closer to the dogs, their teeth bared violently, their mouths bloody, their eyes crazed. My voice came in again, louder:

Are you recording me? Is the camera on? Wait. You have to tell me if it's on. Can you see me in the dark?

My voice cut out. I couldn't make out what I was talking about and couldn't fully accept that the voice on the screen was mine. On-screen, the meat had all been eaten and the dogs scattered away from the bloodstained circle in the dirt.

The image of the road dissipated and we were back in Annandale, in the dorm room we shared: Me in bed alone. The poster from Eden behind me. I was half-covered by a white sheet in a dim room and my voice cut away. My naked upper back filled the screen, my round, dark shoulders, the curve of my neck. The sound of the crickets swelled; the dogs howled. I stared blankly at the screen as it went black and the film began again. I felt cold, though it was summer and the weak fans in the gallery weren't very effective. I couldn't shake the feeling that there was a violent thrust to the video and that something had been done to me that I hadn't asked for. Was it a kind of settling of scores because I'd painted Maria nude? But Maria had succeeded in getting me to destroy those paintings. She had won, had gotten what she wanted without much effort. How many people had seen this video of me? How many more would? Maria took the headphones from me and she did not look smug or self-satisfied, but came across as atoning and even sort of exposed.

"I hope that was okay. Putting you in it. I assumed—"

"Of course," I said, too quickly.

"I know it's strange to see yourself."

"No, it's good," I said. "It's cool."

Everything I wanted to say, I did not say. *Cool?* I thought. *Why, Ruth, would you ever say* cool? I thought it was the most obscene gesture and it would plague me for months. Like, I would be walking down a half-empty city block, remember I had said *cool* at that impasse, and the word would bash me over the head as it might feel to be struck by a falling piano. What I wanted to say was, *Maria, I love you though you hurt me and thank you for keeping that footage, however jolting it was to see myself there again. Thank you for remembering me, however skewed.* But the window of opportunity passed to say anything more at all. Maria looked tense.

"Let's look at something else," she said, placing the headphones back on the television.

When I stood up, I saw a doorway. The gallery extended into another, larger room. It was full of people. Maria walked toward the center. I walked behind her. Trailing in her wake like I had been for a decade plus. In the middle of the room was a large cage, and inside of the cage were a man and a woman in vague beaded, feathered, tribalish clothing. Painted faces, braided hair. There was music and people were taking photographs of the incarcerated couple. On the wall, a large banner read NEVER BEFORE SEEN AMER-INDIANS VISIT THE BIG APPLE and people were taking photographs of that, too. We moved through the crowd, we got closer. We stood directly in front of the metal bars, not saying anything, but watching. People around us watched intently. An older man with a swoop of white hair and a dark wooden cane slid a flannel blanket through the bars of the cage. The man inside of it took it, then bowed his head to the older man. In the air there was the question of the authenticity of what we were seeing. *Is it real?* I wondered. Others wondered, too. People don't quite know how to assimilate things that may or may not be real, and we looked around at one another for confirmation.

The painted man sat down in the corner of the cage behind the clutter of rags, maps, instruments, plants, records, photographs, bottles, oils, and talismans. He turned away from the onlookers, but the caged woman looked on. Bright light washed over the man's green face. Images danced on the flat surface of it and there was no expression in his body or mouth or eyes. He was watching television. The woman turned her back to us. I saw her bones move under the surface of her oily skin. She sat down and watched television with the man. Her husband? I was in awe of it all. My mind wandered as I watched the couple watch TV. I believed it was real. It was like certain books, cryptic and mimetic. Performance was almost never like that. But then I didn't know if it was a performance or if that was just what it presented itself as. *Is it real?* I asked myself again. I turned to Maria.

I looked at Maria and she looked bored. She pointed her head toward the exit sign and I followed her back to the door. She spoke to me without looking back. I was almost in a trance over the man and woman.

"She's a hack," Maria said. "I mean, I knew it'd be bad, but the face paint?! It's atrocious. I ran into her in a bar last week and she talked my ear off. I'm sick of this postcolonial garbage. It's just navel-gazing."

"Yeah," I said reluctantly, but it took me a while to register that it was all fake. None of it was real. But I had believed it. Some children believed in stories longer than others, that was what that was. That was the difference between me and Maria. Where I saw incarceration, she saw bad performance art. What I saw as ethnographic, she rightfully wrote off as artifice. I would have been content spending the rest of my life walking behind her, but we reunited with Ed and Sheila. We resumed our roles in our respective partnerships. Just moments ago, I thought Maria had made the video to memorialize me, but standing next to Ed, it occurred to me that Maria had her own reasons for doing things that didn't take me into consideration.

We started off to a Chinese restaurant where the food was served on a spinning tabletop. It was BYOB and cash-only, so Sheila, Maria, and I each held a bottle of cheap white wine wrapped in brown paper. Ed bought a case of beers. Enough alcohol for a small party. As we moved farther downtown through rows of dressed-up, dark silhouettes, we made small talk about people we hardly knew. All there was to do, it seemed, was talk about other people. To talk about ourselves, our shortcomings, our bad books and bad paintings, our parents who we were not talking to, these significant others who we were treating badly, would have been too much. So Sheila went on and on about the man who owned the gallery where she worked the reception desk. He was extremely addicted to cocaine, she said. It had smashed his first marriage apart, estranged all his children, alienated his oldest friends and clients. The usual, and yet he couldn't stop.

"It's one thing to be a functional addict, but if your septum is all torn up and you're twenty pounds thinner all of a sudden and you haven't spent a day of your life in the gym..." Sheila said.

"I've never understood coke," said Ed. "I wanna be less alert, not more. I love a downer."

"I'm with Ed," said Maria.

"I don't do drugs anymore," I said. "They don't agree with me, I guess."

"Always so puritanical, Ruth," Maria said.

"Well, we can all like what we like. It just has no place in a professional environment," Sheila said.

"It's a gallery, hardly a professional environment," Ed said.

Maria laughed at Ed's joke, but I didn't believe her laughter; it was for my sake. Across the street, I saw a man who looked like James, but as a car sped by and illuminated the familiar stranger, I saw she was a short-haired woman, not a man. The speeding car startled the stranger and her plastic bag of groceries spilled onto the road. Apples and cracked glass jars rolled toward the gutter and the woman looked indifferent, somehow composed as she bent down to collect what she could. Moments later she turned the corner and walked on, blending back into the night around her.

At the restaurant, we drank, and Ed ordered. It was very bright and fluorescent inside, so that you could see everyone's faces. I hated dim restaurants and the way they made everything feel clandestine, like the meal was part of some larger conspiracy. Our conversation shifted to movies and books we had seen and read but not enjoyed. We were all very good at articulating what we hated and why. It was almost a full-time job, keeping yourself abreast of all the detritus churned out each season. I stopped pretending to know what was going on. Watching people rant about what was new, as if in a foreign tongue, was enough exposure to this culture that floated above me, a reminder that there was simply too much, more and more of it all the time. Somehow, maybe naively, I still wanted to paint. No such thing as oversaturation when you want to contribute, too. Just as the ever-present facts of death, sickness, and bleak outcomes didn't stop the world from pushing out babies every second of every day, the probability of failure didn't dissuade me, either. Wanting to was enough.

The waiter set the plates down all at once: a lacquered duck split in half, nesting in a pool of dark liquid on a floral dish; a small pile of clams; slender, long broccoli that were like tall grass. We all ate ravenously and when we were finished, we left only the bones. While we waited for the bill, Maria burped and laughed to herself slyly. Then she leaned into the table as if she had great gossip.

"I learned my gallerist has been stealing from me, thousands," Maria said.

"That's awful," I said. Ed nodded in agreement.

"No, it's actually wonderful, because Sheila's boss has some dirt on him about a baby he had on the side with one of his artists in Italy. His wife has no idea. So I'm going to blackmail him first thing Monday morning and get back all my money and more. Sheila set up the whole thing."

Maria looked delighted and Sheila looked very proud of the plan. Sometimes there were momentary glimpses into how a couple justified one another's misdeeds, how they enabled the inventive, bad behavior we relished as people trapped in our own lives and bored of them. I wondered if I should behave badly to enable myself to paint, the way it seemed most talented writers were at some point alcoholics, philanderers, or both. But no, I couldn't. I was who I was. I wasn't someone who behaved badly. When Sheila and Maria stepped into their cab at the end of the night, I didn't feel even a pang of jealousy.

23

◇◇◇◇◇◇◇◇◇◇◇◇◇◇

ED COULDN'T KEEP supporting me on one income. He didn't say so, but I knew. The nights out were fewer and fewer. And he never bought new clothes anymore as he had previously liked to do each weekend. He was taking any work he could get on the side, tutoring, copy writing, and he was talking about getting another job teaching on top of the adjunct situation he already had. Asking his parents for another loan was out of the question, he wouldn't even discuss it. Apart from that, I needed money of my own for the inevitable split. It was hard to say out loud, but Maria's success made me ashamed to go back to working in a restaurant. If she walked in for dinner and I had to seat her again, I'd die on the spot.

I remembered that Moser had told me to call him if I ever needed help. Folksy, salt of the earth, generous. The way it was for so many couples, Moser played the innocent and Hildy acted out the base impulses dormant in him.

"I really mean it. You're a good person. Let me give you a hand. I've got friends," he had said. Naturally, I vowed to never call Moser and didn't believe he would help me even if he could. I was so cynical. I didn't believe in anything at all, despite all the good luck I'd had finding a boyfriend and a place to live. In the beginning, when I told Ed I'd quit my job at the restaurant to focus more on painting, I expected him to throw me out on the street, but he did just the opposite, embraced me and told me to take my time. We could make do with the little savings he had and what he made working freelance until I found something else. I couldn't assimilate his kindness with my expectations that the world was a constant disappointment until you died.

The next morning, I called Moser and when he answered, he launched into how glad he was to hear from me and asked how I was. The first adult that had ever really been kind to me for no reason at all. After some friendly catching up, nice talk, I told him I needed his help after all. Could he help me find some work? He said he would keep an eye out and asked me where he could reach me. I gave him Ed's landline and thanked him, goodbye.

Two days later, Moser called me with an address to a painter's studio in Chelsea. A young woman artist whose name sounded familiar. Moser had put in a good word. I was to go there for an interview. *When?* That afternoon. I needed money, didn't I? I thanked Moser and told him I'd stay in touch. I told Ed the good news and said I'd take a cab, but he insisted on driving me. He put his work aside and we went out into the cool April day, stopping for heros on the way, drinking sodas in the car, Ed wishing me good luck and telling me to make sure to look the artist in the eye. I evaded eye contact and Ed had noticed this early on. He said it was something I should correct while I still could. In America, Ed said, eye contact is everything. When he spoke that way, I thought he'd make a good father, so absolute, sure of what was good.

I rang the doorbell and a young dark-haired woman with a middle part came down. You could see her ribs, the sharp bones beneath her cheeks and forehead. She had porcelain, almost reflective skin. There was a little dog cradled in her left arm and her T-shirt was covered in red paint, the thin cotton loose against her thin frame.

"Ruth?" she asked. I nodded.

"Emily." She adjusted the dog, and gave me her hand to shake.

We took a big freight elevator down to her studio. It was a dark space; there was very little natural light and she made up for it with these harsh, industrial clip-on lamps everywhere with flickering bulbs that needed to be changed.

It's impossible to describe Emily without noting that Adderall was very new those days. It was only beginning to be widely available. But it was all over the news and plastered in the subway stations. Advertisements making many promises: Soar confidently into the new school year, meet your true potential. Similar drugs had been around for lethargy and depression, weight loss, dread. But Adderall, "ADD for all," with its talk of inclusion and its appeals to innate human potential, could not be more of the moment. I'd taken it only once to finish a big art history final but didn't find it conducive to the work of looking at photographs in an empty corner of the library. It only made me want to go to the pub to drink and talk for hours. Adderall seemed better for partying or manual labor. It hadn't been for me, but I could spot people on it from a mile away. College had been full of these types.

Emily was one such case. Her eyes darted everywhere. There was literally writing on her walls. Large scrolls of text in varicolored ink written directly on the white surfaces. Long red lines that connected one note to the other. If I hadn't known she was a painter, I would've thought she was down there writing a manifesto. There were easily twenty-five completed paintings propped up in the studio and more works in progress stacked in the back corner. Her dog's trembling resembled her own and she spoke at a rapid clip, without taking a breath. First recalling an old boyfriend she'd had who had gone to Bard, then talking about the caged birds her grandmother kept in South Africa when she was a little girl.

Emily was pale, her undertones harsh with shades of pink and blue. Her studio was that of a hoarder's, materials piled everywhere, tall mounds collecting against the yellowing walls. That I could smell the cigarettes over the stench of oil paints with the closed windows made me wonder how Emily's poor heart and lungs were still going. The Adderall couldn't have helped. She had a look that was somehow both spacey and hyperfocused; her mind wandered but she always circled back to her original point.

"My old boyfriend was Moser's student. I hated him, the boyfriend, but Moser was really fantastic. He's a good guy. Shit painter, great guy. He spoke very highly of you."

Emily's candor shocked me, but I smiled and nodded. I made eye contact as Ed had reminded me to do.

"So, tell me, Ruth, do you know how to stretch a canvas?"

"Yes."

"And you're fine with dogs? And simple math?" she asked.

"Yes, to both."

"I do a bit of research, so I may need help cleaning up my notes." She pointed to the writing on the walls, the stack of books piled on the old schoolhouse desk. "Do they cover spelling and grammar at Bard?"

"Yeah, they do," I said, standing up straight. Looking her in the eye.

"Just a joke," Emily said, smiling, her yellow teeth bold against her skin. "You've got the job. You know, I think we'll have a fun time. I usually work alone, but, um, you have to know when to ask for help. Isn't that right, Guy?" she asked, petting her dog's matted hair.

As she spoke, describing the job in further detail, I couldn't stop staring at the writing on the walls. She had all these numbered sentences piling up over one another and I knew she had written them in earnest:

TAKE GOOD CARE OF YOUR BODY, KEEPING IT CLEAN, TUNED, AND WELL OILED, LIKE A CAR.

EMBLEMS CONCEAL. MAKE SURE THERE AREN'T ANY "SYMBOLS" IN YOUR PAINTINGS.

ALWAYS GET A SECOND OPINION—DOCTORS, GALLERISTS, ETC.

USE THE SHAME TO MAKE PAINTINGS THAT MAKE MONEY. REPEAT.

FIND A VERY CRAFTY ACCOUNTANT. FIND A "GUY" FOR EVERYTHING.

DO NOT LET SEX GET EXTREME WITH MEN YOU DON'T KNOW.

There were easily a hundred sentences like that scrawled on the walls. Some were incoherent, while others made their own strange kind of sense. I didn't want to write her off, or say it was just the drugs. There must have been a logic to what she was doing since it had made her able to work so athletically. If she were a man, it might not have seemed so crazy. Her scrawls might have been collected in a book of aphorisms with a serious foreword. She saw my puzzled stare and explained.

"Those are just my ideas," she said, as if that clarified anything.

I was eager to tell Maria about my new job. I'd be sure to make it sound impressive, but I'd have to call her first, that was the battle. Maria and I hardly saw one another unless I initiated the plans. I promised myself many times over that I would not reach out to her again, and I broke that promise just as often, calling her to see if she wanted to go out to eat in Little Italy, where she loved to go for sandwiches, or, when I woke up missing my mother and had this strong urge to get my nails painted, inviting her to join me for a manicure. When I asked her to meet me somewhere, she said yes, somewhat unenthusiastically, always seeming very busy and troubled by the weight of her professional obligations. But I didn't mind. Any yes would do, no matter how lukewarm. She extended invitations to me only when they involved going to one of her shows or going to her studio to see what she was working on. Maria, perpetually in need of an audience, a quiet witness.

24

◇◇◇◇◇◇◇◇◇◇◇◇◇◇

WORK WITH EMILY was stable, rigid. She paid me on time and told me I could use the studio for my own work, on off days. She blasted prog-rock albums over the loudspeakers and worked the same hours that I did. Her instructions left nothing to chance. She constantly asked me if she was underpaying me or overworking me and she brought me out with her friends to readings and openings, on the rare occasion that she went out at all. Emily was very successful for her age. It was always a bit surprising when I remembered she was only five years older than I was, but could afford a studio and an assistant, and that she lived entirely off of her paintings. But she wasn't megalomaniacal as one might expect. Once, while I was stretching canvases, she approached me and asked if I wanted to join her for lunch. Strange, considering I'd never seen her eat. Not once had she ever mentioned food. Emily took me out for dim sum in a small restaurant whose only patrons were elderly Chinese couples. She promised it was very authentic and asked me about my life on the way: where was I from, did I like New York, what sort of music did I listen to. Surprisingly difficult questions to answer. My identification with Kenya was faint. My identification with everything was faint. I knew where I had lived, where I'd gone to school, the essential facts about myself, but had little to say about myself. Living in Rhode Island and the years at Bard and my being a woman were not things that made me feel very talkative. But I liked Billie Holiday, and I liked New York when its weather was in transition: fall and spring, when we were all on the precipice of something and were fittingly romantic about the future and the past.

Emily told me things with her ex-boyfriend from Bard were plaguing her. He was a writer and lived in the neighborhood. He popped up at events where he knew she'd be, but when she approached him to be cordial, he gave her the cold shoulder, once turning around so that his back was facing her while their mutual friends spoke nearby. He spread horrible rumors that she was a sex pest and an addict. Her ex-boyfriend was half-Chinese and claimed that Emily was a racist, but how could she be? She thought Eastern cultures were far superior to Western cultures. He was doing it to ruin her name because she was more successful than he was. Even though, she admitted, he was the bigger talent. While explaining this to me, Emily only ate one half of a piece of shumai, but she drank enough for the both of us. *Aren't boys the worst?* Emily asked. To appease her I told her an abridged version of my story with James. I laid it on thick, drawing out his emotions about feeling suicidal, but to tell the truth, I didn't feel anything toward James anymore. *His life, his funeral,* I thought, whenever he came to mind. It was a big consolation for Emily to hear about the mysterious tryst with James. Did I really think he'd done it? "It" being both the suicide and the theft. His big promises and lies. My story with James, it made her feel better about her own situation, I could tell. She assured me I would get a raise and told me she'd pay for my health insurance, too. The conversation shifted to artists we liked and, weirdly, I brought up Maria.

"Maria? The lesbian...from Cuba?" Emily asked.

"Panama...but yes, that's my old friend. We grew up together." When Maria came up in conversation, I hardly ever explained the extent to which we really knew one another.

"Is that right?" Emily pushed the food around her plate. "She's a real *it girl,* isn't she?"

"You know her work?"

"Yeah, well. We have all the same friends, but when I see her out, she pretends she doesn't know who I am. She's got that hot girlfriend," Emily said.

"Oh, do you mean Sheila? Maria can be kind of...cold, but she means well."

"Well, good for her. Black artists are really hot right now," Emily said, waving the server over for another beer. She was more impatient. Her disposition was less friendly. She started to tap her fingers. I could tell she wanted to stay on the topic of Maria a bit more and air her grievances. A part of me wanted to defend Maria and another part hated that she was someone my boss saw as an equal, as competition.

"I don't think Maria ever really had the spirit of an artist; she likes the attention. Privately, I don't know if it's *real,* you know," I said.

"She *definitely* doesn't have the spirit. I mean, let's see who's around in ten years. When this fad dies down."

"Sure," I said.

"Come to think of it, I might've seen you in one of her videos. In that group show a few months back. I thought that piece was really manipulative."

"Honestly, I had no idea she used that footage. But that's how she is. Whatever Maria wants...She's always been that way since her mother killed herself and all. She's a black hole of a person."

"Right, that'll do it," Emily said. "Step over anyone's head... You know, Ruth, I'd love to do a studio visit with you."

I looked at Emily more closely. She had a glint in her eye. I'd mistaken it for curiosity before, but it looked more like greed. I smiled and said we should plan a studio visit for the coming week.

Ed picked me up from Emily's studio and asked if I wanted to go out to a movie. I hoped that what I'd said about Maria wouldn't get back to her. He asked me how work had gone; I didn't want to talk about it. We walked down the narrow sidewalk full of streams of people headed out for dinner, for drinks. I felt a violent rage for all these people on the street. Anger over the fact that I was unsuccessful, doomed. A one-way ticket back to that little apartment in Pawtucket, Rhode Island, where all the days were the same, slow torture. Rage for my jealousy over Maria and my love for her, no void big enough to place that. That I could tell Ed all these grim feelings and still be accepted was all the more reason to keep them to myself. I didn't want to spoil our fun or scare him away.

We saw an interesting-looking movie on the marquee and bought two tickets. He bought us popcorn and sodas. In a dim movie theater, he placed something cool and round in my palm. I squinted at it in the dark. A silver ring. I watched a silver car explode on the screen, killing a man. I put the ring on. It wasn't possible to say yes or no in the quiet theater. We were at that small cinema in Greenwich Village where everyone in the audience was always over eighty years old and some kind of connoisseur. You felt bad if you drank your soda too loudly in a place like that. We walked out into the spring night and ducked through the traffic toward a bar on the other side of the street. I thought about the engagement. I really had no choice but to say yes. And at the same time, it didn't feel like Ed was forcing me. He was older than I was and wanted children. If anyone I knew could afford to have a child, it was him. Ed was a fundamentally conservative person, risk-averse. It would have been unfair to say no and leave him stranded, having to start over at thirty-five with another woman after all of his goodwill and generosity toward me. I believed, basically, that a person deserved to recoup on their investments. Not to mention that I loved Ed and had come to depend on him being in my life. *Remember that, Ruth, that you love him.*

We went into a pub near the theater. I left him at the bar where he ordered two High Lifes and shared his good news with a drunk woman in the corner. I found a pay phone and meant to dial my parents' number, but just instinctively called Maria's apartment instead. Sheila answered and handed Maria the phone. I explained it all in its simple unfolding: darkness, silver, the bang, the ring, the night. I believed I was responsible for the silence that followed, that it was mine, not hers. Had Emily spread a terrible rumor? Or was it the engagement Maria disapproved of? I took her silence as displeasure. I saw the world's silence as similarly watchful and unsympathetic. Since the ring was already on my finger and could not come off without undesired consequences, I did not stop to consider that maybe the disapproval that emerged in our silence was my own.

"How do you feel?" Maria asked.

"Happy," I said.

"Well, did you say yes?" she asked.

"Of course I did. What else would I say?"

"You have a say in the matter, you know."

"How would that look?" I asked. "If I said no?"

"How would that look?" Maria paused. "That's the quintessential question of your life."

There was another silence. We exchanged pleasantries after that and said we'd get together soon for a dinner. Maria rushed me off the phone, congratulating me, her voice almost convincingly warm but beneath the surface frigid. Ed held my hand as we crossed the road where the car was parked. I thought the speeding traffic would kill us, frankly. Consecrate our love by running us over. This image of us jaywalking together in the congested avenue became an emblem of the future. I was never to be alone again.

But I should not assume that the couple, the old unit, would be a circumvention of danger. Of course, the cars would still come. Ed was not stronger than the world and he didn't purport to be either.

So, I was engaged. We celebrated with a party lit up by dollar-store candles and characterized by a high level of drunkenness and belligerence, which was new to me in its length and volume. Less self-control than I'd had in college. Art was there. He said I was well on my way. It is difficult to say what changed after that, aside from everything. The privacy between Maria and me that had been dissolving for a long while vanished. I tried to get her alone at the engagement party while she poured herself another glass of wine.

"Thanks for making it out," I said.

"I wanted to see if it was the real thing," she said, then she smiled and congratulated me. Standing next to her, it didn't matter if I was ten years old or twenty-four. I had no chance, no power. I went home that night too drunk to take off the white slip I had worn to the party. I spoke to all of Ed's friends that night. My friends now. But the only thing that stood out in the crowd was talking to Maria by the bar for less than a minute. Ed pulled off my dress and threw it in the hamper. He told me that Maria and Sheila would make great bridesmaids.

A few days after the party, Maria called me to tell me she was leaving town for Venice (Italy, she clarified) next week and wanted to treat me to a nice dinner before she went overseas. I met her after work and told her to wait down the block so that there was no awkward run-in with her and Emily. I saw her in the intersection before she saw me. She was dressed nicely, in linen trousers and a sheer blouse, and I wished I had gone home to change. My plain dress was faintly paint-stained, but I'd washed off what I could in the studio sink. We embraced on the sidewalk, ducking away from the foot traffic.

"I like your dress," she said.

"I meant to bring a change of clothes, but work has been so busy."

"You look good," she said. "You look like yourself."

There were no prices on the menus and we were the only Black guests as far as I could see, from the most central table, which Maria had insisted on. She had berated the sleekly dressed maître d' for seating us by the bathroom. I was afraid, listening to the way Maria spoke to the hostess. She was stern and severe, but spoke softly. She threatened never to come back and mentioned someone's name whom I did not know and did so in a restrained, even way that made it feel even more menacing. As she spoke, she touched the hostess's arm like they were old friends. The woman went away apologizing and promised us a free glass of wine, moving our menus to a table in the middle of the room. Where did Maria's authority come from? While I was amassing self-doubt, she had built up great reserves of power that she could dispense quietly without appearing to. She apologized for being rude; she was rarely rude to servers, but the mistreatment accumulated, and she couldn't just say nothing. It wasn't the first time it had happened. Once or twice you could forgive, but she was tired of it and had to complain. I told her she didn't have to apologize and thanked her for inviting me out. It had been a long time since I had been anywhere like this.

"It's my pleasure, but I have to say I hate coming to these expensive restaurants. They act like they're doing you a favor. I mean, this place is empty and they put us by the bathroom."

"But you're the one who suggested we come here," I said.

"I wanted to bring you somewhere nice."

"I would have been happy anywhere," I said. "It's hardly ever just the two of us—"

"Sheila's the one who suggested it. She's always dragging me out to these kinds of places. I mean, the *way* that woman spends money."

"I can imagine."

"She spends a hundred dollars in a restaurant without thinking and barely touches her food. And I tell her how badly I'm treated by the servers in these places and she says she doesn't notice. The crazy thing is that I'm so used to it when I'm around her that I wonder if I'm just imagining it. It's just, I don't recognize myself when I'm with her and her friends. They just don't think about money like the rest of us. Finally, I'm making a bit of decent income from my work and I'm spending it all on clothes and in fucking restaurants where they seat me by the toilets." Maria clutched the table, working herself up as she spoke.

"Have you told her how you feel?"

"Either you understand or you don't. And she *doesn't*. I mean, it would have been inconceivable for me as a child to live the way she expects us to live. You of all people know. You know how I grew up."

"I know."

"And she just expects me to buy her gifts constantly and dinners. I mean, she doesn't say she expects it, but she buys things for me and then if some time goes by and I don't return the favor, then her mood shifts and I just know it's because she needs me to put a bit of money in to keep the ride going, basically."

"Maybe you don't have to see it so...transactionally."

"But it is a transaction. She makes it fairly obvious: 'Now that your career is taking off, we can go here and eat there...You've just sold these photographs and you're working on that campaign and you'll definitely be able to afford to spend a month here.' I try to explain to her that other people don't live that way."

I nodded and gave her a sympathetic look.

"Look at you. You're so content with simple things. An ordinary life. You don't care about coming to restaurants like this. I tell Sheila, 'Look at Ruth and Ed. I mean, Ed must have money stored up somewhere since his books haven't sold in years, but he's not burning through his cash. He lives in a modest little place uptown.

Ruth works as a studio assistant. What they spend on rent, we're spending on martinis!'"

"I'm not an assistant. I manage her studio."

There was more I wanted to say, but a server came by and filled our glasses. I thanked the server, and he gave me a shy smile. He was young and nervous. He lingered for a moment. Maria waved him away, telling him we needed more time with the menu.

"Things are just changing very quickly. It's hard to know how to adjust to this world when I had so little as a child. Do you know what I mean?"

"I can imagine," I said.

"Sometimes I feel like the only constant, unchanging thing in my life is you. I can depend on you to be who you've always been. You don't want more and more and more. You don't have this bottomless ambition and greed people seem to have here."

I took a sip of water, looking down at my lap. Was it true that I had no ambition and would always be the same as I was? I couldn't remember much of what we ate after the second course because of all the wine Maria kept pouring for me. I noticed that the waiters wore bow ties and that the oak-colored shiplap walls were bent from my drunken perspective. Outside, in the middle of the sidewalk, I hugged Maria goodbye with a half-hearted "Have a good time in Italy. Take lots of pictures."

"Thanks for listening to me complain about Sheila. I didn't mean what I said. I just needed to vent. Sometimes I'm afraid of how close I've gotten to her; I've never been able to get so close to anyone," Maria said, then she looked me in the eye and said, "Thank you for always being such a friend to me."

I held her more tightly then. I stumbled back off the curb when I pulled away. While standing in the road, I noticed a taxi approaching. I offered Maria the cab. I had planned to take the train because it would be too expensive to take a ride all the way uptown, but she insisted I take the taxi instead, and I guess I was just too embarrassed to refuse. She said she could walk home from the restaurant. She needed to take an important phone call and she could take it as she walked. She showed me her new cellphone and laughed at its novelty. I hadn't gotten a cellphone yet, but I had thought about it. As I reached into my pocketbook to make sure I had enough money, she handed me some cash and tapped the hood of the car, sending me off. I was dejected in the taxi home. I didn't know why I felt the way I did. She was only trying to be kind, taking me to dinner and telling me how she valued me, what a dear friend I was to her. I must have looked gloomy enough to warrant my driver's attention because he asked, "You alright?" over the sound of his Yankees game on the radio. It didn't help that Art had just written a big profile about Maria, a hagiography that went on and on about her videos and photographs. I wasn't serious and Maria was one to watch, according to Art.

At home, I slipped into the apartment silently.

"How was it?" Ed asked, standing in the bedroom as I set down my purse, rolled down my ripped stockings. He was glad to see me, but I couldn't return his enthusiasm. I pulled my hair back into a scarf in the mirror and I looked at Ed's smiling reflection. I sighed.

"Did you have a bad time?" Ed asked.

"No, it's only that...I love Maria. I'm so happy for her success, but sometimes you just wish things were handed out more fairly."

"Well, there isn't anyone handing anything out. That isn't how the world works, but it's alright to feel jealous."

"I'm not jealous that good things are happening to her. It's just that I wish something good would happen to me, too."

"Good things have happened to you."

"Like what?" I asked, incredulous.

"Like falling in love. Getting married."

"I'm not talking about planning a wedding, Ed. I'm talking about being an artist."

"Don't you think Maria wishes she had a mother? And a father? Someone more substantial than Sheila to spend her life with? She's probably at home now thinking, *I wish I were more like Ruth*."

"Of course she isn't. She's going to Venice for the Biennale with important people, and I'll be here in New York with all the lepers. She even has a cellphone!"

Ed tried to hide his laughter. "I think you might have just had too much to drink. Just get into bed, I'll bring you an aspirin."

"It isn't funny...You have no idea how it feels to work and work and work. And no one cares. And the only people who'll buy my paintings are your philistine friends!" I ran into the bathroom and locked the door behind me. I fell asleep on the toilet. Later I was woken by the sound of Ed picking the lock, then consoling me and carrying me into bed.

In the morning I woke up thinking that the previous night was a bit of a cold shower. I had to do something with my life, otherwise I'd never have the career I wanted. Maria would leave me behind. I remembered that each year my alma mater awarded a prize to an early career painter. It offered a sizable cash prize and a position teaching for two semesters as a visiting artist. The next morning, I pulled myself out of bed and took some photographs of my portraits in the spare room: the seven paintings I thought represented my best work. Ed edited my cover letter and made me sound certain of myself in a way I wasn't. I didn't have much to put on my CV, but he convinced Art to serve as one of my references and we figured that would give me a better chance. We went out for coffee and walked down to the post office on 110th Street, where I neatly filed the photographs and documents into a padded envelope. I paid for the postage for the materials, still unsure if I would send them or not. I wasn't qualified and I didn't know how I'd face the rejection. I held the envelope over the drop box in the post office and looked at Ed nervously.

"It's alright," he said. "Just send it off and hope for the best."

So, I did. And as we walked to go taste cakes for the wedding, I prayed for the first time in years, silently in my heart. I hoped God would give me the fellowship, as well as a gallerist and a nice write-up like Art had done for Maria. If it wasn't too much trouble, I also hoped He would give me a nice sheer blouse like the one Maria had worn to dinner when I saw her last. But I was afraid God wasn't listening to me and that He had already decided before completing the earth who would do well and who would always be just an assistant and a housewife without even a cellphone.

25

ON MY WEDDING day, I sat alone in the small, mirrored back room of the church basement that Ed's parents and mine had rented. The high pile rug was a washed-out shade of maroon with faint brown stains and I imagined this was the color of the inside of a person. My mother shuffled around upstairs, anxiously ensuring everything proceeded on schedule for our very special day. Though I was nervous about the wedding and all that it marked the beginning of, I was more nervous about hearing back from the school about my fellowship application. I hadn't told Maria I had applied, and for some reason, this felt dishonest of me. Had she applied, too? If she was also a candidate and also awaited a response, but had failed to mention it, then what did that mean? It felt strange to be paranoid of my friend of so many years and at the same time want her validation so. *Does one of us need to lose so that the other can win?* I asked myself, and suddenly it seemed I was no longer talking about the fellowship. If only the art department could choose two artists for the same role and we could go together, back into our recent pasts. Older, having seen more, on the other side of the classroom, but still together. Where was Maria, anyway?

I sat back waiting in the tall, velvet-lined chair where, before me, many priests must have smoothed out their robes for service or looked over their sermons with varying levels of conviction. I stared up at the clock. Sitting alone amid my dress and veil made it clear how much I had neglected the project of friendship and instead placed too much hope and trust in this person who couldn't bother showing up at the agreed-upon time. But of course, she was on her way. She wouldn't just not show. Not unless something terrible had happened to derail her. I stood up and practiced walking, one foot in front of the other, as I'd go down the aisle. Just then, Sheila walked through the door holding a wooden crate piled high with white flowers. I couldn't see her face clearly behind the heap of baby's breath, but I would know Sheila's hair anywhere and it was almost down to her thighs. Sheila turned and set down the arrangements and I saw Maria charging in behind her, holding coffee and a bag of bread.

"God, we were held up with the florist. He was just impossible," Maria said. "Plus, I was up all last night editing and I overslept, so Sheila had to run back and get my shoes since I forgot them."

"She forgot them. They were right by the door," Sheila said, like an echo.

"But everything's fine now. We ran into your mom outside the church. Sheila's going to go up and join her."

"I'm going to head up now and help your mother with the flowers."

"I'll help you get ready. Here, I brought you a cup of coffee."

"We figured you'd want coffee," Sheila said, picking up the box of flowers and balancing it carefully on her hip. She pushed the door open, leaving us alone. Maria nodded and handed me the coffee. She had all these bags on her shoulders, little ones and large ones. She set them down and started reeling off all of the things we had to do and what we needed: hair spray, bobby pins, champagne, double-sided tape. I wanted to say what a frightening and large milestone this was for me, getting married, and that it hurt me that she had kept me waiting, but there wasn't an opportunity. Plus, I already felt more relieved having her there, and truthfully, the momentous morning hadn't seemed real until she'd arrived and created this air of busyness in the room. She was so adept at taking charge and making the endeavor seem serious. Even when we were children, Maria had a way of making our play seem serious. She sifted through her handbag for some lipstick and held my face still as she painted it on with great concentration.

"I don't think this color will do," she said, as if she were standing over a cadaver with this grave, attentive look. She wiped off the gloss, then pulled another lipstick out of her bag. She squinted at me, turning my head from one side to the other with my chin in her hands. There were expensive powders and creams and she pressed those into my face, too. I didn't know where she'd learned to do all this because I'd always seen her as very easy about her own appearance—beautiful, but unaugmented. Clearly, that wasn't the case. Pleased with her work, Maria helped me into my dress, squeezing the secondhand gown over my tan Spanx and rigid bra. She pulled at the thin white straps on the halter top and once she'd fastened them, she rested her hands on my shoulders. I gasped. She didn't mean anything by it and I wasn't uncomfortable, but it was a shock to feel her hands firmly against me. Not a sexual shock, I told myself. Just the body having its own inexplicable response to something ordinary.

"Too tight?" she asked.

"No," I said.

"You look good, Ruth. Like the real thing."

There were our strained smiles in the mirror. She had grown

out her hair, had it blow-dried, and she was wearing the same shade of lipstick she'd painted on me. Her dress was long and black, with countless narrow pleats. It was the first time in years I had seen her done up this way. A reversion to a former self, covered up and inoffensive. I'd grown accustomed to Maria's severe, self-serious look and saw it as an armor for the new self she was forming: rootless, self-made, worldly. But this woman reflected back to me was just the opposite, as quaint as anyone on the street. I looked more out of place, like I was wearing borrowed clothes. She untied the bow at my neck and retied it, gently looping one end of the fabric over the other.

"Why are you shaking?" she asked.

"Nerves. I need a drink."

"You don't have any reason to be nervous. If you're doing something you want to do, then you shouldn't be nervous."

"No?" I asked.

"No," Maria said. "And it isn't too late to back out now. Not saying you want to, but if you did."

My mother knocked on the door of the small room and let herself in. I quickly stepped away from Maria. Maria folded her hands behind her back. We were embarrassed, like we'd been caught in the act. My mother kissed Maria hello on the cheek. We huddled around one another warmly, rattling off all the sweet platitudes: that I looked beautiful, that it was unbelievable how quickly the time passed, that just yesterday she was waiting for us outside the schoolyard, hanging our uniforms out to dry. Something dangled between those memories, too unsayable. I wondered at certain turns what my mother suspected. I didn't underestimate the strength of a mother's suspicion. A silence settled in the room, then Maria pulled away from us.

"I'll give you two a minute. I should go check on Sheila and the flowers anyway," Maria said.

My mother watched the door shut behind Maria and looked at

me again, her smile fading. She ran her hands over my bare arms as though trying to warm me up or make sure that I was real.

"Maria's a good friend, isn't she?" she asked.

"Yes," I said.

"But now it's time to move on to other things, isn't it?"

"Sure."

"Are you ready?" she asked.

"I don't think so."

"I got married to your father in the courthouse with a hand-me-down dress on. I couldn't afford a wedding at the church. I was an orphan, like Maria is," my mother said. "No one came to hand me over. My mother wasn't there. She drowned on holiday."

"I know," I said. "You've told me. But I'm not you."

"No, you aren't. I'd never have my arms uncovered in a church."

I laughed. I drank a glass of wine, spilling some of the faint yellow drops on my dress and hoping they would dry clear. My mother took the glass and bottle out of my hand.

"Don't think too much," she said, before saying goodbye and finding her place out with the other guests.

She sat next to Ed's mother, Suzanne, who was fair-skinned, heavily sedated, and looked like she had always had money and would always have money. Ed's father was even less expressive but looked just like his son. Everyone's faces turned to watch me.

It was a small wedding, littered with faces from a past that wasn't distant, but was estranging all the same. Emily was there in a scary-looking dress, tapping her feet; Moser was there with Hildy, and Sheila and Maria were in the second row. Art sat beside a woman who wasn't his wife. Before my father and I stepped down the aisle, I crossed myself. A ridiculous reflex. Sometimes stepping out the door on the way to run an errand, I moved my right hand over my forehead, then my chest, then my right and left shoulders. Reaching for that illusory, triangular protection. I stood in front of Ed, who wore a rented tuxedo. I stumbled through the overwritten vows in the too-empty church basement in the Financial District. Everything else had been booked. I looked at Maria, who mouthed the vows along with me, betraying no emotion, focused solely, like a director, on the effectiveness of my delivery. She had helped me write the words for the occasion, urging me to cut out the jokes since I wasn't a funny person.

*Thank you for your unrelenting support, love, and generosity. I feel like I've known you my whole life...*and so on.

Ed sobbed and that moved me, but only slightly. I wiped his face and couldn't believe it was my life, even though every dollar my parents had spent and every hour spent in grade school had been in preparation for this. My father cried into a plaid hand-kerchief, tears of relief, I thought. No more school fees, one less mouth to feed. My father loved me but never seemed to want all the responsibilities foisted on men born at the stage in history that he happened to appear in. He could entrust me to Ed. To him, Ed was less a person, more an ideal: capable, beautiful, strong, gentle, devoted. And a writer, not someone who would be forced to wreck and age his body with physical labor, as my father had done, but someone who would sit comfortably at home in a plush chair and work with his mind. Very desirable qualities but ultimately pow-erless against the scrutiny I'd put them under. We would wait and see. I reminded myself to smile.

We went to a restaurant in Midtown. The service was slow, the food cold. Maria shouted at the hostess on our behalf. Not very long ago, I was the hostess being shouted at. But to see her come to my defense was refreshing. Our close friends and families came back to our apartment for coffee, nightcaps. I was tired by that point, still wearing the dress. Ed was kind and did the talking for both of us. Everyone went home, except for my parents. My mother sat on my bed and picked lint off my duvet while I hung up my wedding dress and changed into a T-shirt and flannel pants. She and my father were staying at a budget hotel in New Jersey. When

I told my mother they could stay on the pull-out couch instead of driving back at night, she said it was our first night being married and that she didn't want to impose. She couldn't have thought we had waited until marriage? I sat down next to my mother, and we were quiet. She looked at one of my paintings on the wall. A small nude portrait of twins sitting on a sofa I had painted in school.

"Ruth," she said, then paused. "That painting is really vulgar. You should take it down."

26

·◇◇◇◇◇◇◇◇◇◇◇◇◇·

MARITAL BLISS. ALL my hours spent making paintings that I never showed anyone. Going to the movies at night with Ed and trying not to nod off as he played the cinephile (how he kept up energetically with these four-hour subtitled movies about the terminally lonely and depressed, I didn't know). Never going to see any art. Crossing the street if I walked by a gallery with paintings hanging in the window. Those days, I thought the only people making any work worth mentioning were primitive artists. Little education, no designs about New York. Obscure types who painted because they "had" to. Yet another one of my romantic fantasies, holdovers from the girls' school days. *What do you want to be when you grow up? An artist.* That revisionist history: I really wanted to be a nurse. A few steps up from a secretary. I tried to be shocking and smart. I simply wasn't. I was a sweet, simple person and that wouldn't fly in this place. I had that impulse shared by many women to advertise my failures and ask anyone around to commiserate, then resent them for having looked too closely.

In the end I was my mother's child. I wanted a good-looking

husband to shield me from certain realities. I wanted a credit card at Macy's, solid wood furniture, a reliable dry cleaner. To dislodge myself from the sad childhood. My mother never let me forget how young she was when her own mother died. *You'll miss me when I'm dead,* she would say from down the hall, when I'd left a mess in the living room. I supposed I would. Or maybe I wouldn't. She and I hardly spoke those days. We got along. Maybe the conditions by which we got along required not speaking, not seeing one another for all the same reasons a person evades the mirror in the morning after drinking.

When I was a child, my mother never touched me: no kisses or pets or hugs. Feeling guilty once, she pinched my cheek after reading me a bedtime story from the illustrated children's Bible. The story of Job. The next morning, I woke up with a faint bruise on the side of my face; she'd been too rough. My mother had hugged and kissed Maria regularly. Maria was a little orphan and had certain entitlements to love. I wished once that I was an orphan and that my mother was another person so she would touch me, too. Then I couldn't stand myself for letting my mind go there. Roundabout ways of fulfilling simple needs. But I shouldn't have blamed my mother. It was tedious the way everyone rushed to pin all their deficits and all their pain on their mothers. It wasn't her fault I felt lost and inferior. It could have been the school, it could have been the stars I was born under, it could have been the fact that I was failing as an artist or that I had rushed into marriage or that I'd read too little or too much. It could have been Maria who made me feel so inferior.

Lately, I avoided mirrors. I painted in low light from cheap candles that burned out quickly, from the dollar store down the road. I could scarcely see what I was doing. I'd have liked to have been one of the early men drawing on the insides of caves.

27

◇◇◇◇◇◇◇◇◇◇◇◇◇

IN JULY, I called Maria and asked if she wanted to get lunch. She'd been on my mind. *Okay,* she said. On the train ride to the restaurant where I was meeting her, I read a short review of a group show that compared my portraits to those of a painter I couldn't stand. It was a small art newspaper, but just seeing my name in print was a shock. That feeling quickly subsided and I found myself annoyed by what I was reading. The artist the essay likened me to was a woman close in age, who pretended, each time we met in passing at parties, that she couldn't remember my name. I suspected she was faking her accent, because it had a different quality each time she introduced herself to me. The more I reread it, the more irritated I became. I wasn't very used to having strong opinions. There hadn't been room for them in my life. I had to go along, acquiesce, be grateful. Even then.

The place I'd chosen was a newish cafe in Chinatown that still wore the original sign in Mandarin of the social club it had replaced. Maria was a regular at the restaurant and I thought it would be a good place to tell her that I'd gotten the fellowship upstate. I had quit my job with Emily. Thank God. It had been tedious to be around her now that the floodgates had been opened for her resentment of Maria; it was all she wanted to talk about. At first it was comfort. I had never expressed my jealousy about Maria directly before and here was someone who shared it, but it grew old as I remembered the other dimension of our relationship and my sense of protective-ness took over. I'd come to really dislike Emily. I thought the drugs she took made her paranoid and considered telling her so to spite her, but I took my final check and left on good terms instead.

Ed and I were leaving the city next month. He was thrilled. Me, I didn't know. The moment I got the call, he started looking for houses to rent in Dutchess County. Ed had cleaned up his act considerably and wasn't all that invested in his bohemian friends in Manhattan anymore; many of those dearest to him were having children and moving to New Jersey anyway. Even Art stopped drinking and was on a kind of apology tour for all his exes and other people he had burned along the way. Ed started mentioning kids and so that was another thing I had to deal with. The traffic and poverty and violence and pollution were really starting to wear Ed down, he claimed. He had romantic fantasies of writing in the woods, so it was one of those rare situations when both halves of a couple benefitted.

Still, I hoped our lunch would be a tearful departure, with Maria telling me how she'd miss me badly, even though I was only a two-hour train ride away. I wanted to make the most of the fel-lowship and I didn't intend to travel down to the city each weekend to drink with people I didn't know or like. If she cared to see me, she'd have to make an effort, I told myself. I felt older and less will-ing to be a doormat for other people. It was a bit of a breakthrough to be going back to the college with a clearer head. I hardly ever thought of James, and when I did, I was glad I hadn't been given what I thought I wanted. I hoped he wasn't dead, but didn't people die each day, people far more decent than James had been? Climbing up the stairs out of the station on Grand Street, I found that for the first time in my life I was glad that I was myself and not another person.

This spot wasn't so far from the pub where Ed and I had held our wedding reception. When I walked down the street where we celebrated after the wedding, I felt something in me harden and shatter. I smiled at the hungover hostess and took a seat facing the door. The windows in the restaurant were dirty. Part of the charm? Maria came in late and sat down. She looked beautiful, but I didn't tell her so. Some women you tell they're beautiful and they say, *Thanks, you, too.* Not Maria, of course. The lunch was about me, I decided. The server brought us a carafe of water and a basket of dinner rolls.

"I hate this restaurant," Maria said, tearing at the bread.

"I thought you came here all the time. I wouldn't have picked—"

"Yeah. The food's awful, but they have the most beautiful waitresses in New York. Last time I was here with Sheila, we had a server who said she'd arrived from Cairo three days before and just walked in here. They hired her on the spot. No questions asked. She looked like an angel. She barely spoke English. These girls really make it worth your while."

"Ah, Maria, the great feminist," I said, opening a square of butter. "That's what I read in your review. You're a very important feminist artist. Haven't you heard?" Maria winked at me and nodded in the direction of a server in a tight, low-cut blouse, her long curls halfway down her back, her jadeite eyes scanning the room. Deep, deep brown skin any number of women in this city would pay for.

I had no sense of whether or not Maria had other girlfriends. She and Sheila still lived together. Pretty domesticated. They had just bought a loft in Soho, but Maria regularly traveled alone and would offhandedly mention "friends" in other cities. I didn't ask any more and she didn't elaborate.

"Sheila and I are very unhappy. I'm thinking about ending things. I want an equal and she wants to be a disciple. That gets old."

"But you two seem so in love," I offered.

"I don't think I've ever loved anyone. I don't care much about other people."

I didn't believe her and didn't want to entertain these big assertions she had always needed to make about herself. All feeble attempts at getting around the business of feeling what she felt. Maria, ever the actress, figured if you said the lines enough times, others would believe them and then you would, too. *Have you considered analysis?* I asked Maria. When I started the job with Emily, I went to analysis three times per week. Not because Emily exacerbated the trouble I had, but because out of guilt or real benevolence, Emily reimbursed me for the sessions of analysis. I worked my way down to once per week, seeing myriad improvements in my life. I finally enjoyed sex with my husband and wasn't plagued by terrible dreams, for starters. My fixations about Maria had greatly diminished. But Maria was still the first thing I thought of when I got up in the morning and the last thing I thought of before I went to bed at night. My analyst wondered if Maria wasn't a stand-in for my artistic ambitions. Was she the echo I thought of so that I didn't have to think of the thing itself? I didn't think so. Mostly, I went to therapy because the sound of my analyst's voice was so consoling, so motherly, it scratched the itch, basically. I didn't mention these details to Maria. I knew she'd laugh.

"Therapy?!" She rolled her eyes and waved her hand in the air, casting the idea out of the room. "Pay hundreds of dollars to find out what I already know. Surprise, you're fucked up because your mom hanged herself. How much do they charge you for those brilliant observations?"

"My analyst told me I'm parentified, that I always emotionally supported others, namely my parents, but they never reciprocated. I began to feel responsible for their moods…"

"*Parentify* is a really stupid word. Corny." Maria flipped through the menu. "What do you think of the grilled trout? Does that sound any good?"

"Trout sounds fine," I said.

"Fish in America," she said, "isn't really fish."

Part of me was afraid to leave her. The other part was glad. Two p.m. and she ordered a liter of wine. I was drunk by the time the appetizer came out. Something to do with snow peas. I didn't really follow these new restaurants, didn't understand. The next course was octopus. Maria ate a few bites and then told me she felt that after eating something as intelligent as an octopus, all that was left was to eat human beings. Then she helped herself to some more.

"So what's the big news?" Maria asked.

"Oh, I got a job."

"You have a job, you're a painter. And a housewife."

"I'm not a housewife," I said, indignant, swallowing the peas.

"Don't be sensitive. What's the job, then?"

"Yeah, just a residency. At Bard. Teaching two classes. Just for the year."

I downplayed my excitement at being chosen out of a pool of what I assumed were talented, young candidates. All less talented than me, I was proud to consider. Plus, teaching was noble, I'd thought, though as I looked at Maria, I couldn't be so sure. Our first teachers had been predatory or punishing. Later, they were distracted and permissive. I was beginning to feel doubtful about this job and wondered whether it had been a mistake to accept the offer. I wanted her to say something quickly, one way or the other. She nodded.

"Congratulations," Maria said, calling over a waitress. "It's a start."

By the way, Maria forgot to tell me, her aunt was dead: pills. The downstairs neighbor found her two days after she died. They mailed her the ashes and she had yet to pick them up from her P.O. box. Who were "they"? I asked. She didn't want to discuss it. She just wanted to put all that sordid business behind her. A server with long brown hair and round dark features—black eyes, a shadowy round mouth, and dense eyebrows—poured water into our short glasses. She *was* beautiful. Come to think of it, they all were. She set a grilled fish in the center of the table between us and asked us what we needed. Maria smiled and unconvincingly flirted with her. No, she didn't have any other girlfriends. Maria turned back to look at me and her smile was gone.

"So you two are moving?" she asked.

"We'll have to." I sighed.

"I thought you hated Bard."

"I'm in a better place now."

"Are you?" Maria asked.

"Yes, I'm very happy."

"How long will you be up there again?"

"One year."

"Right, I'll see you when you come back. I still haven't been up to Ed's place."

"It isn't Ed's place. It's ours."

"You know what I mean."

"It's not a big deal, it's just that I pay rent, too," I said.

"Well, then, I'll go to your and Ed's apartment when you two come back to the city."

"Or you could visit us upstate. It's only two hours away."

"Oh, I'm not going down memory lane," Maria said.

We ate the fish in relative silence. I moved my food around my plate and when the check came, Maria handed the waitress a hundred-dollar bill. On the street, waiting for a cab, I told Maria that Ed was having a reading at a cafe in the Village that weekend. I explained that she didn't have to come, but that it would mean a lot to him. Her approval, in short, meant a lot to him. To us. To me. I didn't say this but thought it and she knew it. She nodded inattentively.

"I'll be there," she said, though I hadn't given her the time or address and she hadn't asked.

I stepped into the road and waved a taxi down. It appeared to slow, then sped past us.

"Wait," Maria said. "Smoke a cigarette with me before you go."

"I quit smoking after school," I said.

"Old times' sake?" she asked.

"If I start again, I'll never stop," I said, raising my arm out for another cab.

"Then just stand here with me while I have one," Maria said, digging in her canvas bag. "Who knows when we'll see each other again."

I folded my arms and looked down at her feet. The sky was overcast, about to break open and strand those of us without day jobs under awnings, in coffee shops. I faced Maria, glimpses of the eleven-year-old girl frozen in the face of the self-serious twentysomething before me. The wind gained speed. Maria struck a match, and it didn't take. I cupped my hands around her mouth. A cab stopped before us and the driver rolled his window down. I pulled my hands away and Maria blew the smoke back over her shoulder. She let out a dry cough. I offered her the cab.

"You take this one. I'm not in a hurry," she said.

I climbed in and shifted in my seat. I gave the driver the name of my street. Maria put her free hand on the window, widened her fingers, and exhaled.

"I'll miss you," I said without intending to, through the foggy glass.

"Can't hear you," said Maria, over the sudden rain.

"Shit," she said, turning away, the cigarette extinguished. She struck another match and a waft of smoke rose up around her mouth. The cab sped off and I didn't turn to look behind me.

28

◇◇◇◇◇◇◇◇◇◇◇◇◇◇◇

LATER THAT NIGHT, Maria called our apartment and Ed answered. I overheard her voice as he asked who it was. I hadn't expected to hear from her so soon, as awkward as things had been in the restaurant. Or maybe lunch hadn't been awkward at all and I'd invented the whole thing. In my mind, Maria and I were embroiled in a huge, fatal drama that hardly ever manifested in the way we spoke to one another.

"It's for you," he said. He was suspicious of Maria lately but didn't say why. Ed was proud and hid it behind his humility, as it was easy for him to do. I cleared my throat before picking up the phone in the bedroom. I said hello. Maria's words were slurred on the other end of the line.

"Can you come over?" Maria asked. "Sheila's out of town. Can we talk?"

"Um, Ed and I are about to watch *The Sopranos.*"

"Can't it wait? It's the same thing every week anyway. Someone cheats, somebody kills somebody else."

"I don't know."

"Please," Maria said. "I need to see you."

I rushed her off the phone. Her mood had changed from the coolness at the restaurant. I went in the bathroom and splashed warm water between my legs and dried myself off. It was a strange precaution to take. I did it without thinking. I got dressed quickly and sprayed myself down with a bottle of perfume I'd put on Ed's credit card. It had been his idea. Him trying to make a woman out of me, I guessed. Beneath it all—the partying and everything—Ed was hopelessly old-fashioned. A lot like my mother: strong sense of obligation, serious, materialistic. He liked taking care of me and paying for everything. He was happy when I sat at home and painted and went out to buy new clothes. I wondered what he got in return. He was taken by the idea of me as a kept woman and I thought that it was something wrong with me that that didn't really turn me on. Or maybe it did and I just didn't want to say.

"I'm gonna go see Maria for a drink," I told him.

"Oh, tonight? I already ordered Chinese."

"When I get back?" I asked, my hands pressed together apologetically. "She's having a bad night. She said it was urgent."

"Everything's urgent with her."

"I won't be long," I said, buttoning my shirt.

"Fine," he said, "and you've got some lipstick in your teeth."

He saw me out and slammed the door as I climbed down the stairs. *A real marriage with eye-rolling and slammed doors,* I thought. I hailed a cab and gave him Maria's address. I couldn't contain my excitement to see her. *Twice in a day,* I thought. I should have been embarrassed.

"You married, sweetheart?" the driver asked.

"Yeah," I said.

"That's too bad. Got any sisters?"

"No," I said. "Only child."

"Just my luck," he said. I tuned him out.

We reached her apartment on Mercer Street, and I gave the

driver a big tip. All the cash I had. I was in a good mood, irra-
tionally so. Maria opened the door in her nightgown with a
half-finished beer in hand. She let me in and took my coat. The
coffee table was littered with empty bottles. She had incense going.
She seemed glad to have this brief freedom from Sheila, who made
such a nice home, comfortable, as far as incarceration went. All the
recycling going in its proper place, the floors always freshly vac-
uumed. Potted flowers. A couple of Maria's photographs. A busy
tapestry mounted by the window. Maria had nothing to do with
the apartment. She would be content with a plastic folding chair, a
plain table, and a bare mattress. Had the circumstances been different, she and I could have lived that way. I underplayed my desire
to be there. I hadn't been truly alone with Maria in a long time.
Sheila was always around or Ed was always around. Or we were at
a party, or in a crowded restaurant, where the other patrons were
all eavesdropping on one another, trying to listen for a conversation more salacious than their own. Life in that city was structured
around an elimination of privacy. All boundaries permeable. A
person had to pay a lot, almost everything, for a break from the
constant proximity. It was easy to forget how vulnerable you were.
Another person's hands were never very far from your throat. It
was no surprise that Maria and I had run headlong toward whatever shelter we could find. Her toward Sheila. Me toward Ed. Playing house so unconvincingly, it appeared our early educations had
worked. The poor suburbs we grew up in as much a disposition as
a physical place.

"Why did you call me?" I asked her.

"To see if you'd come," she said.

I sat on the sofa and watched the fragrant smoke spiral up into
thin air. Maria sat beside me and flipped through the *TV Guide*.
My hands were loosely folded in my lap. I didn't want to touch
anything or incriminate myself. I had a feeling I shouldn't be there.
I scanned the room, impressed by how well-appointed it all was.

All these prints and paintings, souvenirs of a well-traveled adolescence, hanging on the wall salon style. The striped wallpaper and brass sconces, the candelabras and rows of books. I'd never seen Sheila read much, but they did the trick as decorative objects. I was eager to see what Maria had in store for me that night, in that beautiful apartment. It didn't look like there was anything terribly interesting being offered on TV, even with all of the extra channels Sheila paid for. Maria opened another beer, then turned to me suggestively and sighed, as if to say we were moving from one act to the next.

"Have you been with any other women?" she asked.

I paused. I shook my head.

"All that time ago, when we were together, did it mean anything to you?"

"Sure, it meant something. But we were kids. And we're with other people. And that's alright with me."

"But what if that isn't alright with me?" she asked, placing her hand on my forearm, her palm slick and warm. "Do you think, Ruth, that we couldn't find a way to live together?"

"Like as roommates?" I asked. I looked down at the coffee table, the incense a pile of ash on its burl wood face, the candles spent, pools of hardening wax.

"No, as...I'm leaving Sheila," Maria said. "We spoke this morning. That's why she isn't here. She's staying with her parents. I think about you all the time. Don't you think of me?"

I nodded. Neither of us said anything for a while. I looked at Maria, who was crying. I toyed with my wedding band, the way I did when I was uneasy. Worse than disappointment was getting what I wanted. She reclined on the sofa and put her hand in mine.

"You're being serious?"

"Ball's in your court," she said. "Don't think about the money. I'll take care of you. Please."

I put my hand over hers and held it. She had told me what I'd wanted to hear since I met her and I had not even known I'd wanted to hear it. She put my hands against her face. That was too much. I had dreamt of this moment many times, in rooms like this and in other rooms. Any satisfaction I thought I'd feel never came, seeing Maria beg this way. She slipped off the couch and got down on her knees and kissed my fingers one by one. Then turned my hand over and put her lips in my palm. She brushed my skirt up to my thighs and put her mouth on my knee. She rested her head in my lap, then looked up at me and pulled at my skirt.

"Go home and pack your things," she said. "We'll go wherever you want to."

"I have to think," I said.

"About what?"

"Whether or not you're someone that…anyone can depend on?"

"Are you really happy? Do you really want to move upstate? With him?"

I looked down at my feet. I told her to get up.

"Go, but if you don't come back, I never want to see you again," she said. "I don't say that to pressure you. It just hurts me and if you go, it would be better for me if we didn't speak."

I sat still for a long while before I spoke. I had to think clearly because Ed wasn't just some boyfriend I was living with who I could treat poorly without a second thought. I didn't think Maria understood the magnitude of what she was asking of me and I didn't want to be a temporary stand-in for Sheila just because they'd quarreled and Maria was lonely. I told Maria to get off the floor so I could look her in the eye.

"I can't implode my life on a whim just because you called me drunk," I said.

"It isn't a whim," she said. "I've felt this way a long time."

"Why are you only telling me now?"

"I didn't have the courage to," she said. "And now I'm worried you'll move away with Ed and have children and there won't be another opportunity."

"And if I stay here with you? What happens when Sheila comes back?"

"I'll tell Sheila that you and I are going to be together. I'll call her right now."

Maria stood up and searched for her phone. She found it on the other side of the room under a pile of magazines she'd been cutting apart. She held the phone up so I could see and dialed Sheila's number.

"Don't," I said.

I straightened out my blouse and pulled down the hem of my skirt. I got up, unable or unwilling to move from where I stood. She put the phone in her pocket.

"Please don't go now," Maria said, blocking the front door. I hadn't planned to leave quite yet and felt I should at least listen to her proposition. I walked to the refrigerator and helped myself to another beer. Maria searched around for a bottle opener, and when we couldn't find one she said we could just go out instead.

"Go where?" I asked.

"There's a diner down the street," she said. I told her to give me a moment to rinse my face. In the bathroom, I stared at myself as though I were looking at a photograph of another person. I often bought old bags of photographs at flea markets and rifled through them for unusual subjects, people to paint. I was interested again in what a face could communicate: a sense of affliction or openness. In each face there were the remnants of all the generations. Sometimes, I chose figures to paint based on the kind of story I could fabricate from looking at these anonymous persons. What did my face in the mirror suggest? This woman was young, married, maybe she was pregnant right now and didn't know it. Maybe she was on the brink of starting an affair. Maybe this affair would be the first of many.

I fixed my lipstick and went out to the living room, where I found Maria lacing up her shoes. We took the elevator down to the first floor and once we were on the street, she slipped her hand into mine. I was devastated by how familiar it felt. We walked down several blocks, her fingers tightly wrapped around mine. I could have been walking in another country where no one spoke the same language and I wouldn't have noticed. I didn't know where we were going, but stared up dreamily at the lights, letting Maria lead the way. I didn't have to make a decision yet. All I had to do now was take one step and then another. I heard someone call my name and I froze. There was someone tall and slim walking in our direction. Long dark hair and pasty skin. I saw that it was Emily. It was dark but she wore big sunglasses; when she took them off I could see why. Her eyes were bloodshot. She looked like she'd gone days without sleep. She was nervous and spoke quickly, giving Maria a cold, sideways glance.

"Ruth, I thought you left town. I've been up all day and night walking. I haven't been sleeping. My new medication is just way, way off. I'm glad to see you. I miss you at the studio. Oh, you two are an item. Alright. Weren't you just married, though? God, I hate that I ran into you while I'm like this. I feel like I'm hallucinating. Do I seem off to you?"

"Emily, you should check yourself into a hospital," I said.

"We have to go," Maria said and dragged me away. I waved goodbye to Emily and pulled my hand away from Maria's. We had turned onto another street before the possibility of Emily telling someone what she'd seen occurred to me. I would call her the following morning to tell her that Maria had been drunk and I was only holding her hand to keep her from stumbling. But maybe there would be no following morning. It was possible that the night would upend my life in such a way that it would not matter who I called or did not call once it was over. We walked into the diner and took a seat in a slick red booth in the back corner, where Maria promptly ordered two shots of bourbon, a coffee, and a pastrami sandwich. She looked at me expectantly and I saw that she had the same expression she'd had as a child of opening her eyes very wide when she was paying close attention. She didn't touch the sandwich when it came but slid one of the shot glasses across the table to me.

"I'm worried Emily might mention she saw us holding hands."

"I'm sure Emily's seen worse," Maria said.

"I just don't want to betray Ed. He's been so good to me."

"I don't feel I'm betraying Sheila," she said. "And you shouldn't feel you're betraying Ed. People should do what they want to. Ed, Sheila, you, me. We should all do whatever we want. You and I want to be together."

When the waitress came by again, Maria asked for another round. I had a bite of the sandwich and a sip of the bourbon in front of me. I wanted to be lucid if I was going to do something so drastic. I didn't want to wake up in the morning forgetting anything that had been said. It was late and people were just crawling out of their apartments to begin their nights. I had been so secure in the enclosure of my relationship with Ed that I'd forgotten the curious sexual and romantic possibilities of a Saturday night. Whereas his consistency had previously seemed like a gift, I wondered if it wasn't inhibiting me. Maria slammed her hand on the table, a little too loudly, seeming rather manic.

"I know!" Maria said. "Let's each say a secret. Something we haven't told anyone. You start."

I looked from one side to another to make sure no one was listening. I emptied my glass and cleared my throat.

"Do you remember my professor, Moser? The one who got me the job with Emily?"

"Yes," Maria said.

"I had sex with his wife. When I went to work for him. James never showed up, so it was just her and me alone."

Maria squinted at me.

"Does he know?" she asked.

"Of course not."

"So you *have* been with another woman. I asked you and you said no. That was a lie." She frowned.

"I'd hardly say I was with her. I mean, she initiated it and, I don't know, I wanted to and I guess I enjoyed it, but…it was over as soon as it started."

"You don't have to lie to me, Ruth. It's okay if you wanted to. What do I care if you had sex with someone's old wife?"

Maria called the server over and handed her cash for the bill. She asked for a box for the sandwich and I took it to mean the evening was coming to an end.

"You aren't upset, are you?"

"No, of course not," she said, counting out the tip.

"What's your secret?"

"Right. You remember how James was so terrible to you? How he just disappeared after sending that email?"

"Yeah, that sounds vaguely familiar," I said.

"Well, when we first moved to New York and you lived with Sheila and me, we started getting all these letters. And they were from London…"

I turned my head to the side in surprise. Maria paused and looked embarrassed.

"You were always at work when the mailman came. The letters, they were from James and I didn't know how he got the address so I just held on to them. Then I read them and they were these long, weird apologies and he mentioned the money he stole and how he was so depressed and ashamed and didn't know how to face you. How sorry he was about saying he was going to kill himself. Just letter after letter saying he loved you and missed you. That he wanted a relationship, basically, and that he'd be back in New York for a summer with his father and maybe you two could start anew. I just kept them, all the letters. Then months passed, and I threw them out."

"What?" I asked. "So he really did steal the money."

"That was always obvious...Anyway, you finally seemed happy, like you were moving on. You had a job and I thought, *He's just coming into her life selfishly and then he'll leave the same way he did before.*" Maria was smiling. "It's so funny now. I mean, can you imagine? He just thought he'd come back from faking his death and you two would shack up together."

"Why didn't you let me decide for myself?"

"You said yourself you were glad he was out of your life. I was looking out for you."

"So he isn't dead?"

"I mean, he might be dead now. But he wasn't dead when he sent those letters. What difference does it make? You aren't angry, are you?"

The waitress came back with the takeout box. Maria stood up and looked out the wide windows. I was a bit annoyed, fairly confused, but maybe Maria had done me a courtesy by intercepting those letters from James. Still, I wondered, in light of Maria's recent confessions, if she hadn't thrown out the letters out of jealousy. My sense of isolation that first summer in New York had been so extreme. And even if James had been a bad boyfriend, it might have been a comfort to have someone to sleep with and go to parties with in the same way that Maria had Sheila. They had fought terribly when I lived with them, but they had been given the opportunity to fight and figure things out as adults. She'd deprived me of that and hadn't given me the choice. Looking at Maria, I couldn't cast any blame. There would always be an air of total innocence and decency emanating from her, no matter what she did. I'd grow jealous and resentful at turns, then sit in front of her this way and all those tense feelings would dissipate. Looking at her, I understood that we needed strong people to make the choices for us that we didn't have the courage to make for ourselves, and that I should be grateful she threw those letters out on my behalf.

"Where to next?" she asked, smiling. She extended her hand and we walked out of the diner together. We strolled for a long time before stopping into a corner store for beers. I didn't know what time it was and didn't care. In such a short time, so much had been revealed. I'd been waiting for this sort of direction and here it was. When I painted, I tried to imbue each scene with a sense of the world's strangeness and opacity, with a sense of my own mystification, in hopes of seeing in a clearer way. Maria had brought a spirit of confession into my life when she called me over to her apartment, and I didn't want to pass it up without really trying to deal with it seriously, without figuring out what it might reveal. Failing to meet her with honesty would be an awful waste. We walked to the river to drink our beers, leaning over the railing and stealing glances at one another.

"Do you think that if you had grown up differently, you would have ended up with a woman instead of a man?"

"You and I grew up the same way," I said.

"We grew up in the same place, but not the same way," Maria said. "I never took anyone's authority seriously. As far as I was concerned, I didn't have parents and no one had authority over me. Things could have gone very badly for me."

"You would've been fine. People like you, they're drawn to you. I remember when I saw you for the first time. I thought you were so beautiful. I was totally taken with you."

"You followed me in the supermarket, then you ran away," she said. "I remember."

"Before that. In the uniform shop. You were just perfect, like a little doll. I don't think you saw me. I doubt you remember."

The moonlight trembled on the surface of the East River. Cop cars rolled by and the sound of their sirens was muffled as though we were underwater. Maria threw her empty can over the railing and we watched it bob like an apple. I thought of the logistics of leaving my life.

"I've known you for so long," she said. "All these things you've been to me. A sister and friend and lover. Is it too much to ask from one person? If you said no, I'd understand."

"If we were to leave now, where would we go?" I asked. "I have a month before I start teaching. We could find an apartment and I could commute up there by train."

"Sheila's aunt and uncle have a house in Pine Plains," she said. "I could tell her I'm staying there to work."

"I thought you and Sheila weren't speaking. Aren't you going to leave her?"

"Of course, but not right away. I have to give her time to get used to the idea. She's been so generous with me. And with you, too."

"Ed's been generous," I said, sitting down on the curb. Maria sat down beside me.

"After you and I got together that night at school, I told Sheila about it. She said she didn't want you living with us in New York anymore. And I told her that if she didn't let you stay with us, I would never speak to her again."

Maria put her hand on my knee. I felt a profound sense of being loved with all its dependency and confusion. Hiding the letters from James so that I could move on, giving Sheila that ultimatum so that I would have a place to live. Maria had been interceding thanklessly on my behalf all along and I'd repaid her by being jealous and gossiping about her with anyone who would listen. I had wasted precious time resenting her and now I could recoup on that lost window of time. Things with Ed and Sheila had all been a mistake, but we didn't need to worry anymore. Maria said we should get a taxi and book a hotel. She could take out cash and reimburse me, but we'd have to use one of my credit cards to book the room so that Sheila didn't see the statement. All the cards were in her name.

"What if Ed sees the statement?"

"I didn't think of that," she said.

We went to a hotel in Midtown where we wouldn't run into anyone who we knew. In the taxi, I asked her if I could use her phone to call Ed. I'd tell him I got drunk and was staying on Sheila and Maria's couch. There was no use in confessing my plans in the middle of the night. He'd insist on coming to me and persuading me to go back home. Maria told me that she'd left her cellphone back at her apartment because she didn't want the distraction. She wanted to just be alone with me.

The lights were dim in the hotel and there was bad live vocal jazz playing in the bar. Maria asked the concierge if she could pay with cash and they said they'd allow it so long as she left a deposit for incidentals. She opened her wallet and counted out the money, setting it on the counter. The elevator was covered in mirrored panels and as we rode it up to our room, many versions of ourselves were reflected back to us from all sides. The towels on the bed in the center of the room were folded like swans. I set my purse down and sat in the love seat opposite the bed. My head spun and I was glad to be sitting still. I made a mental note to call Ed before falling asleep. I fished around for aspirin in my purse and asked Maria if she wanted any herself. I heard the water running like heavy rain in the next room. She hadn't heard me. I called her name again. When she came into the room she was undressed. She stood by the desk and wrapped a towel around herself. She had strong shoulders and small feet. Her coarse, curled hair was cut just below her ears in the style she'd had since we'd left college. Feet, hair, shoulders—nearly universal, ordinary features. Why did they feel endlessly symbolic when connected to someone you loved? Suddenly there was a lot of meaning in the slenderness of their feet, the curve of their shoulders, the way they wore their hair.

"Will you join me?" she asked. I took off my clothes and tossed them on the floor by the toilet. Then I took off my wedding band and my engagement ring. Maria lathered me with soap in the shower and as the water ran over my head, I cried without making any noise. She didn't notice or didn't say. We did not dry off before getting into bed, peeling back the stiff, white sheets. Our bodies were very alike and I wondered, cradled together, what we looked like from above. I slid my hand between her thighs, but she pulled away and clasped her legs together tightly. I felt rebuffed. She noticed and turned to comfort me.

"It's not that I don't want to," she said. "It's just that so much has already happened tonight. And there'll be time for all that later. As much time as we want."

I smiled and kissed her hand. We lay side by side breathing slowly. You could hardly hear the sounds of traffic from below. I felt we were floating high above Manhattan and had no worldly responsibilities. That errands and appointments and meetings and careers were things for other people. We spoke in clipped sentences, not needing to elaborate. We drifted on shifting terrain, not quite awake or dreaming. I listened and I couldn't tell whose voice belonged to whom. We fell asleep listing cities we might run off to.

"What about Los Angeles?"

"No real seasons."

"Montreal?"

"We don't speak French."

"Rio?"

"We don't speak Portuguese, either."

"Philadelphia?"

"Are there galleries in Philadelphia?"

"Venice?"

"Istanbul?"

"Boston?"

"No, not Boston."

We woke up in the morning to heavy knocks on the door. We had overslept. It was past checkout and a cleaner was there to see us out. We quickly gathered our things and rushed down to the lobby. Neither of us knew what to say, clutching our belongings to our chests, like we'd just had a first date and didn't want to scare the other away with declarations of strong feelings. I didn't know what Maria was thinking as she took back the deposit and stuffed the cash back into her wallet. We stepped outside and the sun bore into us unrelentingly. She shielded her face and her hand cast a dark shadow over her eyes.

"Maybe we go home and straighten up and meet here later today," she said.

"Yeah, okay. I'll have to tell Ed."

"And I'll have to tell Sheila," she said.

"Where should we meet?" I asked.

"Right here, at this hotel."

She walked me to the train and we descended two flights, splitting up finally with a polite kiss on the cheek before I walked toward the uptown train and she crossed over to go farther south. I watched her from across the station. She didn't see me and I noticed her take out her cellphone, the cellphone she had said she left at home, and check the time. Then she looked up at the fluorescent lights and sighed. She moved through the crowd, finally disappearing behind a metal column and then she was out of view.

29

◇◇◇◇◇◇◇◇◇◇◇◇◇◇◇◇◇◇

I TREMBLED THE whole way home. As I walked from the station to the apartment, the familiar storefronts and avenues were rapidly cementing into a past I knew I would look back on cynically someday soon, no matter what I chose to do. I felt there was still a choice to make. The night before had made it apparent to me that in each moment consequential decisions awaited us and that it was only out of convenience that we neglected this perpetual responsibility and went along as though we were on a fixed course. I crept up the stairs quietly, hoping Ed wouldn't hear me come in. Of course I found him home, sitting at his desk, writing longhand. He was wearing over-ear headphones and I could hear the loud jazz he listened to through them. I tapped him on his back and he startled. He stood up and stepped back, looking at me uneasily.

"Where have you been?" he asked. "I called Maria's all night."

"I got drunk and fell asleep. I hadn't eaten. I slept on their couch."

"Sheila called me last night and said she couldn't reach Maria, either. So where were you?"

"I don't know what you're insinuating," I said, "but I'm tired and I need to lie down."

"What happened to your rings?" Ed asked. I felt very sick. I shrugged. Ed told me I was interrupting his work and that if I wanted to turn up in the middle of the day, smelling like alcohol, after being gone all night, I shouldn't complain when he does the same to me. He told me I should get away from him and to clean myself up because I stank.

"You smell disgusting," he said again. "I can't look at you."

He sat down and I turned away and ran. I locked the bedroom door behind me and decided that however long or loudly he banged, I wouldn't open it. I pulled a leather duffel bag out of my wardrobe. We had financed the dresser and Ed was still paying it off since it was so expensive. I must have wanted it because it was the kind of thing my mother would describe as *built to last*. Wedged under its engraved mirror, there was a picture of Ed and me feeding one another cake at our wedding. Where was my passport? My dresses hung from cloth hangers. My sweaters were folded up on the top shelf. Ed's jackets were neatly tucked into the corner, beside my own. I looked at the Tiffany lamp on my nightstand and the narrow Persian rug at the foot of the bed, the books on the windowsill, the old wooden blinds. The duvet I'd ordered from a Nordstrom catalog, the carafe on my vanity, my colored glass perfume bottles, the display case where I kept my small accessories: the costume jewelry and the thin gold necklace from my mother with the eighteen-carat Virgin charm bought at an Indian jeweler in Mombasa. I could live without it all. You only needed all these flimsy consolations when you knew you were living a life you didn't want.

I placed whatever dresses and sweaters I could fit into my bag. I could shower once I got where I was going. Later, I would go to an

ATM, take out a few hundred dollars, and not think about the rest. I would go away with Maria and live differently. There wasn't any infrastructure in place to stop me from doing whatever I wanted. People abandoned their lives all the time, didn't they? The next step I took would color my life, one way or the other. All I needed to do was pick up my bag, get past Ed, and walk down to the subway station, ride the train to the hotel, figure out where to go, purchase the ticket. She was waiting for me. She had already set our plans in motion. By then, Sheila would know. I walked past Ed and went to the kitchen drawer where we kept spare cash. I needed money for a taxi, then I'd get more out later. Ed shouted at me, but I didn't listen.

"I am going to my mother's house," he said, "and if you aren't here and cleaned up and ready to apologize when I'm back, then you need to get out of my apartment."

"What?" I asked.

"You're disgusting. You smell awful. I don't deserve to be treated this way. You think the world owes you. I swear, Ruth, if I come home and don't find you here, I'll leave you."

"Then leave me," I said. I rushed out the door and heard Ed call down the stairs. A neighbor opened the window to watch me. I must have looked strange, running down the street like that. I flagged down a taxi that was speeding toward the opposite direction. I chased it down until it slowed to a stop, my bag hitting my side as I ran. I gave the name of the hotel where I'd been the night before. I paid the driver and slid out of the car, scanning the street for Maria. I didn't see her. She was probably running late. It was hard to pack when you didn't know where you were going. In the lobby, I asked for the housekeeper who had cleaned up our room. She was a short pale woman with stringy gray hair worn up in a tight bun. I asked if she had seen any rings.

"I didn't find anything," she said.

"The rings were on the counter."

"I wiped the counter. I didn't see anything," she said with a shrug.

She wiped her nose with the back of her hand, then placed her hand on her hip. Her look was smug and impatient. I handed her a few bills. She sighed and pulled the rings out of the apron at her waist. I slipped them back onto my finger and walked back out into the sun. I didn't know why I'd gone through so much trouble for the rings now that I didn't need them. I sat on the edge of the stone planter outside the hotel and ran my hands over the bright clumps of begonias. Maria would be there any moment. I'd place a flower behind her ear. Once settled, I'd paint her in various poses. That would be my new work. Lately, I couldn't understand why anyone painted figuratively. I couldn't understand just wanting to paint a person anymore, but sitting in the sun, swinging my feet and waiting for Maria, I understood. It would be like before, when I first painted her as a child. Soon, it wouldn't matter that I'd discarded those precious early paintings years ago. For a long time, I had been devastated that I agreed to put those paintings of Maria in the landfill. *You shouldn't have parted with the evidence of your past so easily, you shouldn't have thrown yourself away so carelessly,* I chided myself, now that I was older. But not to worry, it was all being restored to me. As it was written in the Bible, "God will restore everything you've lost." Everything was being restored.

The tall, olive-skinned driver was still parked in the same spot where I'd left him. He leaned against his shining yellow car and smoked. He looked at me without appearing to look at me, like he had been hired to keep watch.

"Do you need a ride back the way you came from?" he asked.

"No," I said, "but do you have the time?"

"It's one thirty," he said, putting out his cigarette and getting into the driver's seat. He looked back at me again to ask if I was sure and I waved him off. Maria must have been held up back at her apartment. I could have gone to find a pay phone, but there wasn't one on that block, and if I left, I might miss her. I sat there in the sun feeling my color deepen. I didn't know how long I waited. Finally, I was hot and needed to get off the street. I went to the front desk and booked a room. I put it on Ed's and my credit card since I wouldn't have to answer to him anymore. I asked once, and again, that they make sure the window of my room faced the street. I needed to be able to look down and watch for Maria. They placed me in a room with a balcony and I sat outside with wide, tortoiseshell sunglasses on, looking over the edge of my magazine for a woman who looked like Maria from above.

I imagined she was getting into it with Sheila, calling everything off, packing up her clothes, and that she was making her way to me, through the heat, through the traffic. There was sweat sliding down my neck. I was eager to see her. To be with her on the balcony, on the sofa, in an airplane, on a high-speed rail. Watching the street, I would see a black head of hair pass over the gray sidewalk, I would throw my sunglasses off to look more closely, then I'd notice it was a man or a tall, slender teenager. Finally, I called Maria's apartment. No one answered. The numbers on the alarm clock shone 6:05 in lime green. Things must have gone terribly with Sheila; I called again. Again the phone rang and rang, but no one came to it. I pulled the cord as far as it would go so I could both watch the street and continue to call. If only I knew her cellphone number. Worried she had been derailed, I called again. I left a message asking Maria to please call me at the hotel. I left increasingly frantic messages.

"If anything has happened, if you've changed your mind, gotten cold feet, or are otherwise stuck and can't make your way here, please call me and I'll come and get you. I'll give you the number again so you have it."

"Maria, please, it's me. Remember our plans?"

"Ed is very upset at home with me and I might have ruined things irreparably with him, so if you're going to back out at the last minute, you have to know what an impossible position you've put me in and that this is my life, not a game."

"You're selfish. You've always been selfish. What's the matter with you? I hope Sheila never finds out the kinds of things you've said about her throughout the years...I'm sorry. If you're still coming, call me so I know. I've been waiting for hours."

I went into the mini-fridge and pulled out a small bottle of vodka. I portioned out a heavy pour and took a sip. My stomach was empty and the liquor was cheap, so it went down badly. I threw the rest back in one swig, then I ran myself a hot shower, scrubbing myself until my skin came off in dark clumps under my nails. I dried myself off and lotioned my body meticulously. Then I changed into one of the clean dresses I'd packed to desert my marriage. I did a final scan of the room to make sure I hadn't left anything behind. Then I walked down to the subway station and went home. I struggled up the stairs, holding the banisters for life. Pulling myself up the steps, I felt I'd narrowly escaped something grave. But from the outside, I knew I looked like any woman walking up to her apartment after an ordinary day of errands, on a summer night no different from any other. When I turned the key and pushed the door open, I found Ed had locked it with the chain. I tried to force the door open, pulling it back and forth, but the lock wouldn't give.

"I know you're in there, Ed. Please, let me in!"

"I told you that if I came back home and you weren't here, I didn't want to see you."

"I took a shower. I'm all cleaned up. Please let me in and talk to me."

I saw Ed's brown, bloodshot eye through the sliver in the door and his staticky halo of black and gray hair. Men in his family grayed early. Yellow light spilled out from the apartment. I felt if I didn't gain entry, if he didn't unfasten the chain, I'd just cease to be. He blinked and stepped back. I thought he would open the door. I heard him rummaging in the next room, then he came back and started madly stuffing my belongings through the gap. He pushed them toward me—my mail, my jewelry, a bundle of paintbrushes—and I wouldn't take them. I pushed them back inside, pleading with him to let me in.

"Don't you think, Ruth, that I've had women take interest in me since I met you? Don't you think I had opportunities to step out on you, too? That's the problem. You're young and you think you invented everything. You didn't invent cheating. You aren't that clever."

"Nothing happened, Ed. I just felt trapped, I needed space. I was alone in a hotel, that's all."

"Oh, right. What do you take me for? Take your shit and go."

He shoved my hand away when I tried to slip it through the door. He pushed one of my sandals through the crack, but the heel was too long and snapped in half.

"It's your own fault you don't paint. It isn't Maria. It isn't your mother. Or Art or your old boss. Or me. It's that you're lazy, self-pitying, directionless, insecure, spoiled. You walk around like you're so persecuted. Please," Ed said.

"Do you think women don't throw themselves at me? I'd never treat you how you treated me. Where exactly did you think you'd run off to? With what money? You don't have a job until September, remember?" Ed said.

I bent down on my knees in the pile of my crumpled and broken things. What was the logic to what he chose to pass through the door? Whatever would fit? I knelt on top of my necklaces, scarves, unpaired shoes, and credit card statements. I clasped my hands and begged, but I didn't feel a trace of regret. I banged my fists against the door and wall, moving myself to tears.

"If you let me in and forgive me, Ed, I'll spend my life making it up to you. It's awful what I did. You're right, I am lazy. I do feel sorry for myself. I've been so, so ungrateful and behaved so terribly. I don't know what came over me. I've been so foolish. I'm ashamed of myself. There's nothing I can say to excuse my actions, but please know how remorseful I am. Please. Please, let me in. I need you."

He opened the door and I fell forward into the entryway.

30

◇◇◇◇◇◇◇◇◇◇◇◇◇◇◇◇◇

UNTIL WE LEFT New York, I didn't call Maria and she didn't call me. For a time, I was paranoid that she had called when Ed was home and he'd failed to pass her messages along. Maria had admitted to intercepting my mail before and maybe it was possible there had been frequent messages from the world for me that had never reached me at all. It was possible I'd been living on wildly incomplete information all along. I woke up for several days after last seeing Maria believing something terrible had happened to her, but no news came and I took the silence as confirmation that nothing had changed.

Art met us in a restaurant to say goodbye before we moved upstate. We got to talking about Art's plans for the week and he mentioned he was going to visit Maria's studio the following day. I lit up but didn't inquire. When I didn't say anything, Ed changed the subject, noticing my sore expression. It was merciful of him. I understood his sense that if he just never mentioned it directly again, we would move on more easily. I felt that because Ed had his writing and had a separate, imaginative place he could go to and basically live in, it was easier for him to assimilate things that displeased him by just writing them out of the narrative. I imagined it was how he had survived his parents' criticisms, which seemed to have no effect on him and hadn't made him similarly critical or cruel. Though sometimes Ed gave me a fretful, sideways glance and I wondered if he wasn't quietly building his case against me.

Still, Ed seemed glad we were leaving the city and the morning we were to drive up, he woke up early. A family of four had lived in the house in Tivoli before Ed and I arrived. A mother, a father, and two girls. We were only renting the house; they owned it. They were moving to Europe, for culture, they said.

"There's a second bedroom and an office, perfect size for a nursery. Perfect for when you decide to grow your family," the wife had said during the tour.

"My husband will take the office. I'll probably just use the other room for storage," I replied. The words "my husband" were strange coming out of my mouth; they made me feel like a child bride, but it wouldn't have looked strange. I was more than old enough.

"I didn't mean to overstep," the wife said. "It's a woman's right to choose, of course."

"To women's rights," I said, raising my empty hand in a toast. The woman didn't laugh and instead encouraged me to look at the knobs and window fixtures; they were all professionally restored and original.

The house was a ten-minute drive from the college. We started to unpack the day we drove up from the city. We didn't have enough belongings to even come close to filling the first floor, let alone the second. The contents of our apartment hardly filled our new living room, but once the crates from my studio arrived, it would feel less sterile, I hoped. Our apartment in New York had felt so full, a physical manifestation of our time and tastes. Art was subletting our old place as he finalized his divorce. The end of his second marriage appeared to cause him no distress. He'd become quite zen since he'd stopped drinking; things didn't faze him. Besides, there was no making women happy, Art said, there was no knowing what to give them as they themselves didn't know what they wanted. That had been his explanation over lunch, the unappeasable nature of women. Art, on the other hand, was very easy to please. The apartment was perfect, he said. It was plenty of room for a bachelor and Art was never home, anyway. He floated from cafe to restaurant to cafe, no doubt already restless and scoping out his next mark. On the other hand, Ed and I were always home, always just a few feet away from each other, relegated to the little furniture we had. The sparse home Ed and I were meant to live in looked like a holdover, a temporary post until the rightful owners came back and brought life back into it. Nothing a few rugs couldn't fix and a few shelves, I told myself, listening to the echo of our voices. We'd paint the walls, buy some art. What else did couples do with all of that time to kill?

There was a shed in the yard where the girls had stored their bicycles and Hula-Hoops and the father had stored pesticides and his ax. I'd seen all of those things in the walk-through of the house two weeks ago, but now it was empty. We knocked down some of the shelves and christened my studio.

As he swept the dust from the floors, Ed looked at me with a question on his mind.

"What?" I asked.

"Maybe we have a kid?"

I made a humming sound like I was considering it. I kicked the dustpan over to him and kept scrubbing down the windows.

"It doesn't have to be the way it was with our parents," Ed said. I did love Ed. If I ever reproduced, he'd be my first choice, but

I didn't understand why each and every generation thought they would parent best and differently. Why wasn't he dissuaded by my infidelity? Now that something frightening about me had been revealed, he seemed eager to force it back into its place with the physical presence of a child. I thought of how Maria had said that if I moved upstate with Ed, I'd leave her and have children, how effortlessly she had made that prospect sound undesirable.

As he poured me a glass of wine in the kitchen, and himself a glass of water, Ed made the suggestion again, this time alluding to how much space we had. What a terrible shame it would be to waste all that space. That time I pretended I didn't hear him. The doorbell rang just in time. I went out to collect the pizza. I met the driver halfway, so that he didn't have to walk through the tall grass we hadn't mowed. Ticks were something to worry about. I tipped the young, pimpled deliveryman and stood in the warm summer night for a while, staring up at the white colonial, the black shutters that looked blue in the photographs from the realtor. I was panting. Since leaving New York City, when alone, I found myself out of breath. *This is my life,* I thought, standing in the driveway, weeds growing through the grooves in the cement. *I'd better deal with it and quit acting so surprised.*

For half a year, I waited for Maria to visit me or call, at the very least. She sent two cards: one right after we moved for my birthday (which she'd missed by a week) and one curiously on Christmas (which she did not celebrate—she was atheist). I figured they were Sheila's doing. I suspected they were still together, that Maria had never had the conversation with Sheila that she'd threatened to have. I kept up with Maria's career in spite of myself. There was a spread in *Hyperallergic* about these portraits she'd taken of mental patients freshly discharged from Bellevue. Underneath the photographs, Maria had written these short captions that had come from conversations she'd had with the subjects, little excerpts from heart-to-hearts that had apparently lasted as long as two hours on the street. The prints were hanging in a gallery in Soho. One captured a rail-thin woman, her silver eyes and shy smile, with the sentence THE VOICES ARE ALL BUT GONE printed beneath her. A woman who looked, from afar, like a distant relative of Maria's late aunt. This show was doing very well and the natural connections to Maria's childhood and family history were woven into this piece in the magazine. I was initially angry, jealous of how easily this had all come for her. *Cheap, manipulative* was the general direction of my response. But as I scanned the photographs again, I noticed tears falling onto the glossy pages. Who were those tears for? For Maria, I suppose, for the sort of tranquil, remote beauty in the eyes of the insane; for myself, in part. For her aunt Jocelyn, a bit of a patron saint of irreparable situations, like the one I found myself in now. I wiped my eyes, shut the magazine, and put it in the recycling bin.

In spring, while marking artist statements for my thesis students, I called Maria's apartment. Sheila answered and rattled off some made-up reason as to why Maria could not come to the phone. She was home but tied up. So they were still together, after all. I didn't force the issue, but it depressed me. Sheila promised to pass along my messages, but I knew what that was. I admit, I called five or six times after that. When she answered, Sheila gave me the stock response: Maria was busy but was glad to hear from me and would return my call soon. Sheila made a good secretary. I tried to force it all out of my mind. I occupied myself. I painted as though on a regimen, planted bulbs in the lawn. Rabbits dug them up, nothing grew. Around that time, I got an email from James congratulating me on my inclusion in a group show of women painters in London, where I presumed he was living, since his email didn't say. I always knew you could, his email began, and it continued in that vein. He didn't neglect to mention (before signing off) what a toll it must have taken on me, his failed suicide, and maybe that was why I didn't respond to his letters all those years ago. If I was around, he wrote, he'd love to get a drink. P.S. Was I married? It was characteristic of him not to disclose which continent "around" referred to. I read the email once, then deleted it. Reminded of Maria's assurance that I was better off with him gone from my life, I called her apartment again. I thought of how glad she'd be to say, "I told you so," and I couldn't help myself. Sheila answered politely, but I didn't know to what extent it was okay to confide in her. I didn't know what she knew. Her tone over the phone didn't betray any animosity, but it wasn't as friendly as I remembered. The final time I called, it was a Wednesday evening and I'd just gotten home from campus. I had a stack of papers to mark. I stood over the kitchen counter and dialed Maria's number. Sheila answered, but her voice was different then, tense:

"Maria told me what you did. That you asked her to leave me." She spoke quickly.

"What I did?" I asked.

"You've always been obsessed."

"Sheila, I think you have the wrong idea."

"Don't call me or my wife anymore."

Wife? I thought. That was new. So, I stopped calling. Ed busied himself with work and didn't notice my change in mood. It would have been too much to explain to him anyway, where to begin. There was no way to recount it all without betraying my doubts about our marriage. I didn't want to drag Ed into all of that and I didn't want to be a distraction to him. He'd become stable, basically sober. AA meetings more than once a week at the Unitarian Church one town over with all the blue-collar men he got along with just fine. I hadn't even known he had a serious problem. He didn't drink more than anyone else I knew. Was it possible I had been too selfish and distracted to notice the man I was living with was an alcoholic? Sober, he felt he could finally write.

After disavowing all of his early work, Ed finally felt he'd figured out what he wanted to say. He couldn't give me a hint as to what that was, since it was all in the forthcoming novel he was working away at.

Until then, I hadn't seen Ed as being as needy, as turned against himself, or as torn in two as anyone else. He had been such an anchor to me from the night we met and somehow, I hadn't seen him as capable of the same discontentment I felt. Perhaps I hadn't been able to see people very clearly, until the pivotal moment that clarity would have prevented. Knowing all this, I couldn't unburden myself on him then, just when he was starting to see things clearly himself.

Every morning at seven a.m. I went out into the studio and didn't leave until the two-hour timer went off. Not a minute more than two hours, not a minute less. The house could be on fire and I'd still obey the timer. For the first time, it appeared to be possible for me to live off my paintings and my teaching, to contribute equally with my husband. I had a show in Germany opening in September and I was proud. My paintings sold for good money and important people wanted to be friends with me. What more could I have wanted? I got lost in the work of teaching. Toward the end of the semester, my student Poppy, a figurative painter who had "fled" a large Mormon family (as she put it), asked me what she could do to ensure she got an A in the class. Poppy still had a very simple way of viewing the world. A black-and-white sense of things I recognized from my own childhood. Everyone who did the work got an A. It was my policy, I explained. There was nothing you could do or could not do, apart from showing up.

"How do I know if my work is any good? Or if it's better than anyone else's?" said Poppy, antagonistic. She reminded me a bit of Maria then.

"If everyone gets an A, it's worth nothing?" I asked. "Is that what you're saying?"

"Well...exactly," said Poppy. "I just don't understand what we're supposed to be learning. What are you supposed to be teaching us?"

"I'm teaching you to trust your impulses...as artists."

"Then what do we need you for?" Poppy asked.

She was terse and I could tell she was in distress. I had no impulse to comfort her. I saw in Poppy someone who had been calloused by their upbringing. Everyone had to be fought. Stupidly, I thought I might save Poppy by being stern, cruel, but in service of what I believed were higher ideals than Mormonism and conventionality, bootstrapping, etc. I could also see that she didn't respect my "authority" and wanted to let me know that and I felt threatened. But it wasn't my authority Poppy was acting out against, it was God's. I understood because I'd tried to act out, too, and been thwarted. And there I was.

"If all you want is an A, then you probably aren't a painter. You might want to try your luck in the economics department," I said. "Maybe they'll have something to teach you, since you feel I don't."

She never came back for office hours after that. Spring was at its sad climax. I remembered being in school in May as a girl and sweating through my heavy polo shirt. Our Lady had no air-conditioning, just fans that circulated hot air. Yet we were still expected to wear the heavy shirts through those hot Rhode Island afternoons, when the sun shone through the tall windows unrelentingly. Sometimes sitting at my desk at the head of the classroom now, taking attendance, I would find myself sweating and I would feel afraid. Then the class would end, and I'd hurry out to my car like I was being followed. The semester was over as quickly as it had started. I sat through the long critiques, listening to students air their personal grievances cloaked as constructive criticism. Over the course of the semester, couples had disbanded, infidelities had come to light, friends had grown to hate one another. It was a small program in a small school, incestuous. I'd forgotten how teenagers were, how sad and shy. I tried not to notice. One particularly sensitive student cried and stormed out of the classroom. A pious vegan in the class got on his soapbox over Poppy's painting of a butcher shop that depicted mutilated poultry and the intestines of sheep. A play on the Dutch masters that Poppy never stopped talking about.

"My father was a butcher," said Poppy.

"Doesn't matter," said the vegan. I hoped for a day when I'd be so emphatic for any cause. During the next round of crits, Poppy smeared the floors with blood from free-range chickens she'd bought live from a nearby farm. She bled them in front of the class, coloring her T-shirt and jeans. This was her way of doubling down. She had this gleeful, irreverent look on her face that moved me. But just as quickly, I was irritated by the mess. I couldn't say anything or hold it against her, because I had told the class that performance was allowed. Otherwise, the days were unremarkable. Before summer came, I brought the students to the local bar, an Irish tavern that served plant-based bowls and burgers on the small concrete patio in the back. The town was different from the way I remembered it when I was a student. For some reason, it was dark in all of my memories. Someone was always passed out on the pavement and needing to have their stomach pumped at the hospital. It felt calmer and more idyllic, sitting there with the class, listening to their gossip. I paid for one round of their drinks and then slipped out before any one of them could corner me in a private conversation. When I told Ed I had taken the class out for drinks, he frowned and asked if I was crazy.

"What's the matter?" I asked.

"They're underage," he said.

I wondered why none of them had said. But then again, why would they? They were definitely already drinking anyway; there wasn't anything I could do to prevent it. Was I doing right by these people entrusted to me? Had my teachers done right by me? Teaching convinced me I was finally doing something with my life, but I couldn't be certain to what end. On the last day of the semester, as I walked past the empty buildings on the north side of campus, draped with ivy and marked with plaques commemorating this or that donor, this or that founder, I felt unconvinced. Despite all this confirmation that we were part of a storied tradition laid out for us in the service of a higher ideal, I wasn't sure who I was meant to pass the baton to—I wasn't even sure that I was holding it. Earlier in the semester a student had told me she was so glad to finally have a Black woman teacher who cared so much about her students. It was a long few minutes before I realized she was talking about me. I'd applied for and gotten a full-time position at the college. Moser had really advocated for me. He had gone through a lot of trouble on my behalf. I told myself it was what I wanted.

I braced myself for the years ahead of teaching perennial crops of students these skills I wasn't sure could be taught. I read reviews that proved my pantomime pleased its intended audience. While I was driving home on that final day of the semester, my back seat full of monographs from my office, my engine gave out and I steered my car to the side of the road. I opened the hood and it started to smoke. Eventually, the smoke was so dense and black that I couldn't stand to be near it. I opened the back seat and took what books I could carry. I decided to abandon the car. I walked quickly down 9G, the narrow grass shoulder precarious and muddy in places. Eventually, I abandoned the books. The walk was longer and more tedious than I had expected when I set out. As I neared our driveway, I saw Ed's car parked in the street. He was home and I found I couldn't face him. Alone, I walked past the row of standalone houses and past the limits of the small village. My arms were crossed at my chest, my few belongings pulled close: wallet, keys, lipstick. I walked a long while, past the farm stand run on an honor system, full of eggs and bell peppers. A large hand-painted sign above the run-down wooden shack: ORGANIC, NON GOM, a typo, the kind of charm people moved to the town for. I turned down a road I'd never taken. In the distance there were grazing cows and picturesque grassy hills. I came to a lonely man tabling on the corner of an almost-empty intersection. He wore aviator glasses and a black trucker hat. I was no stranger to proselytizers. His handmade signs were illegible, scribbled in bad handwriting. He stopped me and waved his arms, the makeshift cardboard cross behind him blowing in the breeze, a drawing of Jesus with bloody teardrops scribbled in red permanent marker.

"Ma'am. Have you heard the good news?" he asked. "Jesus loves you. He died for you. Whatever you've done and whatever you do, He'll never turn away from you. Whatever regrets you've got. However badly you've been hurt or hurt somebody else. Lay your troubles at His feet. You don't have to carry them alone."

I remembered there was money in my pocket. I walked three-fourths of a mile down to the German pub advertising a happy hour special: Get two drinks for the price of one. I proceeded to get pissed. I struck up conversation with anyone who would listen, like a person with a broken heart. A man with many faded tattoos covering his weather-beaten knuckles took some pity on me. I told him I had had a friend and that we had been as close as two people could be, had loved one another in the all-consuming way young people do, but that it wasn't cheap or naive, that it had matured as we had, had withstood all the troubles and changes that accompany really knowing someone. I could tell he understood, that he was no stranger to that sort of knowledge. I explained that this friend had confessed their love to me, had given me a genuine opportunity to go all in, committing totally to one another, since it would plague us if we didn't try. Then something changed and ruined it all, and I didn't understand how or why. That since their confession and the subsequent unraveling of things between us, I hadn't been living, but sleepwalking through my life and there was nothing I could do. There wouldn't be another opportunity. I'd squandered everything. I told the stranger that while I loved my husband, I couldn't deny the terrible regret I felt. Denying it would only make it grow.

"If this friend is really serious, he'll take you back. Have you told him how bent-up you are about him?"

"He won't answer my calls. His wife picks up the phone. She says he doesn't want to speak to me."

"Tough. But it'll pass. I'll buy you another drink. Take your mind off it."

We drank and drank, watching the bar clear out gradually. The light was orange through the dirty windows, then it was dark blue. I felt warm and receptive from drinking. I was heartened by the fact that there were still people in this world, like this strange man, who listened kindly to the afflictions of women they didn't know. Little angels who gave, expecting nothing.

"Do you want to get out of here?" the man asked. I nodded, since it was getting late and Ed was expecting me. I had walked a long time and it wouldn't have been safe to go down those dark, unfamiliar roads again. The stranger's car stunk of menthols, but I didn't mind. I struggled to remember the directions to my home and we drove in circles before I saw a road I recognized. I felt safe in the car of this man whose name I didn't know. He was so patient. I never got a good look at his face, but in my mind, it was just bathed with light. We reached my driveway; the lights were on through the window. I was so glad to be home after everything. Life was tiring, it never seemed to relent. But at least there was this possibility of going home. There was that mercy, at least. *That's it,* I said, *that's my home!* The stranger slowed to a stop and I gathered my things, the few things I had. When I turned to thank the man, I saw that he was unbuckling his seat belt and opening the driver's door. I saw the erection through his jeans. I finally understood, he was expecting me to invite him in. I'd given him the wrong idea. I ran to the gate and ran up to the door. He shouted after me, calling me a tease, a whore, and a cunt. *This is how a person gets murdered,* I thought. I stumbled into the kitchen. Ed sat at the table with his chin in one hand and the house phone in the other, with the careful look a person has just before they break terrible news.

"You should sit," he said, barely a whisper. Vomit came up: notes of bourbon, sour mix. Then I knew it was Maria.

ACKNOWLEDGMENTS

Thank you to my parents and my brothers. Thank you, Elijah, for your true companionship. Many thanks to my agent, PJ Mark, for your belief in and support of this book. Thank you, Hannah Assadi, for your wisdom and generosity. Thank you, Gary Shteyngart, Dinaw Mengestu, and Alexandra Tanner, for reading my novel with such generosity. Thank you to everyone at Little, Brown and Company who worked on my novel in any capacity. I'm glad to have done this for the first time with you. Jean Garnett, Vivian Lee, Morgan Wu, Peyton Young, Karen Landry, Carla Benton, and Susan Buckheit, your insight, attention, and experience were invaluable. To the many people I haven't had the opportunity to acknowledge directly whose contributions had a hand in making this book, thank you. Lastly, thank you to all my friends. This is a book about friendship, and I wrote it with you in mind.

ABOUT THE AUTHOR

STEPHANIE WAMBUGU was born in Mombasa, Kenya, in 1998. She grew up in New England and now lives and works in New York.